RIDE OR DIE

RIDE OR DIE

D. D. BRAITHWAITE

Ride or Die by D. D. Braithwaite

ISBN: 9798355664831

ddbraithwaite@outlook.com

Cover design by DDB Designs

Firehawk logo property of D. D. Braithwaite

First Edition

To all those who believed in me,

Thank you.

ACKNOWLEDGMENTS

There are so many to thank for getting me to this stage over the years either directly or indirectly. Without your support, advice, friendship and everything else over the years I wouldn't have been confident enough to even do this, thank you all. Sorry if I have forgotten anyone.

FAMILY

My wife Gillian and son Corran, my niece Nicole, my father Norman, my mother Catherine, my brother Douglas, my father in law Stewart, my mother in Law Alison, my brother in law Gordon, all my aunts, uncles, cousins and second cousins who have been there for me at various times, most notably Benita, Rachel, Ifor, Wendy, Thomas Nicola and cousin in law Tracey. Also my sons Godparents to whom I consider family as well, John "He-Ro" Scott, Jay Gallacher, Jade Austin and Elizabeth Scott.

SPECIAL THANKS

Anthony Greene, Aileen Gormley, Stacey McDonald, Jason "Rifleman Harris" Salkey, Angela Thomson, Angela Hamilton, Kirstin Turner, Sharon Scally, Marco Piva, John Nelson, Kharin Klepp, Rachel Taylor, Jack Berry, Stephen Cameron, Kwaku Adjei, Suzanne Rust, Matt Weston, Phil Marriott, Gareth Holland, Debbie Craig, Lauren Fox, Tracey McCulloch, Siobhan Robertson, Stuart W. Little, Iain MacIntyre, Linda McCabe, Frank McKenna, Marco Calleri, Daria Cotugno, Kimberly Benson, Richard Divers, Alix Brown, Colin Waldie, Keith Campbell, Scott Crombie, Chris Brown, John Sneddon, John Corry, Alex Nicol, Sister Martina, Father Gerard Maguiness, Kitty Gahagan, John Bell, Mo McCourt, Rhys Kay, Luke Murray, Claire McCafferty, Bianca-Louise Little, Sinclair McCall, Brian McLaughlin, Gerry O'Donnell, Ian Gowrie, Haider Dar, Alister Speedie, Chris Cowie, Kimberley Ferguson, Amy Speirs, Gary King George Thompson Smith, Peter Dunne, Chic Anderson, Scott Walker and everyone I worked with in security and with the regular staff especially at the Esquire House Glasgow and at Tesco Extra Wishaw.

CHAPTER 1

It was another dull cloudy Friday morning in Glasgow as Darren Douglas looked out the window on the seventh floor of the Glasgow College of Building and Printing. Running his hand over his close-cut brown hair as he sighed. As always he was early for class but he blamed that on the bus timetables, although he did admit that it allowed him to check a few things online as he had to contend with a slow dial-up connection at home. Darren went back to his seat and checked on his emails, the only noise in the room was the sound of the computer cooling fans.

The silence was broken by Darren's friends Linda and Jason arriving, Jason was nineteen, the same age as Darren and with his ill-fitting baggy clothes and mop of ginger hair with a beard more resembled a homeless hippy than a college student, Linda was a thirty two year old mature student and was usually the one to talk sense into the other two to limited success. The three of them were all in the same HNC Electronic Publishing course at the college and despite their differences were quite close friends.

"One of these days we will get here before you." Jason said as he crashed out on the nearest seat, clearly out of breath, Darren looked unimpressed, as did Linda.

"He ran up the stairs again didn't he?" Darren asked, Linda nodded and took her seat next to him.

"I even offered to hold the lift door for him but he insisted," she said shaking her head "halfwit."

Soon the class filled with students, today's lecture was on Photo Manipulation for Desktop Publishing and the assignment looked interesting, it was to digitally restore a graveyard headstone and the lecturer was an eccentric Yorkshire man by the name of Howard Preston smugly remarked that this was probably the single hardest piece they would probably do on this course, though Jason had enough trouble remembering today's date.

"Is it the fourth or third today?" he remarked.

"It's the fourth of February... Two thousand just in case you're wondering." Linda remarked and looked at Darren who just shrugged, Jason was a smart guy, he just didn't always show it. As the morning went on Darren was way ahead of the others, he seemed to have a natural eye for detail and an uncanny ability to think outside the box, something that drove lecturers mad as he usually found different and ultimately easier techniques to do many of the tasks given. Howard stood up and tapped his desk to get everyone's attention.

"I apologise for this but I forgot to mention before that there is a departmental meeting I have to attend but I should be back before you all finish. now I will stress this," He said looking directly at Darren. "If you find a way to complete the task that is not in the official instructions you must put in the report what you did and why" now the reason he looked at Darren is not just because of his idiosyncratic way of working, it was more the fact he had a strong willingness to assist others in the class which is what the Lecturer was driving at. Howard had barely left the class before Linda and Jason looked at Darren intently, then Linda started counting down from five with her fingers, she got to two before there was a call from across the class.

"Darren... I need help." came an all too familiar voice to Darren, he looked at the other two and shrugged before getting up out of his seat. The voice belonged to one Lucy Bannatyne or Blondie as she was known as thanks to a lecturer calling her it on her first day at college and it just stuck. There she was lounging on her seat wearing her usual footwear of choice, beat-up Doc Martens that had bright purple laces with Denim shorts and a Nirvana T-shirt (Darren secretly doubted she ever listened to the band personally) and of course her strikingly blonde, naturally curly hair. She smiled as she saw him approach.

"Hi Blondie, how can I help?" he asked.

"Darren, how do I do this part?" and she looked at the instructions given "I know what it says but every time I try it won't work, what am I doing wrong?" she then looked at him like a sad puppy, Darren had a feeling she hadn't really tried but the truth was ever since they were in the same NC Print Production course a year and a half ago along with Jason, he had a crush on her and was always willing to prove his worth. Darren tried to explain how to do it but he could tell that she wasn't understanding so he just sighed and decided it would be better if he just did it for her.

"May I?" he said gesturing to the computer, she slid her chair over and he squatted down and started "Blondie, what are you going to do when you get a job and I'm not around to bail you out like this?" he turned around to see her reading the Glasgow Herald of all papers, it wasn't something he thought she would read but she quickly put it down and seemed a little flustered about it.

"Sorry, was distracted there. Darren, I'm sure with your guidance I can cope one day," and she put an arm around him "Until then I will need as much help as I can get." Darren finished doing the part Blondie was having difficulty with and stood up.

"There you go, the rest is easy." he said.

"Thank you." Blondie said with a wide smile. Darren went to walk away but had a thought, he made a vow in the new year that this new millennium will be different for him and he was going to do the one thing he had been putting off and even then he had been procrastinating, he was going to take the plunge.. and ask Blondie out on a date

"Erm, Blondie?"

"Yes?" she said not looking up.

"I was wondering, only if you want that is, after college... maybe going for a drink or something? nothing fancy..." His nerves were getting the better of him but he was determined to finish ".. It would mean..."

"Uh oh," said Jason to Linda "He's actually doing it, he's asking her out." Linda rolled her eyes and put her head in her hands. she could tell it wasn't going well for him.

"Is it going as bad as I think?" she asked, she could just about hear it happen but couldn't bear to look, Jason nodded.

"he's going to crash and burn, she has the how do I break it gently to him look on her face," he told Linda "oh no, now she is giving him the sad eyes.."

"Aww Darren," Blondie said as she turned around to face him, looking sad "I'd really love to but I need an early night to get up in time for the protest." she shrugged apologeticly.

"What protest?" he said, confused, her eyes flashed with frustration at his comment.

"Against the Strathaven Foxhunt, didn't you see the posters all around college?" she ran her hand through her hair, letting out a sigh and patting his arm "I'm sorry Darren, it's just every year they do this, get on horses, release packs of hounds to tear some poor innocent fox up all in the name of sport and nothing is done about it.

It's barbaric and we should all do our bit to stop this sort of thing happening, it's just wrong.." she trailed off then added softly "I wish more people cared about the bigger picture. I've heard too many people say it doesn't affect them so why bother, sorry I shouldn't have taken it out on you. I know you're not like that, narrow-minded I mean."

"No, I'm definitely not," he said almost nervously "And it's okay, I understand, we can always go for drinks another time." he suggested, she smiled at him before returning to work. He walked back to his desk, opened up internet explorer and looked up the Strathaven hunt on Yahoo to find out the location and start times.

"Darren, no. Don't even think about it," said Linda the minute she saw what he was doing "You are not going to that protest are you?" Darren said nothing "Darren?" she said again "It's a very bad idea, trust me." Darren turned to face Linda.

"Look, I know you mean well Linda I really do but How long have you been with Ellen? Jason, you have been with countless women in the time I've known you." His voice had a hint of desperation "I'm nearly twenty and I have never been in any sort of relationship, I really like her and if going to this protest gets her to think of me as someone other than the guy who helps her in class then I'm sorry but I am going." Jason nodded.

"And even if you don't win her over there might be some other hot girl there looking for a geeky sci-fi fan for a boyfriend." he quipped, earning a slap to the back of the head from Linda.

"Don't encourage him" she said to Jason sternly

then turned to Darren, took both his hands in hers and got him looking into her eyes "Darren, I'm your friend and I am just looking out for you, I'm just worried you will get hurt. I know all too well what it's like to have feelings for people that don't think the same way. Imagine how I felt, I realise I'm gay while still in high school and found myself falling for girls I knew would probably never see me as anything other than a friend at most. Just promise me you won't do anything stupid, that's all."

"Okay I promise." Darren said softly then smiled "Linda, trust me. If I do this and she still isn't interested, that's it, not going to chase a lost cause." Linda smiled back and nodded and turned to continue working.

"That's all I ask Darren." Linda said softly

The rest of the day went without much incident and when it was time to go home. Knowing the the lifts would be busy and usual full of people, Darren decided to take the stairs.

"Darren!" shouted Jason as he burst through the stair doors "Got a minute?" Darren stopped and gestured for Jason to continue "I know you are going to that thing regardless of what Linda or I think, just try keep an open mind..if some hot protestor shows interest, promise me you won't turn her down." Darren laughed.

"Okay, okay. I appreciate you and Linda looking out for me, I do. I'll tell you how things go when I get on MSN Messenger after it, okay?" Jason seemed satisfied with the answer and walked with Darren down the stairs, wishing him luck as he ran to get his train and Darren headed to the bus station.

Meanwhile, Blondie was walking to get the train with her friend Julia, a rather tall natural redhead who spoke her mind.

"You could see the disappointment in his face when you said you couldn't meet up with him," she said absently "why do you even bother with him anyway?" Blondie adjusted her bag and thought for a moment.

"He's useful, you see how willing he is to help. Who else should I ask out of the ones that know what they are doing? Jason is a horny sleazeball, Robert is creepy and smells odd and then you have Mark who is a bloody know it all who has to tell you how brilliant he is, with Darren all I ever need to do is throw just enough affection his way and he will do anything I want without fuss," she said smugly "you just have to be careful how you let guys like him down when they do ask you out so they are still interested."

"So are you really going to the protest or was that just an excuse not to go out with him?" asked Julia with a raised eyebrow.

"Oh" Blondie replied, "I will be there, that wasn't a lie. Are you going?" Julia shook her head.

"Sorry but my fiance is taking me to see his parents this weekend or you know I would be there, people still talk about what we did at the Faslane peace camp last year," Julia said smiling.

"Oh I remember, and that big protest last summer.

I will try and avoid getting arrested this time though, I promise." Blondie said as Julia gave her a look of total disbelief

"Oh come on, it's not a good protest if you don't" Julia said as her grin widened "I just had a nasty thought, what if Darren turned up tomorrow at the protest, you did give him a compelling little speech." Blondie just looked at her.

"Don't joke about that, he wouldn't anyway. He's probably going to be too busy watching Sci-fi or playing games online with his little group he has or something, besides I might not be here much longer." she added.

"Oh you mentioned something about that last week," Julia said with interest "tell me more."

"I wish I could Julia I really could but nothing is finalised yet, but if it all works out I might not need to come back to college and Darren can find someone else to have a crush on, might even be you." Blondie said with a laugh as she watched Julia's face contort with disgust.

"If he does I will just kick him in the balls and tell him where to go." They both laughed.

Buchanan Street Bus Station was a few short minutes from college and after a short wait in the queue at the information office Darren was able to find out the bus times to reach Strathaven, he knew the hunt started at eleven in the morning and the bus would get him there about half an hour early. Darren smiled as he boarded the bus for home, he had a good feeling about this.

CHAPTER 2

Darren's journey home to the small town of Wishaw was largely uneventful, luckily for once no one sat next to him, he hated when a stranger would sit next to him and take up too much space or worse have a conversation with someone in the seats across to, in front or behind him. It just seemed oddly rude to him, like being included in a conversation he really didn't want to hear. A couple of university students were talking behind him.

"... Sometimes I wonder about the other girls in my class." said the girl.

"Oh," the boy said, "why?"

"Well one seems to hit the sunbeds all the time, another is a policeman's daughter who won't bloody shut up about it as if it's some big deal and I'm sure another said something about going on a hunt whatever she meant by that but apparently she lives is some big fancy house with horses and stuff. I could go on, the guys are worse." she seemed cynical about her classmates.

"Hey, you chose nursing." the boy replied.

"I know, a noble profession, I am well aware of all that," she retorted "anyway, going out with the boyfriend tonight.." and that was Darren's cue to put his headphones on and play his portable CD player. Due to various factors in Darren's life, he found public transport an uneasy experience and thus would always have his CD player handy to essentially block out the rest of the world, especially conversations that he had zero interest in hearing.

Darren got off the bus as it stopped off at the local Tesco to get supplies for the next day, he decided on Lucozade orange as he felt it would be a long day and he would need the energy and then wandered around seeing what else to buy. Darren chose the luncheon meat for the sandwich filling as he liked it himself and although he wasn't sure what to get if he did convince Blondie to give him a chance, he knew she wasn't a vegetarian plus the meat as it was on offer anyway.

The queue was relatively short and the employee on the checkout was Elaine, an easy going cheerful girl who usually spoke to Darren whenever he was in helping his mother with the weekly shop.

"Hey Darren, it's unusual to see you in yourself, how's your mother?" she asked.

"She's fine," he answered "I convinced her to go out tonight. It's her first night out in years so I have the flat to myself."

"Oh nice, lucky you," Elaine said as she started to scan Darren's shopping "I'm here until closing time," she shrugged "living the dream I suppose." Darren laughed as he packed his shopping.

"I'm sure you'll do alright, I hope it's not too busy tonight. Are you working tomorrow night?" he said.

"No." she looked relieved "first night in ages that I'm not studying or working so I decided I'm going out with my boyfriend, don't know where yet." Darren forced a smile, hearing about others going out with loved ones was yet another reminder of the fact he didn't have someone like that in his life.

"Have fun then and see you probably next week." he eventually said, Elaine smiled and quipped.

"Well, you know where to find me." and then she shrugged dramatically. Darren smiled back and headed out, zipping his jacket up he headed home.

He returned to the flat he shared with his mother Kate, who already had his dinner ready. When Darren said she was going out it was kind of true, she was going to see her friend that night and was just waiting until he came in before ordering a taxi, probably a good thing she was going out as he believed she would have tried to talk him out of the protest too.

After he had eaten his rather bland macaroni and cheese, it was made the way his brother always liked which wasn't to his tastes but a bit more salt and some sauce livened it up a little bit. Darren decided to look out what he was going to wear tomorrow, he figured it would probably be cold wet and muddy so decided on his well worn comfortable Reebok trainers and his old jeans. However the choice of what to wear on top was tricky as anything he wore had to be something warm but comfortable. After some thought it had became clear to Darren what the best thing for him to wear would be.

In his football shirt box was a selection of goalkeeper tops, they were lightweight but very warm so they would be perfect, he had the Republic of Ireland national team, Aston Villa and Newcastle United ones but there was only going to be one option. It was the Celtic goalkeeper shirt from last season, metallic grey, black and white it was the perfect mix of warmth and lightness but this wasn't any old Celtic goalkeeper shirt, this was the one his brother had given him for Christmas nineteen ninety eight. This shirt had the name Warner and the number thirty four on the back after the goalkeeper Tony Warner who was in goal for the now infamous game last season against hated rivals Rangers when Celtic won by five goals to Rangers one. It was also Darren's lucky shirt, every time he wore it his team in five a sides didn't lose.

"Let's hope you bring me luck tomorrow." He said out loud as he put the shirt on a hanger and hung it on his bedroom door, the jeans were slung over the door too and the trainers were left next to the bed. He had a Marvin the Martian t-shirt laid out as well for going under his top, he was more or less all set and lay on top of his bed in deep thought enjoying the peace and quiet, eventually his thoughts turned to Blondie.

Blondie and he weren't friends immediately, in fact, she barely acknowledged he was there but that changed one day when they were doing a desktop publishing assignment and she was having a hard time with it, especially couldn't get one part of the assignment to work at all and Darren did it for her while the lecturer wasn't looking. Ever since that day, they had enjoyed a steady if odd friendship but tomorrow that was going to change.

He checked his emails on his computer, he could use the Internet as his mum wasn't in to ask him to keep the line clear no matter how many times he would explain it automatically disconnects whenever a call is incoming, most were junk but one was from Linda further reminding him not to go tomorrow. He decided to wait until tomorrow to reply to her

As Darren was going to take his portable CD player he burned a couple of mix track CDs for the bus trip, most songs downloaded from Audiogalaxy, a site recommended by one of the lecturers. Once that was done he went to the kitchen and prepared around eight luncheon meat sandwiches and wrapped them in tin foil before packing them in his bag. Darren then packed the two large orange Lucozade bottles and some mint aero bars and he was all set. Just then the phone rang, it was Charlie, Darren's older brother.

"Hey, coming out tonight?" he asked hopefully, he was six years older than Darren but they were still close, even if Charlie sometimes ordered Darren around a bit.

"No, going to have an early night and I'm not sure mum has a key to get back in." Darren replied.

"Oh come on, we haven't been out for a couple of drinks together in about a month, it will do you good," Charlie sounded a little concerned, he understood Darren preferred nights in on his computer but Charlie at least tried to get Darren to go out at occasionally, then if it was just to the local pub "You don't need to stay the whole night." he added.

"Charlie," said Darren trying not to sound too hopeful "I am going out with a girl tomorrow morning, that's why I'm not going out, I'm nervous enough as it is." it wasn't a complete lie, just not the whole truth but by his brother's tone of voice it seemed to work.

"Really? That's great news. I knew you could do it brother," Charlie said gleefully "What did I tell you? Now just remember play it cool, as I told you. Just don't force anything, if it happens it happens, anyway I better let you go, tell mum I phoned." and he hung up, Darren decided to have a bath, to help relax as much as it was to wash.

Once again in while he was the bath his thoughts turned to Blondie, she never really spoke about her family much, but he did know she lived with her mum in the Knightswood high-rise flats in Glasgow but apart from that she never really spoke about her past about and would find creative ways to avoid the subject. He wondered if something really bad had happened and it's something she is still coming to terms with. It wouldn't be the first time he had seen something set her off in a rage over small details. Darren knew she was a bit odd at times but he thought she was beautiful and clever young lady, granted she didn't really use her intelligence much at college but he figured it was more due to her not really trying that hard for whatever reason as opposed to anything else. Darren just wanted a chance to make her happy and maybe tomorrow she might open up more about things if they were away from college.

By nine thirty he decided to get an early night, after all, he had to be ready for the next day and what that would bring. Unfortunately, it was a restless night, he kept wondering about the little things, what if Blondie had a boyfriend and just had not told him? What if she isn't there, every little fear he had rushed into his mind so he did the one thing he knew to relax, he went to play one of his games online, after an hour of gaming he started to feel tired and did manage to doze off eventually, he heard his mum come in but nothing else.

His alarm woke him up early and he wrote a note to his mum who was still sleeping that he was going out, once again he thought if she knew his plan she would not agree to his plan to win over Blondie's heart. He put his black bomber jacket on and headed out, grabbing his bag as he did.

It was still dark and the only people out were the milkman and some dog walkers. Darren walked along the pavement wondering what happens at a protest, to him it just seemed like a bunch of people standing about waving banners and shouting catchphrases while they freeze in the cold, he doubted that the people taking part in the foxhunt were going to go out and take a look at the protestors and simply go back in and cancel the whole thing and there were probably better and more effective ways to go about these sort of hunts. Darren admitted the whole thing wasn't his usual idea of fun but he had to try for Blondie's sake, all he was hoping for was a chance.

As usual, he was early and the bus trip was eventful, Darren overheard an odd conversation that he doubted he would ever forget, an older gentleman was on the bus and a few stops later aother older man who must have been his friend got on too.

"Hey Jack, is that you off you the bookies." said the friend.

"Aye," said the first man, who Darren now knew was called Jack "Mick, you haven't seen Davie lately have you. Not seen him in the pub." the friend, Mick, without skipping a beat simply replied.

"He's dead jack." now the delivery of the news wasn't what worried Darren as much as Jack's reply did.

"The bugger owed me twenty bloody quid, ah well not getting that back now am I."

"Nope." said Mick then changed the subject but Darren decided to get out his CD player and headphones to avoid being shocked further.

Strathaven itself was a nice little town with lots of old

buildings and a large park, Darren never really came out this way but took a mental note to come back again, stopping someone on the street he asked for directions to Netherfield House and her reply was curt.

"Find it yourself, I know why your type is here." Darren was taken aback and it seemed several people had a similar opinion, it was obvious he wasn't there to hunt but to protest and they didn't want trouble at their doorstep and they weren't for or against it, just against the trouble it could bring.

Fortunately he found one person, a fourteen year old kid told him in the directions in exchange for five pounds, the time was a quarter past ten so he paid the boy and headed toward the big house and the protest.

He could hear Linda now telling him he is mad for doing this and Jason reminding him to look at other women but the fact is Darren knew he needed to do this for his own sake and sanity. It was a nice walk, the trees, bushes and fields were all very picturesque and calming, won't be long until it's all busy with foxes, hounds and horses.

As he got closer Netherfield House came into sight. He did stop and think if he turned around now and went back home, got a few hours more sleep and enjoyed his weekend but no, he said he would do this. If it works, it works and he gets the girl, if he goes and doesn't, at least he can say he tried.

CHAPTER 3

Netherfield House, a beautiful Georgian mansion with seventy acres of land was the staging area of this Saturday's hunt and was home to Huntmaster Quentin Galloway. The owner of Galloway Haulage sighed and ran his fingers through his dark but greying hair that matched his trimmed beard. No matter how many times he had taken part, he enjoyed every hunt like it was his first. The countryside always looked peaceful and calm, especially when compared to the organized chaos of the hunt preparations going on behind him. His wife Olivia came up to him and asked if he wanted anything to drink before things got started, but Quentin politely declined gesturing to his red blazer.

"Knowing my luck I would end up spilling it down me." they both laughed and recalled the first hunt he ever took part in when he did just that, just then

Quentin saw his good friend and long-time member of the hunt Edward Campbell come over to give the traditional greeting.

"Good Morning Sir," Edward said with a formality to his cadence that was in stark contrast to his warm smile "so Quentin what's got you so happy today, you look like the hound who caught the fox." Quentin gave a look of mock shock.

"Me? can't I just be excited to lead another hunt?" but he saw Edwards piercing stare "Okay, Tegan is taking a break from her studies and she's joining the hunt." Tegan was his only child and Quentin had every reason to be proud of her and was never afraid to show it.

"Oh," Edward said with a knowing smile "see? I knew it was something. My Sheena tells me Tegan is quite the competitor in showjumping, and rumour has it she is studying to be a nurse just like her mother." word got around fast. Edward was right, however Tegan was following in her mother's footsteps in more than one way as they both regularly enter into equestrian competitions, although Tegan's preference is showjumping as opposed to Olivia's speciality of dressage.

"Yes, she is studying at Glasgow University and we are both very proud of her. Hopefully she will be here soon... And there she is." Quentin gestured to the young lady who just came into view to come over,

"Oh my she has grown, how old is she?" Edward inquired as Quentin's daughter came towards them,

"She's not long turned twenty, she's no longer my little girl Edward, she's a young woman now," Quentin said full of pride at his daughter "Thankfully she gets her looks from her mother."

And what a beautiful young woman Tegan was, the naturally wavy black hair barely controlled into a low bun, her white blouse contrasting with her plain black blazer that she was giving a last minute smooth down with gloved hands. The beige Jodhpurs showed off her curvy legs leading down to her knee high leather riding boots, polished to a soft shine, the metal of the spurs glinting in the morning light. A shy smile was on her lips as she approached her father,

"Good Morning sir." she said in a rather over-the-top formal fashion, Both Quentin and Edward had to fight the urge to laugh, she seemed in good spirits,

"You can call me dad, I'm sure Edward wouldn't be too offended by the break in protocol." he winked at Edward,

"I think on this occasion we could let it slide, just this once." Edward said after feigning deliberation over it, Tegan nodded and said,

"Okay, Good morning... Dad," she said then hugged her dad tight, she turned to Edward "hello Mr Campbell, I hear congratulations are into order, when is Sheena wanting to have the wedding?"

"Hello, Tegan and congratulations are in order for you as well, yet another first place. We saw your picture in the Glasgow Herald," Edward smiled at Tegan as she looked down shyly "You know Sheena, she will have a thousand ideas, all costing me a fortune. She has her heart set on a summer wedding outdoors" he rolled his eyes "I love my daughter dearly but she is her mother's girl. You should see the credit card bill they can run up on a simple shopping trip. Anyway I best let you two chat, I'm sure you have quite a lot to discuss." and he discreetly walked away,

"Is she here?" Quentin asked in a low voice "your cousin, is she here." Tegan nodded,

"She is, I had to loan her some of my old riding clothes but she seems happy to be here." She replied with a smile.

"Good," Quentin was glad Tegan and her cousin reconnected, they were close before he and his brother Ronald had a falling out over money, then a few years later Ronald committed suicide, he offered to help his sister in law but she bit back that it was too little too late "the issue was between me and your uncle, not between the two of you. You did the right thing reaching out to her. I am so proud of you." he then straightened up a little more "Now if you will excuse me, I have guests to greet." and he pointed to the new riders coming up the path, Tegan kissed her dad on the cheek and left him to be the gracious host.

As soon as her dad was out of her line of sight, she went over behind one of the outbuildings and leaned against the wall with her eyes closed. She needed a moment to herself and try to calm down, ever since Tegan could remember she had been an introvert. Sure put her on a horse, with a patient or in a university lecture she was fine but in social gatherings? Clubbing? Student parties? Forget it, she actively avoided such things. She loved to ride and was looking forward to the hunt but not being the focus of so much attention as she was prone to have anxiety attacks like she was having now. Tegan used to have a nervous habit of humming a tune, usually Loch Lomond, if she had a really bad attack. Thankfully she wasn't getting the urge to do that, well not yet anyway.

The only things stopping her from hiding in the stables with the horses until the last moment were the fact her dad was so proud of her and her achievements, of course, he wanted to show her off and be the proud father. She also was looking forward to spending time with her cousin again,

"Tegan," she said to herself softly "you can do this. The hunt will start soon and you will be riding with your cousin, your cousin you haven't seen in years and wondered if you ever would again.. You got this." and with that, she took a deep breath, wiped the tears that were forming on her eyes away and went in search of her cousin.

It had been a long journey but he was there now and if Darren was honest, when he saw he people at the protest he was a little underwhelmed. It looked like a good turnout but they but looked more like people waiting on a bus than attending a protest.

"Mental note," he said to himself "Once again television has lied to you." there were a couple of people who turned out to be from the local newspapers standing off to the side.

"They don't seem very lively." Darren observed, one of the photographers, gave him an odd look.

"First protest?" he asked, Darren nodded "Just wait, when this lot see the first hound... first horse... Anything to do with the hunt, this lot will come unglued, trust me kid, been covering these for thirteen years." Darren shrugged and walked on until he saw a few people he had seen around the college.

"Hey guys... You haven't seen Blondie anywhere," he asked but none seemed to know "come on, Long curly blonde hair, always in denim shorts and doc martens with purple laces." one of the girls replied.

"Oh... Her? No, she never said she was coming, she did ask a lot of questions when I was putting the posters up though." If he was honest Blondie not being there, at least not yet did not surprise Darren as she was notorious for being late for pretty much everything.

"Shes probably running late as usual" he shrugged "So can someone fill me in on what we are supposed to do here..."

It was getting difficult for Tegan, it seemed everyone wanted to seek her out and congratulate her on the awards for showjumping or for choosing nursing as a career, sometimes both and all of it was driving her to distraction. At least shaking people's hands meant they couldn't see hers trembling, luckily her mother stepped in and took Tegan to one side.

"Anxiety again? Tegan, please be honest." Olivia

said softly, she knew her daughter better than anyone, Tegan nodded and sat on a step. Olivia sat next to her and put a comforting arm around her daughter "I know you don't want to disappoint your dad but I know he will understand, more than you think"

"Thanks mum. Was it that obvious?" Tegan asked, her mother nodded and smiled.

"Call it a mothers intuition, anyway I think you have done enough hosting, go enjoy yourself and besides I know who you are dying to see, she is over there talking to Mrs Galbraith, go, enjoy"

Tegan caught up with her cousin and Mrs Galbraith, one of Quentin's business associates and on her fifth hunt, it looked like they were having a great time.

"Ah, Tegan, there you are. Your father never told me what a charming cousin you have, what's your name again?" Said the forty seven year old widow, she was first invited to the hunts to take her mind off her husband's untimely passing.

"Oh, it's Lucy," said Tegan's cousin "Lucy Bannatyne and it was a pleasure to meet you, but if you excuse me. Tegan and I have some catching up to do." Tegans cousin was none other than Blondie.

Not long to go now thought Darren and Blondie had still not shown up, where the hell was she? She attended protests of various things before and while he was sad that it did seem an out-and-out lie just to get out of a date, he was oddly disappointed in her for not attending this after her little speech yesterday, that part bothered him more than anything else.

The cousins walked towards the horses at a leisurely pace talking happily.

"… and now I'm at college," Blondie concluded filling Tegan in on her life up to this point "I do have to say, I'm a little surprised you haven't moved into student accommodation or something." she added looking a little confused.

"I did think about it but this is my home, my parents… and my horse are here. Sure it takes a while to get there and back but at least I get the comfort of my own bed," Tegan said "Speaking of comfort, I see my spare stuff fitted you after all. How does it feel?" Tegan asked, Blondie, did a mock twirl with a broad smile on her lips.

"Well, the blouse is quite itchy and I'm not used to wearing boots that are above ankle length these days so it feels weird whenever I walk." she started to fidget with the blouse collar, Tegan shook her head and looked at her own boots, holding one up off the ground for a better look.

"Really? I could wear these all day long, I admit I feel kinda naked if I'm wearing something not knee high these days." Tegan said then smiled shyly.

"There's an image," Blondie countered dryly "You were always like that though. I also remember getting you in a dress was impossible back in the day." she added, Tegan laughed, her cousin knew her too well.

"I guess but I suppose that might be something to do with the amount of time I spend with horses."

"Still prefer them to people?" Blondie quipped "You still have that nervous look you always used to get, remember your Tenth birthday party?"

"Still trying to forget." Tegan admitted, that despite a lot of money being spent that day, Tegan spent almost the whole thing hiding in her bedroom after having a huge anxiety attack during one of the party games "I'm better than I used to be, well most of the time anyway and if I have something to focus on I'm okay" Tegan stopped for a second and looked at Blondie with a smile "Lucy, I'm glad you're here, I really am and I'm sorry about what happened in the past and I hope we can start afresh, I really missed you." she was sincere about it, she missed Lucy more than she had realized.

"Tegan, We definitely have a lot to talk about after the hunt," Blondie said, stroking Tegan's shoulder "and I missed you too, the whole thing was hard on me too, I would look out my bedroom window at night just wondering what you were up to, wondering if I will see you again," a little tear rolled down Blondie's cheek and she pulled in a slightly surprised Tegan for a hug "Oh Tegan, thank you for contacting me. The problem was between our fathers, not us."

"I missed you too Lucy" said Tegan who was also getting teary eyed, the hug lasted quite a few minutes.

"So, Which horse is mine?" Blondie said to break the silence looking at all the horses awaiting their riders.

"That one," Tegan pointed to a majestic black mare "Thats Lolita, mum injured her wrist and can't ride so She said you could ride her today and that Grey mare behind, that's Princess, she's mine and one of the best behaved horses I have ever known. Though she can be stubborn I couldn't ask for a better horse." Tegan added as she headed over to her horse and Blondie walked up to Lolita as she buckled on her riding helmet, adjusting the chin strap while taking a moment to marvel at Lolita, despite not riding for about six years she got up on the saddle easily and smiled over at Tegan.

"Hey, got up on the first attempt," Blondie stated confidently

"Never really leaves you does it?" Tegan said with a smile. it looked like everyone was mounting up. The hunt was ready to begin.

The minute the crowd heard the hounds Darren finally realized what the photographer meant, it went from a group of people casually talking about their day to seasoned protestors in the blink of an eye. Darren stood near the back as even after the explanation he wasn't really sold on the protest, he just...

"No, surely not," he said out loud largely to himself, one of the riders was familiar, very familiar indeed "Blondie?" He tried to get her attention but either she was blanking him or she couldn't hear him over the chants, it was definitely her though. She was there alright but she wasn't protesting the hunt, she was part of the bloody thing.

CHAPTER 4

As the protestors dispersed Darren just stood staring into space, why was Blondie in the hunt, why not just tell people? Was she trying to preserve her image as a bit of a rebel? What? He needed answers, so he walked over to the gate the hunting party passed through and made his way slowly in the general direction he saw them go. His thinking was they would come back this way after so he could try talking to Blondie, in the meantime, the weather was decent for a winter's day and he supposed the clean air might clear his head about Blondie and what to say to her.

Even though they were near the back Tegan was finally in her element, on a horse galloping through fields, she turned and smiled at Blondie who was equally enjoying herself. It felt every bit as amazing as she imagined it would. Tegan had lost count of the number of hours they spent as kids talking about this exact moment.

The first hedge they were going to jump was in view and did not look like it would pose a challenge, Tegan and Princess made short work of it. Princess was a dapple grey Irish sport horse and Tegan's pride and joy, a gift from her parents and she is the horse with whom Tegan had won most of her showjumping prizes. Blondie's horse Lolita made the jump look effortless though looking at Blondie's face she looked surprised though Tegan wasn't, not only was Lolita a good all round horse but Tegan knew her cousin was as good as if not better than her when they were growing up and it looked like she hadn't missed a step.

"Woah, that was amazing." Blondie said to Tegan, excitement in her voice, her eyes seemed focused on a point beyond Tegan and suddenly her expression. Burst into a broad smile "I forgot how good riding feels." and she galloped to the next jump and leapt over.

As she landed, Blondie started to slow down and it looked like she was shifting her weight on the saddle as if checking something.

"No, not good, not good." she was starting to panic so Tegan stopped and brought Princess alongside.

"Hey, everything okay?" her voice full of concern, she had checked Lolita over with her mum and the stable hand Astrid and none of them had spotted any obvious issues.

"I think there's something wrong with the girth, could be buckles or the straps themselves but that saddle feels loose." Blondie said with a hint of despair in her voice as she dismounted and was checking the straps. Tegan joined her but she couldn't see anything wrong and was surprised and confused as it was her spare saddle and it didn't have much wear on it.

"Let me have a look," she said handing Blondie the reins to hold and easing her helmet off "I don't see any problems, could try tightening them up just a little bit I guess..".

"Hello there ladies," said a voice behind Tegan "Nice day for it." Tegan turned around to see two men, one was tall bald and slightly stocky, the other, who was speaking was of a slighter build and a little shorter than his companion and had short black hair brushed forward. They both wore black jeans and jackets. Tegan's first thought was they were hunt saboteurs, a group who travel to various hunts with the express purpose of disrupting them, she rolled her eyes.

"Excuse me but who are you? I haven't seen either of you around before." she asked puzzled, something wasn't right, hunt saboteurs wouldn't just be waiting about like this and they didn't look like they were helping at the hunt "What are you doing here anyway?" she was sure they wouldn't tell her but it stalled them as she slowly made her way to her horse, hoping her cousin took the hint and did the same.

"Oh just waiting." the shorter man said with a casual tone.

"Waiting? Out here? Weird place to wait, the middle of a field." Tegan said just hoping to keep him talking, get on her horse "you can't be lost surely?" she could feel her anxiety build up in her, her instinct was to ride as far away from them as possible and that was all that was on her mind "What are you waiting for?" she finally asked the man smiled and with an almost cheerful tone replied.

"You." that was it. Dropping her helmet, she ran to Princess. Tegan was just about to put her foot on the stirrup when the horse bolted to the sound of a riding crop, she looked over just in time to see her cousin complete one last swing aimed at Tegan's horse, all she could do was stand and stare, what was Lucy doing? Why did she do that? Blondie just stared at her, a cold smile on her lips but her eyes were burning with pure hate.

"Why?" asked Tegan, her voice almost a whisper "why Lucy?" she was in total shock.

"You are going nowhere... cousin." she replied, her voice dripping in venom. Tegan barely registered the two men coming to either side of her, it was only when they pulled her arms behind her did she snap out of it and struggled.

"Hey!, let go of me! Help!" she shouted as loud as she could, cable ties were used to swiftly secure her hands behind with a couple of quick pulls to tighten them. Blondie walked right up to her struggling cousin and slapped her hard.

"Shut up you stupid spoiled little bitch." she said sternly.

"Lucy, what's all this about?" Tegan said as tears started rolling down her cheeks "If you needed anything my dad would have given you anything you wanted."

Blondie slapped her again as the men held Tegan by the arms.

"Your dad will give me what I ask for," Blondie softly uttered then shouted "he has no idea what I want." she gestured to the smaller man who took out a length of fabric, a large knot tied in the middle and gagged Tegan with it, Blondie walked up and got in Tegan's face.

"You asked in one of your emails why I changed to my mother's Maiden name, Bannatyne?" She said in a soft calm voice as she stroked Tegan's cheek "You think after everything that happened that I'd want to be associated with the likes of you or your family? How could a university student be so bloody stupid." she then slapped Tegan again "Get her out of my sight." and Blondie then turned her back on Tegan, scooped up Tegan's helmet and headed back to Lolita with a noticeable spring in her step.

The taller man hooked his arms around Tegan and dragged her off as she struggled and tried to scream through her gag.

"See Andy, I told you it would be easy," Blondie said to the shorter one, Andy "Where's Frank?" she asked as she mounted Lolita.

"He's back at the van, Pat is enough to handle her. What are you going to do now?" he enquired stroking the horse casually then added "your ass looks amazing in those." referencing the jodhpurs, she smiled and affected a stereotypical upper-class accent.

"Why thank you, I'm going to continue the hunt darling, tally ho and all that. Shame cousin Tegan's horse threw her but the hunt goes on." with that she blew Andy a kiss and rode on, she planned to drop Tegan's helmet further on up to try and confuse anyone looking for her later, Andy jogged over to help Pat.

"Remember tie her feet when we get to the van." He said as he helped drag a struggling Tegan away.

"What the hell am I doing?" said Darren to himself as he walked down one of the many narrow pathways that interlinked the fields "I'm cold and miserable, to hell with it, I'll just ask Blondie next time I see her at college." Now his only issue was how to get to the nearest bus stop as he refused to walk back into town. He walked down one of the lanes in between two fields, still deliberating over how to get home.

An engine noise behind him made Darren turn around to see a black transit van come down the path, Darren decided to wave it down for directions, hell if they are nice enough he might even get a lift.

Frank Quinn, the driver of the van was a stocky man in his early thirties sporting short blonde hair and a goatee side glanced at Andy in the passenger seat.

"Check out this guy, what do you wanna do?" Andy thought a moment.

"Well, could stop and find out what he wants and hope he doesn't suspect anything," Andy offered "either that or run him down. The only danger there is it would leave a body to find," They needed to draw as little suspicion as possible "Let's just find out what he wants shall we?"

"So, you lost or something?" asked Andy casually as the van stopped, Darren sighed and his shoulders sagged.

"Something like that yeah, not having a good day. Just want to find out how to get to the nearest bus stop and get home." Darren said sheepishly.

"Bus stop? Hmm..." Andy said and turned to Frank, "...I think there's one just down the road at the T junction isn't there?" Frank just looked at him blankly but Andy continued "Okay, all you do is..."

Tegan felt the van stop and heard her captors talk to an unfamiliar voice, she had to do something, alert whoever it was out there something wasn't right but what? She inched as best she could to the side of the van and she kicked it with both feet as hard as she could as her ankles were cable tied together. Though thankfully because her boots were still on they weren't digging into her skin like the ones on her wrists, the voices stopped.

"What was that?" said Darren cautiously.

"One of the dogs from the hunt, is injured and needs the vet." said Frank gruffly but he took a little too long answering and Darren remembered something from the websites he looked up the day before.

"Don't you mean hound?" he asked carefully "In a

hunt, they are called hounds." the three men in the van laughed nervously.

"Yeah, hounds... it's been a long day mate and he's new." said Andy pointing to Frank and affecting a casual air about it all.

Tegan listened, in to the conversation, it sounded like the stranger was suspicious of them but the head kidnapper was doing well to explain it away, though spotting the mistake of calling the hounds just dogs was interesting. Maybe another kick will help, she swung her feet to the side of the van again.

there was another bang.

"That sounds like one hell of a big bloody hound." said Darren getting more suspicious.

"Well they can be very feisty and dangerous when injured," said Andy, even though he was showing nerves now "Look we really need to get it to the vet..."

From what she could hear whoever else was out there was certainly not convinced by her captors' explanations, she prepared for one more kick but this time took as deep a breath as she could and screamed into her gag as hard as possible then kicked, she doubted they could explain that away, hoping this stranger would hear…

… he did.

"Okay!" said Darren with a mix of panic and anger in his voice "That's not a..." Frank had opened the door quick knocking Darren off his feet as Pat came round from the passenger side.

"Put him in the back and restrain him, Pat stay in the back and make sure our guests don't get any ideas." said Andy, Frank shook his head.

"Should just kill him." but Andy shook his head as Pat grabbed Darren and twisted his arm behind his back, Darren was in no position to do anything other than comply.

"No, at least not here and not yet." was his reply.

When the vans rear doors opened and Darren was pushed inside, Pat followed and closed the doors behind him as the van started back on its journey.

Tegan assumed that the guy the brutish one she was sure they referred to as Pat was securing with the last of the cable ties by the wrists was the same person questioning them about all the noise, she didn't recognise him but she was glad he wasn't earshot of the other two when they discussed his fate although she was starting to feel guilty about it.

As Pat restrained him, Darren looked over saw the other occupant of the van, judging by her attire she looked like someone from the hunt, She looked quite attractive. Wasn't she riding alongside Blondie? Why was she tied up? Who were these guys? He had so many questions but was gagged before he could ask anything.

CHAPTER 5

Darren and Tegan were propped up in a sitting position by Pat along the side of the van as he sat across glaring at them in silence, Darren looked at Tegan and was trying to work out why a young lady, a very attractive young lady, like her has been taken like this, something to do with the Foxhunt? No, these guys didn't look like protestors and from what he had read online about hunt saboteurs the main goal they had was disrupting the hunts, kidnapping seemed a bit too extreme. Some sort of ransom? Possibly, all he knew was he was in way over his head.

Tegan's tears had dried up for now but her mind was racing, why would Lucy do this? Can't be just for money surely? But then her thoughts slowly turned to something else, she glanced over at Darren and for some reason when he looked back at her she could see a kindness in his eyes. A horrible feeling came from the pit of her stomach, if she hadn't tried to attract his attention he wouldn't have confronted them and wouldn't be here with her, they were going to kill him at some point, they pretty much said so. Her desperate act to save herself doomed him.

At the front Frank looked annoyed, he wasn't so sure about one aspect of the plan

"Andy, are you really sure it was a good idea to bring Pat in on this?" he asked in a low enough voice no one else could hear.

"Yeah." replied Andy, he knew Frank had a habit of speaking his mind "Why not?" Frank glanced over and shook his head.

"Just not sure it's wise to bring a convicted rapist on a job to kidnap a girl like her, what if he gets... Ideas." Frank made a valid point but Andy believed he had the answer.

"You really do worry too much Frank, Pat knows what I will do to him if he tries to touch her... without my permission anyway." Andy said confidently, though Frank still wasn't convinced.

In the back, Tegan noticed Pat was staring at her, looking her up and down with a lecherous look on his face when he'd seen she was looking at her he gave her a wink that sent shivers down her spine. Every so often he would chuckle and mumble away to himself, never taking his eyes off her.

There was something about the way the big guy

was looking at Tegan that unsettled Darren, something disturbing. Now Darren had been testing his bonds ever since he was captured and it seemed that in their rush to leave the area the big bad creep didn't do the cable ties as tight as they could have been, with time he might be able to work loose and if he did get free there was one thing he was certain of, he was not going to leave this girl, whoever she was, with these guys, he just couldn't. Suddenly there was a loud noise and the van seemed to lurch around and come to a stop.

"Damn," said Frank "we have a flat tyre." they went to the back to get Pat and the equipment to replace the tyre.

"Didn't you check them before we started?" Andy asked, a hint of irritation in his voice.

"I did, all four are new so either we must have hit something, or Jim's garage gave me a dud tyre. I'm telling you this is not a good day for us, first, the have a go hero and now this." Frank even by his own admission worried too much but Andy liked that about him, it meant Andy didn't get too carried away, Frank handed Pat the jack "Here let's change this before anything else goes wrong." and he sat at the side of the road.

The abductors were so occupied with their problem they forgot to fully close the back doors to the van, she nudged Darren who looked over and saw the same thing, she made a gesture with her head for him to go. His legs were not bound and hopefully, he could get away and alert someone, although if she was honest she was more concerned with him just escaping as the guilt of dragging him into this was consuming her but either he wasn't taking the hint or something else was going on in his head, why wouldn't he just go?

She was telling him to go, to try to escape but Darren refused, he couldn't take her too and even if he did get out, where was he, where could he go? More importantly what would happen to her? No, he couldn't live with himself if he got away and he read in the paper about her being killed or something, besides he was making some progress with the bonds, not much but the ties might be loose enough to slip his thumb through and if he did that the hand could slide out, no he stayed, for now, for her.

By now she was frantic, begging and pleading with him through the gag to go, she had heard them, he was going to be killed regardless of anything else. She pushed him with her shoulder, used her head to point, everything she could do to try and get him to leave and every time he shook his head, he refused to go.

Darren did the best he could to signal to her if he goes, she does by using his head to point to just him and shaking his head but pointing to both and nodding, he did this until she got the hint.

Tegan was taken aback, here was this guy with a clear chance of escape yet wouldn't because he wanted both of them to go together. Tegan realised that while he may not know their plans for him but she had a feeling when she looked into his eyes that it wouldn't change a thing if he knew and that he would stay regardless, despite the bleakness of the situation, Tegan felt oddly touched by the thought that a complete stranger like him would essentially risk everything, including his life, for her.

"This tyre will be the death of me." Frank complained as he tried to get the wheel off, Pat shook his head and muscled him out the way effortlessly turning the wheel nuts.

"Easy." he said smugly, Andy was standing a little bit away and gestured to Frank to come over, leaving Pat to change the tyre, when Frank came over Andy gestured to the door.

"See that? If that was me in there I would have seen that as an escape route, that guy only has his hands bound." Andy stated but Frank looked confused.

"And?" he said quizzically.

"Something is stopping him from going and it's not the bonds and somehow I doubt it's us." Andy sounded perplexed.

"Relative of the girl maybe? Her boyfriend?" Frank said, thinking to himself that if he was in that guy's situation and if he didn't know the girl, he would have bolted before now. Andy shook his head.

"No, not a boyfriend" he said "She's an only child and very single according to Blondie, could be a cousin as she did mention something about the mother coming from a big family." so that was possible but he doubted it, there was something about the guy that he would need to keep an eye on, they watched as Pat changed the tyre.

"What do you want to be done with this?" he asked, holding the tyre up in one hand effortlessly.

"Just get rid of it." said Andy with a shrug, so Pat launched the tyre into an empty field next to the road like he was in some strongman competition and went to the back as they set to continue on their way. Andy pulled Frank aside once he helped Pat back in.

"Frank, I've been thinking," he said with a confused look

"Yeah?" Frank replied

"Well I just had a look in there and he hasn't even moved. Before we even go any further I say we at least try to find out who he is." said Andy, Frank nodded in agreement.

"Yeah, good point, we need to know something, anything about him. What do you have in mind?" Frank asked the wallet they had taken from Darren had just contained money, Darren had left his bank switch card and college card at home in his separate card holder.

"Oh I have an idea." said Andy with a wicked smile

"Okay, lets go find out then" Frank had a rough idea what Andy had planned and went with him incase it got a little out of hand

Andy made his way to the back of the van and opened the doors, climbed in and went up to Tegan and stared at her intently.

"You," he said staring at her "Do you know this

guy?" and he pointed to Darren, she shook her head "You're sure now?" she still shook her head so he reached into his pocket and pulled out his knife and held it at her throat, "You wouldn't be lying now would you?" Tegan frantically shook her head. Andy was satisfied with her answer, he turned to Darren, holding the Knife menacingly at Darren's throat.

"Okay hero, you have any idea who she is?" he shook his head slowly, Andy stared into Darren's eyes then hung his head and turned to Frank, "I think he's lying." and slowly pressed the blade against Darren's neck, he shook his head with more urgency this time. Andy sighed and put the knife back in his pocket and exited the van, locking the rear doors behind him and they walked away just far enough so no one else could hear, Frank looked at Andy with a bewildered look on his face.

"Something isn't right, if he doesn't know her and she doesn't know him then why the hell is he still here? Why would he stick around for someone he doesn't even know, I certianly wouldn't, you wouldn't. What makes him different?" he said and Andy had to agree.

"You saw how many were involved in that hunt, for all we know he might be the son of one of the others and might be worth something. We will have to wait for Blondie and see if she knows him before we do anything don't want to kill the guy then find out we can ransom him too, you want me to drive for a while?" He added.

"Yeah thanks, could do with a rest if I'm honest." Frank handed Andy the keys "where are we are going anyway?"

"An abandoned cottage in the Lead Hills, Blondie and I scouted it out. Joe is up there already, don't worry I know where I'm going." Andy said as he headed back to the van.

In the back Pat smiled wickedly at Tegan and leaned close, his bad breath alone making her turn her head away from him, that and anything to avoid looking at that lecherous face of his, his hand squeezed her thigh.

"You are such a pretty little thing aren't you?" he said grinning with evil intent, running a finger down hard against her cheek, smiling as she feebly tried to avoid him "Don't be scared, who knows, if things turn out the way I hope, we may get to have some playtime together. I will take good care of you then." he then leaned back again and rested his back on the van and had a humourless chuckle to himself, Tegan, already scared for her life started to cry again in fear of what he meant by playtime, she didn't know why she did this but she inched slightly to Darren and tried to reach out with her hands behind her, she succeeded in grabbing a piece of his jacket, he inched closer to her in response.

Darren looked at just how frightened the girl was and was horrified by the way the big brute across from them was leering at her, he gave her a sympathetic look and wished it would give her some hope, he subtlety got her to look at his hands, as he had been doing everything to twist or stretch the cable ties enough to free and he gave her a wink.

Tegan could see her would-be saviour had been

trying to do something with the bonds, she knew the smartest thing for him to do if he got free would be to save himself but she knew from what she had seen of him he would try and free her, she hoped that it wouldn't prove to be a costly mistake, she just gripped onto his jacket with the two fingers that could reach, somehow it reassured her a little, not much but it was something.

Darren for his part was really unsettled by the big brutes behaviour to the girl, the guy seemed to have... ideas on what he wanted to do to her and looked like that sort that he usually got what he wanted in that sense, before Darren was already determined to take her with him if he escaped and now his earlier choice not to escape and leave her behind was vindicated. Darren could not and would not leave her to whatever fate her abductors had in mind, he had get her away from them at any cost.

CHAPTER 6

Blondie had thought about rejoining the hunt but realised too many people may ask too many questions so what she did instead was after dropping Tegan's helmet at a suitable spot she headed back to Netherfield House, got off the horse just outside the gates and seeing a muddy area nearby did a staged flop into the mud and then walked up to the house itself, affecting a limp.

When she got close enough she saw Olivia run out, face full of concern.

"Lucy, are you okay?" she said looking Blondie up and down "How's your leg?"

"I think I hurt my knee when I fell, its just sore if I try to bend it too much." Blondie replied.

"You better get inside and we can get a good look at it and you can tell me what happened."Olivia told her. Blondie headed to the house as she heard Olivia take

Lolita by the reins and lead her towards the stables.

"Naughty girl Lolita, Lucy is family.. "she heard Olivia say to the horse, she wanted to be away before the hunt returned but didn't want to draw suspicion, after about five minutes Olivia returned, explained that one of the stable hands was dealing with Lolita and asked what happened.

"Well," she started "I had cleared the first jump okay then went for the second... Next thing I know I'm hitting the ground, I tried to get back on Lolita but my knee was too sore so I limped back here, Tegan believed it was for the best, she was worried I might injure myself further." she gestured to herself and the mud " I think I should go change." Olivia nodded but before Blondie went anywhere Olivia insisted on having a proper look at her knee first to make sure she was okay.

"Thankfully I don't think its anything serious," Olivia said after examining the knee as best she could "I'll get you something to help it just to be on the safe side though, Hold on." she left and returned a few minutes later with a tubular bandage "when you change put this on, if it's still sore in the morning see a doctor," she smiled "Don't worry it's your first hunt, these things happen," she leaned closer "I'm my first I was thrown from my horse before the first jump, I went over the fence, the horse didn't... Broke my collarbone." Lucy winced, that sounded painful "ouch, that must have hurt" she said standing up, "Well thank you, Aunt Olivia.." and she limped up the steps to get changed.

When out of her aunt's view Blondie stopped limping and headed to the spare room she used to change in earlier, via Tegan's room.

"So this is the spoiled little bitches room. Hasn't changed much" she said, there was a big double bed, a large television with a video player. The walls were sparsely adorned with various framed pictures and posters. One of the larger ones was a Take That poster, signed by the band of course including Robbie Williams. Another poster she had was of the band Runrig and their Transmitting tour, Tegan had an eclectic taste in music that was for sure, the Sharleen Spiteri signed picture on the wall confirmed that, Blondie hated Texas. A picture of violinist Vanessa-Mae was next to the poster of Sharleen. Blondie just rolled her eyes at that one, to her it was the typical pretentious crap she expected a spoiled rich girl like Tegan to listen to.

Blondie sat on the bed and looked around, she looked over at the bedside table as there were two photo frames one had what looked like a cutting from an old magazine of a guy sporting a short military style haircut wearing some futuristic camouflage gear and armour with a red heart on the chest plate. She was surprised Tegan still had that, she can't remember the actor's name or the character he is in that picture but she knew it was an actor Tegan had a huge crush on when they were younger "Oh yes, him, Corporal.. Something," she half-remembered the character name "You always had to be different Tegan."

The picture next to it was a familiar one, she picked up the pink frame and looked at the picture, it was of Tegan and Lucy, both aged twelve all ready for a day's riding, something about seeing it made her think of the fun times they had together, especially with the horses.

"Happier times." she said with a tinge of regret "Tegan I wish things had turned out different I really do" she took a deep breath and focused, she knew what she was here for, to see what clothes she could take. First, she looked at Tegan's shoe collection, well it was mainly boots, on one side was her large collection of riding boots, some leather, some rubber but all were knee high and black. On the other side, Tegan also had some regular leather boots of various heel heights and styles, all of them were knee high too. Tegan did have a token amount of other shoes and sandals that looked like they had barely ever been worn, also she had some nice Nike Air Max and Reebok but Blondie passed, she preferred her Doc Martens anyway. In the built in Wardrobe was a nice selection of outfits but Blondie selected another pair of beige jodhpurs. Blondie then selected an Ellesse t-shirt and carefully left the room after picking some earrings from Tegan's Jewellery box for good measure and sneaked over to the room that she had changed in before the hunt.

After a quick shower, Blondie put on the clean jodhpurs with her Doc Martens and the t-shirt, carefully putting the dirty jodhpurs in her bag to wash later.

"Andy's right, my ass does look good in these." she said putting on her leather jacket and bag, dumping the riding boots, blouse and blazer just outside the room door on her way out the room. Blondie went downstairs affecting a limp again and this time was also clutching her stomach.

"Aunt Olivia, I'm feeling ill, maybe I should head off home and lie down, see how I feel in the morning," she said sadly "I feel really bad about this." Olivia came over and hugged her niece.

"Lucy, honestly it's okay. It's not your fault and don't worry, I'll call a taxi to take you to the train station if you want." Blondie nodded sadly.

"Thank you, and I am really very sorry," she said meekly "I enjoyed it today and it was good to see Tegan, please let her know I'm sorry." she added as Olivia went to call a taxi.

As they waited for the taxi Blondie told Olivia about her college work, naturally leaving out the fact Darren did most of her practical work. Olivia was impressed.

"Electronic publishing is the future Lucy and such a smart kind young lady you have grown up to be, you have a bright future ahead of you," Olivia said sweetly "I admit when Tegan said she was going into nursing I was concerned. You know how she is in crowds. But by all accounts she is doing well, better than I thought."

"Tegan has and always will be, I guess, a kind hearted girl. It's a silly thing to say but if there was one last sweet in the packet she always let me have it and wouldn't see it any other way" it was true, Tegan did little gestures like that all the time when they were young

"Helping others must focus her I think"

"You could be right there," Olivia told Blondie "she really does mean more to us than anything and we would do anything for her." Oh I know you will, thought Blondie "...and we will do what we can to help you." Olivia added with a warm smile.

The taxi drew up outside and Blondie limped out to it but stopped and had a sly smile on her face, she couldn't help herself, after all, what's one more lie?

"I will try to phone tomorrow to let Tegan know I'm okay, I was thinking of asking her to come with me and some friends to Aviemore for the weekend, just me and two friends and there's room for one more. It's a small group so she will be fine." Olivia looked touched by the gesture and rushed over pressing something into Lucy's hand, it was sixty pounds.

"For the taxi and just a little to help for now, as for Tegan, leave it to me she has nothing on, as far as I know, I will tell her and convince her it would be better than sitting in her room all weekend watching videos inbetween mucking out the stables. Thank you, Lucy, I hope this isn't the last hunt you will join us for." Lucy smiled and got into the Taxi, as it pulled away she could see the first of the hunters return and one had Tegan's horse alongside. They all looked very grim. Part of her wished she could be there when the news is broken that Tegan is nowhere to be found.

The taxi dropped Lucy off in Strathaven town centre and she went in to buy a drink at the petrol station as she pondered her next move when she heard the guy behind her in the queue talk with someone else talking about having to drive down to Dumfries for work and he wasn't exactly sounding excited about it. She had an idea...

She took her time and made sure the guy behind her was close when they left, he was a short slightly overweight man in his twenties with thick glasses and wearing a DHL delivery uniform. She suddenly broke down crying loudly as she pretended to look franticly in her bag.

"No, no where is it, this can't be happening." she said through tears, the delivery driver asked her what was wrong, "I thought I had more money in my other purse but I have lost it, I have no money to go to my aunts now and.. It's not your problem honestly." but the driver who was already in awe of her beauty and at least wanting to be politely asked.

"Is there any way I can help?"he said, showing genuine concern.

"Doubt it," she said wiping her crocodile tears away "my aunt, she lives in the Lead Hills, it's a nice little cottage just off the A702." she looked at him sadly as he seemed to be lost in thought.

"Well it's a bit of a detour but I might be able to swing that direction, whereabouts on it?" He said, subtly looking at her ass although not subtle enough, she saw it and pretended to drop and pick up her purse, letting him get a good look, man these jodhpurs really worked on guys.

"just south of Elvanfoot, near Sandaharr Kennels, I can tell better when we are on the road." she said still letting a few tears flow "she broke her arm and I'm going to help.." The guy put what he thought was a comforting arm around her but she suppressed a shudder.

"Don't you worry, I'll get you there. I'm Jamie, whats' your name?" He said as she headed to the van.

"Blondie" she replied.

"Oh, a fan of the band then?" He inquired, she looked at him blankly for a few moments then nodded, He tossed her a red and yellow DHL jacket "It gets cold in there and the air conditioning is broken." she put it on over her own jacket and got in.

It felt like the longest journey of Blondie's life, the constant compliments that sounded more creepy than charming. The list of celebrities he had delivered to was long and the stories sounded embellished, for example, she doubted the story of the Rangers player Jorg Albertz inviting him on a night out in Glasgow with him and goalkeeper Stefan Klos was genuine (he apparently had to refuse due to work commitments) and she was pretty sure Blythe Duff did not offer him a small role in 'Taggart' and definitely did not try and sleep with him, (once again.. Work commitments) the thought of the little troll of a man touching any woman made her feel sick, but her diplomatic response was.

"Well, you are truly dedicated to your job." and she shook her head. She oddly thought what Darren was up to, probably on one of those online games she supposed. The thing she could say she actually liked was his compliments at least sounded genuine and were, for lack of a better word, nice. Another thing was he didn't care how pathetic he sounded he just told things like they were. She won't be seeing him again if the ransom comes through. She might email him someday... Maybe... Then Jamie started talking again.

"Hey you know, if you got the right haircut you'd kinda look like," And he pulled a magazine cutting out of the glove box and handed it to her, it was a rather beautiful blonde lady in what looked like a wrestling or boxing ring "You would look like her, Tammy Sytch, also known as Sunny.. The things I'd do if she let me." Okay, that did it...

After ten minutes of squatting at the side of the road being sick, she finally had the stomach to get back in and after twenty excruciating minutes she saw the house in the distance and got him to let her out but not before he wrote his number and said.

"Phone me on Thursday." and blew a kiss as she slammed the door. Blondie then waited until he was far enough down the road and tore up the paper with his number and threw it in the air like confetti.

"Never going to happen! " she shouted as loud as she could and then realised she still had the DHL jacket on, she shrugged and she made her way to the cottage. Everything should be ready by now and she also hoped that Pat didn't get any ideas about Tegan... Yet.

CHAPTER 7

The safe house was a dump of a place, a weather-beaten and faded for sale sign stood slumped on the wall of the house. To Andy, though it was the perfect place to hide the girl, miles away from anywhere, hills, trees and everything else in between, in the unlikely event she gets away she would not get far. Even then they had backup plans just in case. Joe came out to meet them.

"Was it a success?" He asked, Joe Murphy was a no-nonsense type guy, his black hair close cut, Joe was the most reliable one of the group if Andy was honest.

"Yeah, plus a spare," Frank said shaking his head "don't ask, it's a longer story than it needs to be."

They first brought out Darren and then Tegan, making sure Pat wasn't alone with her as Frank didn't like the way he was looking at her, Joe had Tegan in a fireman's carry and Frank lead Darren into the small farmhouse. The inside was as rundown as the outside but looked like it had been tidied up as much as possible. Darren's bag was dumped in a cupboard and Frank made him sit in a corner.

"For what it's worth," said Frank half admiringly "You have some balls kid, I would have run away at the first chance I got." Tegan was dumped next to him and she inched closer, somehow just being in some contact with him helped, not much but it helped. Darren continued to try and free one of his hands subtly.

Tegan didn't know what to think, she wished Darren would escape, her guilt over his abduction still tearing her apart, she had value to them and he didn't. Why did he even care about her safety despite saying he didn't know her, maybe he was a very good actor to fool the abductors but she kind of doubted that as there was something about the way he looked at her. A real part of her, a very real part of her wished that she could at least find out why he is doing all this.

Darren for his part had a grim determination, he had no clue who she was, his only thought was to get her out of here somehow.

It had been a few hours of nothing happening and Frank went to clear his head and was outside pacing, he always had Andy's back in the past but something about this job felt wrong, this girl wasn't some rival in the criminal underworld and neither were her parents, and as for the

have a go hero, Frank couldn't fault the guy and there
was something about the kid he couldn't quite work out.
Andy came up to him after sensing something was up.
"Frank, something on your mind?" He asked.

"Yeah, Blondie actually, there is something about
her I don't trust," he saw Andy's face harden "Hey I
know she is your girlfriend but you have to admit this is
not our usual operation here. We have kidnapped some
rich kid on a horse just because Blondie wants to hurt
her parents, this is more like the sort of crap the Lyle's
would do." Frank just thought best to be honest, the Lyle
crime family were known for excessive violence.

"Her father is the founder and owner of Galloway
Haulage, we've intimidated businesses before, this is just
higher stakes, you worry too much Frank." Andy said
trying to reassure his friend, Frank had a habit of this, he
could be too moralistic for a life of crime at times but
was a good hand because he never let Andy go too far,
though this time was different.

"Andy, The hero... I might sound crazy but I kinda
wish we had a guy like him on our side, he has to know
what's going to happen yet we have had bigger men
literally pissing themselves and begging for their lives
and they haven't always known what we have in store for
them, not him." Frank had to get that out there.

"I know, I hope Blondie can shed some light on
this, I really do." then up the path in the now fading light
of day came a familiar sight to Andy...

"Blondie!" Andy ran to the blonde in the DHL
jacket, Jodhpurs and Doc Martens "How are you?" He
said as he kissed her "We have a slight issue."

"It's Pat isn't it? he better not have.." she started, suddenly looking fierce, Andy thought she looked kinda sexy when she got mad.

"No nothing like that. We just picked up another hostage but she doesn't know who he is and he doesn't know who she is." Andy then explained everything from the initial encounter to his failure to run when he had the opportunity, Blondie looked perplexed.

"Hmm, I suppose I should see this guy, lead on." She said with a dramatic gesture.

Darren heard voices, including a female one... A very familiar one... Then who walked in? non-other than Blondie, he hung his head in despair, of course it was her, the way his day was going it had to be her.

"You! of course, it had to be you, didn't it? what the hell are you ever doing here Darren?" She said angrily with her head in her hands, she turned round to Andy and said "This is the guy I told you about, the one I get to do my course work." Andy looked surprised.

"So, care to explain why is he here?" He asked eventually, Blondie thought a while then shook her head and sighed.

"I think I know why, Darren... I wasn't inviting you to the protest you moron, you are great with computers but you don't get subtlety do you? Even if you were interesting and attractive I would have said no as I have someone," and she kissed Andy on the cheek "Andy Donnelly, meet Darren Douglas. Darren, meet Andy... my boyfriend." Oh, that was a name Darren remembered from stories Jason would tell, the Donnelly brothers were a big time crime family in Glasgow, extortion, drugs, murder... You name it they do it, makes sense now how they pulled this off. His heart sank a little, if she had just said she had someone at least he would have accepted it and moved on or was Blondie worried he wouldn't help her as much if she did. The sad thing is he still would have as he did think of her as at least a friend, until now of course. If only he wasn't gagged then he could have told her that, not that it would have made much difference.

Blondie came up closer to Tegan and Darren and grabbed Darren's head and looked him in the eyes, her look was one of anger and hate.

"So basically even if I was single, you and I? Was never, ever going to happen, you were good for one thing and one thing only. Doing the stuff I couldn't be bothered doing." and she took a step back swing her foot and kicked Darren square in the crotch with a kick David Beckham would have been proud of. Darren was nearly doubled in pain and fell to the side as Tegan looked on in shock at the cruel attitude of her cousin.

What no one saw was the fact that when she decided to use his balls for penalty practice was that was his reaction to it gave him the force he needed to pop his hand out the cable tie, he had just enough wits about him to grab his hand by the wrist before it was obvious what happened, he also noticed there was a broken chair leg near, must have been brushed to the side of the wall when the place was cleared up and could be useful, damn the friction burns on the right wrist hurt a lot, not as much as his balls though. Tegan however had seen his hand get free and fell awkwardly on top of him as if he was the one propping her up in order to hide it from the others.

"Aww, Poor Tegan." Blondie said, switching her attention to Tegan with a sneer as they both did their best to sit back up as she sat on the table and thought it best to explain. She found the visual before her amusing as there was Darren, eyes closed in pain and Tegan glaring at her as if horrified and disgusted by her cousin's cruelty.

"Oh Darren, the girl you had that lovely trip in the van with is my lovely cousin Tegan Galloway. You see her dad and mine used to run a business together but in nineteen ninety, my dad had struck out on his own. Set up a small, but successful firm. A recession hit a year later but my father weathered the storm but when the end was in sight it all caught up. He needed help so he reached out to her father," Darren noted the lack of the term Uncle.. It seemed like Blondie really hated Tegan's dad "anyway, apparently her father offered him everything but what he really needed, a loan just to tide him over until things were sorted." Blondie was starting to tear up but was still channelling her anger. Tegan tried to say something through her gag, but Blondie silenced her with a look.

"We lost everything, we had to go live in council accommodation, I had to move school, everything I knew ripped away from me. My father had to take up a job in a supermarket to make ends meet, a Galloway working in bloody Tesco? Yeah, then even they sacked him," Her anger receded as she recalled the events "It was an overdose of prescription medication apparently. At the time all I knew was my daddy wasn't moving, slumped on his chair," She shed a few more tears "Tegan, something else died that day, the Lucy you knew and loved, ceased to be from that moment on." she numbly got up and walked to Tegan anger building up again, she dropped to her knees and got in the girls face and and pulled out a newspaper clipping, it was Tegan's picture in the Herald.

"Look, perfect little bloody Tegan and her prizes, you and I both know I was a much better rider, and more confident with people. do you still like to hide away in the trailer before your turn in a show? Still hum 'Loch Lomond' when you get really nervous? Well do you dear cousin?" her face was one of pure hate, then out of nowhere Blondie kissed Tegan's cheek "Oh Tegan, I will make your parents pay, they robbed me of a father, I think It's only fair I rob them of what they love most." she then slapped Tegan hard twice before she stood up, suddenly back to regular old Blondie.

"You okay?" Andy asked her, Blondie nodded.

"Yeah, got anything to eat? How are we working things here?" She said looking about as if the last few minutes hadn't happened. Joe shook his head and slapped his head sheepishly.

"Damn, I knew I forgot something"

"It's okay, We will go get some supplies. Frank, Joe, Shopping trip, Pat, treat anything Blondie says as if it's coming straight from me, got that?" He headed out. Blondie followed him but first turned and said to Pat.

"Pat, no touching the hostage, okay? I'll be back in a few minutes" and with that she went outside with the others.

"Are you sure leaving Pat there is a good idea?" Frank said to Andy but Blondie answered.

"It will be fine, Andy, I been thinking, I should probably take care of Darren while you are away. It is partly my fault he's here. Anyway, I need to kill someone after the trip I had... Tell you later" Andy sighed and pulled out his knife, the blade was a decent length.

"Here, she's been freshly sharpened... Remember the way I showed you? While we are away I will use a payphone to make the ransom call" He said but Blondie was confused.

"Why not that one in the house?" she asked but he shook his head.

"It's too much of a risk using that one unless it's an emergency, not for the first call at least. trust me I know what I'm doing." he kissed her and got in the van and they drove off.

The minute the others left Pat brought out his little folding knife, which was nowhere near as big as Andy but had a bone effect handle and the initials P and C, his surname was Collins, after admiring the blade for a few seconds he then walked over and squatted next to Tegan. Pat then held the blade to her throat menacingly as he put his hand on her thigh.

"She says don't touch but I gotta have a little sample, you won't tell anyone? There's a good girl." His hand slowly went up her thigh and he intended on getting under her blouse when he felt another hand on top of his, he looked down, followed the arm with his eyes all the way up to a smiling Darren, no longer gagged.

"Hi," Darren said with an almost cheerful tone before his features hardened "Now get your hands off her you bloody pervert" and with his other hand swung the chair leg he had picked up at the side of Pat's head, connecting with the bigger man's temple, the force of the hit slammed Pats head to the other wall and he slid down, clearly knocked out, Darren briefly checked the big guy was still breathing then picked up the knife, he took Tegan's gag off her and started to cut the cuffs from her hands.

"Run!" She said in a panic "please just go, if you don't run.. They are going to kill you." but Darren wasn't listening, he sighed as the knife finally cut through her restraint.

"No, not without you," he said with determination "Not leaving you behind with sleeping beauty there." he gestured to Pat.

"Oh Darren, I should of known. Always there to help others in need... You are ruining everything." said a voice behind him, Blondie was back…

CHAPTER 8

Blondie stood at the doorway shaking her head with a look of mock disappointment.

"You couldn't just stay at home and play your sad little online games with your sad little pals could you?" Blondie stalked towards Darren, who had just managed to cut Tegan's wrist restraint and quickly palmed the folding knife into Tegan's hand then he stood to face Blondie as she ran thrusting the knife Andy gave her towards him in anger. Darren moved out the way and she nearly run into the wall, however she dropped the blade when she put out her arms to stop herself. This gave Darren a chance to grab and try to subdue Blondie but she was more than capable of holding her own and there was a struggle, he briefly looked over to see Tegan cutting the cable ties on her ankles.

Tegan took advantage of the distraction to cut her ankle restraints, looking over in horror a the struggle going on infront of her

All Darren wanted was to distract Blondie enough for Tegan to escape but he did hope she would see sense as he managed to pin her to the wall.

"Blondie, come on you know this isn't right, whatever happened. It's not her fault. Please stop this now... She's your family, Please." Darren said. Blondie smiled, that lovely sweet smile he saw nearly every week for a year and a half and then her eyes went hard.

"Like hell I will." and she drove her knee into his groin, the pain, a second time in such a short period, dropped Darren to his knees, Blondie got a spare length of cable that was lying around, probably from the phone line and wrapped it around Darren's neck, pulling hard.

"Goodbye Darren," she said coldly as she gave the cable an extra pull as she watched the fight fade out of him " Sweet dreams."

No, thought Tegan, she couldn't let this happen to him. Her cousin, Lucy, Blondie... Whatever name she went by now, the one who kidnapped her, left her with hardened criminals and sought to ransom her was now trying to kill this guy whose only crime was he wanted to go out with her? No, She couldn't let this happen, Tegan got up... The knife she had used was still in her hand…

He tried to fight but he couldn't breathe. This is it he thought as he glanced where Tegan had been and saw she wasn't there at least that was some comfort as he struggled for breath, suddenly he heard what sounded like someone breathing out after a deep breath, the cable loosening and the sound of something heavy hitting the floor, he turned to see Blondie on the floor, the folding knife sticking out from the base of her neck and blood pooling on the floor. Her eyes were lifeless, she was dead.

Once he got the cord off his neck Darren turned to see Tegan standing frozen to the spot, hands over her nose and mouth, just staring at Blondie. They had to act quickly and get as far away as they could, he grabbed his backpack from the cupboard and swiped what looked like a folded map from the table. For some reason, Darren also relieved the still unconscious Pat of his watch too. He was about to leave when he turned and saw Tegan hadn't moved, She was rooted to the spot in shock. Darren grabbed her wrist and ran outside with Tegan in tow, picked a direction and just ran.

They ran for all they were worth over the nearest hill and and then, without stopping, over another. They were halfway down this particular hill when they came to a sheer drop that would have probably been caused by a landslide in the past, the adrenaline that had gotten them this far was starting to sap out of them as they tried to walk round and down, Darren looked back up the hill and decided.

"We can at least rest up here against the sheer face, if they look at it from up there they won't see the drop and its high enough for us to be hidden" Tegan agreed, the light was fading fast anyway and she didn't like the idea of wandering in the dark.

They came to a section that slightly bevelled inwards so there was a slight overhang. Tegan leaned her back against it and slid down the reality of it all suddenly hit her hard.

"Oh god, I killed her, no, is this all happening, the kidnap, that guy... You, all of it." she burst into tears.

Darren wasn't faring better, the girl he planned to impress this morning is dead after she tried to kill him and now he is on the run with her murderer, who was her cousin whom she kidnapped, what the hell was going on? He sunk to his knees in shock

"What do we do?" He heard Tegan say.

"I don't know, but we killed Blondie, you may have stuck the knife in but I was there too." he said trying to process it all.

"It was self defence!" Tegan shouted through her tears "she was trying to kill you." He understood what she was getting at but he remembered reading something about that a while ago.

"that only works if she attacked you," he got up, walked forward and crouched down in front of her "Look, neither of us are thinking straight, its probably better to wait until the morning and work out what to do then." she looked at him through her tears and nodded.

"Okay," she suddenly noticed how badly the skin on his right wrist had been damaged by the cable ties." Oh God, does that hurt?"

"A little bit yeah." He replied, The trainee nurse in Tegan came to the fore and she stood.

"Take your jacket off and sit," She said with enough authority that Darren did as he was told. Tegan saw the back of his shirt "Warner? Really? Okay." she said to herself as he sat down. Tegan had taken off the fabric around her neck that had been her gag taking time to unpick the knot so it could be used as a bandage of sorts, she then quickly checked his left wrist to see if it needed bandaging too, it wasn't as bad and didn't need one.

"What are you going to do?" Darren said sitting down.

"Arm," she said tapping his right arm and sitting crosslegged next to him "Please," she added and he held his arm up, his sleeve pushed up to the elbow and she started to bandage his wrist in a very specific way. "So where are you from Darren?" she asked as she continued to adjust the makeshift bandage.

"Wishaw," he said watching her with interest, it was clear to him she knew what she was doing,

"Wishaw? I know a girl from there, her name is Heather Donaldson but we don't really talk to each other that much if I'm honest" she said as she finished

"Hmm, it's not a name I'm familiar with" Darren admitted, he then gestured at his bandaged wrist "How do you know how to do that?" he asked as she tied a knot in the bandage

"I'm at university training to be a nurse." she said as she reached behind her head to tease her hair out of its bun "It's not ideal but it will have to do, is it too tight?" He shook his head and wiggled his fingers to show her it was fine.

"Its fine, thank you." Darren said as he pushed his sleeve back down. Tegan knew what she wanted to ask and this was as good a time as any,

"Darren... Why?"

"Why what" he replied.

"Everything, why and how are you here... With me." she said as she let her hair hang loose and sat next to him with her back to the sheer face, so he started from the beginning, about him asking Blondie out, turning up at the foxhunt protest thinking she would be impressed and then went wandering and hoped to see Blondie and ask what was happening.

"Wait," said Tegan looking baffled "you were only there to impress someone? Impress Lucy? You weren't there to actually protest?" Darren made a face that suggested it did seem as stupid as it sounded.

"I admit knowing what I do now it was a pretty dumb idea, even when it was explained to me why they protested I still wasn't convinced to join in properly. I lingered around hoping to talk to her when the hunt returned. That's when I stopped the van, after they said dogs and not hounds and then the second kick you did I knew something was up, just not sure what exactly..then you screamed." Tegan looked at him curiously.

"Why did you stay when you had a chance to go?" This was what she really needed to know "What was it that was stopping you?" Darren shook his head.

"You don't want to know." he said sheepishly.

"I do, is it because of who I am? My family? Hoping for a reward?" she said getting irate, she needed to know, Darren threw his arms up.

"Okay, okay. You really want to know? I saw this beautiful girl," he started carefully "this very beautiful young lady, bound, helpless and scared. I couldn't leave you, Tegan, I just couldn't.." he trailed off but Tegan could make out tears "then I saw how that big brute was looking at you, guys like that eventually find a way to make sure they get what they want and he wanted you, I wasn't going to let him touch you..." he didn't get much else out as Tegan just threw her arms around him.

"Thank you." was all she said through fresh tears.

After a while Darren looked in his bag and produced sandwiches and a bottle of Lucozade orange.

"Hungry?." he asked as he handed her a sandwich, Tegan accepted graciously, the meat was cut too thick and the margarine was thickly spread but it didn't matter to Tegan. Taking a few mouthfuls to drink felt way better than it ever should too.

"One more question, well two questions I guess, you obviously figured out my family must have money, but you have any idea who my family is? Do you really not know who I am?" she just needed to know.

"I'm guessing Galloway cheese and before you ask, I don't want money. I didn't do any of this for a reward." Darren said with a sigh, he really doesn't know she thought, admittedly a few people in her past have assumed her family were the cheese company but to her, this made what he did and the risks he took mean a lot more than they did had he have known her identity.

"No, my father owns the Haulage firm." she said, Darren had a flicker of recognition.

"Oh, I see those trucks and down the motorway, that's your family?" she nodded "As for your sporting achievements, the only famous kid from a Haulage company around here that I know of is the racing driver David Coulthard, his family are part of the firm Hayton Coulthard. I'm Sorry, but unless it's on a football field or going around a formula one track, I don't pay that much attention." something piqued Tegan's curiosity.

"Oh, you follow Formula One? David Coulthard fan? I was at Silverstone last year and I got to meet him before the race so it was kinda hard not to be a fan after that." Darren smiled, they needed this sort of chat, she needed to relax, there's enough time to talk about things in the morning.

"I like DC, he's Scottish so I kinda have to but I support Schumacher." he said, Tegan made a face that suggested she wasn't amused.

"Michael.. Really?" She replied.

"No... Ralf." Darren corrected her, now that was surprising she thought.

"Oh, different I guess," then her mind drifted a little "Darren, back in that van when I was telling you to go, it was because I didn't want you to die because of me. I blame myself for you even being here. At least my parents could pay a ransom and get me out of there.."

"Tegan." Darren said softly.

".. I'd be free, oh sure I'd need a lot of therapy and lord only knows what else..." she continued oblivious.

"Tegan!" he said again, a bit louder this time.

".. But you, they were just…" Darren pulled her close to face him looking deep into her dark brown eyes and tried to tell her as calmly as he could what the more likely scenario was going to be.

"Tegan, they were never going to free you for the same reasons I'd be killed, I'd be able to identify them as I went to college with Blondie but she is... was your cousin after all and she did say something about robbing your parents of what they love."

"I thought she meant money." Tegan said softly, the realization just hitting her, Darren shook his head.

" No," he said "It sounded more personal. Your parents live in a big house and I bet you never wanted for anything like horse related stuff. I'm sure they also put you through university, that sort of thing. Are you close to your parents?"

"Yes, always have been, Although they both ride horses themselves, my mother is the more serious rider of the two so I spend a lot of time with her in the stables and out riding but my father always makes sure he has time to spend with me too, especially at the weekend when he is not in the office." she replied. Darren looked directly into her eyes and smiled.

"It seems like you are very special to them, am I right?" she nodded then replied.

"My mother lost several before they had me, even then I was kept at the hospital for observation, I'm their little miracle, my mother is more like a cool big sister and my dad, the proud look whenever he…" she just started to cry again, she looked up at Darren," It was never really about the ransom, was it? That's just a bonus... Wasn't it?" Darren pulled her in close.

"I can't say for sure but I promise you they will not get the chance." he then reached into his pocket and looked at the watch he took off Pat and put it on as he looked around "It's getting late, we should get some rest." he said.

"here?" she said as she looked around confused.

"Yes here, I agree it's not the most ideal place but it would be dangerous to be roaming about this late" he used the watch, which was a digital one to set an alarm for seven in the morning "we get up just before first light make plans and go but for now.." he went close to the sheer face and tried to smooth the ground as best as he could, Tegan got down and tried to get comfortable and he laid his jacket on her "Here, keep you warm." and he sat next to her looking up at the stars.

"Darren," Tegan said patting the ground next to her "you need rest too, come and lie down.. Please, we really need to share body heat in this weather and we are quite exposed to the elements here as it is." she said to try and reassure him that it was okay so he lay down, cautiously at first, once he had settled Tegan gently spooned him. He could feel her body quiver and shake, could be the cold or fear and possibly both and soon he felt her arm go round and she inched herself closer.

"What were you looking for up there?" She asked innocently.

"You see those three stars close together? That's Orions Belt, most people look for the North Star or the Big Dipper. Not me, it's strange if I see a night sky I look for the Orion's Belt, it's like a weird sanity check I do…"

Tegan knew it was Orions Belt but let him talk as he rambled on about various little details about the stars, space and everything else, his voice was oddly soothing and hearing him talk made her feel safe and protected, she cuddled into his back closer, taking a mental note to ask about why he has Tony Warner's name and number on his shirt, nuzzled in and to her surprise found herself comfortably drifting off slowly to sleep.

Darren felt her get comfortable behind him and noticed she had a death lock on his waist and was cuddled up into his back.

"Tegan," he said thinking she was fully asleep "I won't leave you, I promise you I will do everything I can to get you home and safe." the fact she seemed to pull herself closer still to him suggested she heard, he just lay there, thinking of what to do in the morning.

Tegan admitted to herself that after hearing what he said and knowing he thought she wasn't awake, couldn't help but be touched, how could Lucy, or anyone else for that matter, take advantage of a guy like that? She pressed her ear against his back so she could faintly hear his heartbeat, something about the rhythm of his heart beating helped Tegan off to sleep.

CHAPTER 9

Andy had the number of Netherfield House ready, they had decided a phone box would be better at least for first contact, he dialled it up, it was answered quickly by a panicked Quentin.

"Hello... Tegan?" He asked flustered.

"No," said Andy "But we are enjoying your beautiful daughter's company.."

"Don't you dare harm her…" Quentin shouted.

"I dare anything I want," Andy said "But no she is not harmed.. Yet, see here's what you are going to do, first no cops and no reporters, if I see anything about this in the papers or on the news you will never see her alive again." there was a long pause.

"Okay." he said finally.

"Secondly, I am a fair man so you will have until Thursday at noon to put together the ransom money, it's just five hundred thousand." Andy smirked.

"Five hundred… Okay, okay. Is she okay, can I talk to her... Please." his tone was pleading.

"She's fine but you can't speak to her, not tonight. Will phone again tomorrow at the same time, if you don't answer she will die." he hung up and went to the Van to help Joe and Frank pack it with various microwavable meals, burgers and snacks they had bought, he noticed a few crates of Tennents Lager.

"There is a microwave there isn't there Joe?" Said Frank ever the sceptic "I don't want to eat cold burgers for the next few days." Joe just looked at him.

"There's two actually," he said, obviously annoyed "remember? You asked for a backup one?"

"Quit your bickering you two and get in the bloody van," Andy ordered "Blondie is probably trying to pull Pat away from the girl by now."

"I suppose," said Joe "He is a big liability, you do know that." Andy stood and shook his head.

"I know, I know but I have my reasons, and for some reason, Blondie gets on well with him." He tried to justify his choice but the expressions on the other two suggested they still weren't convinced.

"We better get back." Joe said to break the awkward silence.

The drive back was awkward in the dark.

"Andy, do you think she has done the deed yet?" Frank said with a tinge of regret, he was glad he wasn't there to witness it.

"Oh she would have, Blondie can be ruthless when she wants to be, probably did it in front of her cousin to freak her out," Andy replied, "she has a mean streak like that."

"Charming," Joe said, rolling his eyes and looking at Frank "I'm guessing we will be on grave digging detail." Frank shook his head and then hit the brakes, they nearly missed the driveway turn off.

"Damn, it's these country roads," Frank shouted, "they all look the bloody same."

"Frank you should get your eyes tested," Andy quipped "either that or better headlights for the van."

"It's a bit quiet," Frank noted, avoiding Andy's comment as they stopped "No lights on." they decided to unpack the van after they checked things out, something wasn't right. Joe went in first and put on the light but as Andy went to follow Joe stopped him.

"Andy, you don't want to see this trust me," he said calmly but Andy pushed past "Don't want to see what?".. Then he saw it... Saw Blondie in a pool of her own blood... Dead.

Andy ran over to Blondie's corpse and started to cry as he held the body close.

"No, not now... We were so close... So close." his hand brushed metal on her throat, he looked down and saw Pat's knife in her sticking out, he looked over at Pat who was trying to regain consciousness with Frank and Joe's help, the stupid bastard, he tried something on with that girl, she must have gotten free or something, a dozen scenarios played out in his mind making him angrier and angrier so much so he walked up and started to repeatedly kick Pat in his crotch, or just knife him. Andy wasn't sure what would be more fitting.

"You bastard, you couldn't wait you couldn't wait for the ransom.." Frank pulled Andy off him as Joe took Pat away to lay him on one of the camp beds they had set up in the bedroom. Pat should go to the hospital but there would be too many questions.

"Calm down, the guy has a bad concussion and we don't know what happened," He looked into Andy's eyes "Blondie is gone but we still have a job to do, she would want to see it through," the fight in Andy's eyes dulled just a little "Andy, think about it, about the ransom. All that money."

"Your right," but then Frank saw Andy's eyes go cold and hard "When we get them back, I will kill them both... after he is made to watch Pat enjoy her," and an evil grin came over his lips and leaned closer " The he dies too, Frank I was going to ask her to marry me after all this, let me have my revenge." Frank nodded slowly, he wasn't so sure about this but decided it's best to go along with it when Andy gets in these moods.

"Joe," said Frank "Contact the nearby farms and other residential areas, let's put Operation Detox into effect." Joe had the same idea and was already on the phone.

"And what about him, what do I say about hero boy?" Joe asked, Operation Detox was a backup plan if she escaped and was one of Joe's more inventive ideas.

"Be creative, then get some more of the boys from Glasgow just in case we need extra help finding them, maybe ask Malcolm to come too, he has experience of hunting..." Andy said to Joe.

"Andy, get some sleep, we need you fully rested okay mate?" Andy nodded, "Don't worry we will clean the place up." interrupted Frank

Andy reluctantly left the room and everything was cleaned up as best as they could Joe sat on a seat head in hands.

"Frank, what the hell happened here?" He said, then decided to rephrase the question "what do you think happened?" Frank sighed and sat down himself.

"If I had to guess our hero boy has a lot to do with this, I would bet you anything at the very least he freed himself and the girl." Frank answered.

"Oh," Joe said but Frank explained the situation when they changed the wheel, Joe nodded "Sounds like he didn't run because of the girl, he wasn't going to escape without her. At least that's what I think." he said, Frank agreed, it did make some sense now he thought of it and if he was honest Frank had even more respect for the kid for making sure he took the girl with him.

"Sounds like the guy has some very strict morals." Frank eventually said, Joe nodded thoughtfully.

"Well, we have a big day of planning in the morning, I'm going to call it a night." said Joe stretching.

"Me too." Frank agreed.

Andy felt a bit numb as he walked into the bedroom and collapsed on the nearest camp bed, seeing Blondie, the girl he loved, lifeless on the floor like that was a sight he wasn't sure he could ever get over. It's not like it was his first corpse but it was still a huge shock. he didn't even remember falling asleep.

"Come to bed Quentin, it's late." Said Olivia as she stood at the entrance to his study at Netherfield, He looked at his wife, her black hair showing signs of grey, the slender body covered in her bathrobe. It was obvious who Tegan took after in the looks department.

"I should have known something wasn't right," he said as much to himself as to Olivia "there is no way a rider of her talent and ability would have fallen at the fence near where we found her helmet. Somehow they knew she would be there, I don't know how but they did" he buried his head in his hands "I have to pay, there's no other way or risk losing her forever." He said with a helpless tone in his voice. Before the phone call, he and a few friends from the hunt were out and retracing their steps and found nothing, though one of the other riders did remember seeing a black van in an odd place when they rode past it during the hunt and it wasn't there now but apart from that, nothing was found. Quentin was about to call the police but then Andy had phoned with the ransom demand.

"I'm worried too, especially with her anxiety and panic attacks." Olivia said as she sat on the desk.

"She still gets those?" Quentin asked, puzzled "I mean as bad as she used to, I know something like that doesn't simply go away."

"Oh yes," Olivia replied, "not as bad as before I admit but she still gets them, she had an attack today I think, she was more nervous and on edge than I saw her in quite a while, luckily seeing Lucy helped her calm down."

"I did talk to Lucy for a bit and introduced her to Mrs Galbraith, who made her feel very welcome. Lucy has matured into a lovely girl, I'm glad Tegan and her started talking again." Quentin sighed.

"I know, Tegan noticeably relaxed when she saw Lucy," Olivia had a few tears in her eyes" We raised a kind, loving daughter Quentin and we have a lot to be proud of her and I hope and pray she is safe, I don't want to think of the alternative." He got up and held her close.

"I will get her back I promise, they want half a million, then that's what I will do, I just want Tegan back."

Darren couldn't sleep, it had nothing to do with Tegan's death grip on him, if he was honest Darren was afraid the kidnappers would be out to try and find them, he couldn't sleep, he couldn't fail Tegan, eventually, oddly his thoughts turned To Blondie, he really thought she was different. She did truly give the impression that she genuinely did like him as opposed to putting up with him the way other girls did, instead, she played him like a fiddle and he let her do it in the slim hope he could turn the situation around. Something about seeing her walk in, seeing him bound and gagged and her reaction to him made him wonder if he ever really did know her.

Then there was Tegan, no one could ever convince him she deserved any of this. He felt her weight shift slightly and she moved in her sleep and it felt like her cheek was resting on his arm, her arm still wrapped around and holding on tight he repositioned himself on his back gently to get more comfortable, she sleepily readjusted her position again so she had her head on his chest, one arm and one leg over him. Darren repositioned his jacket that she was using as a blanket to cover her better. They were lucky it wasn't raining and there was only a slight wind.

He found himself looking at her face, she was a very attractive young lady with a natural beauty who didn't need makeup, hair dye or anything a lot of others her age would do to change how she looked in order to look pretty, yet because of that he imagined she would probably get overlooked a lot as a result. He wrapped his arm around Tegan tight and protective, she responded by snuggling in deeper. Darren had to get her safely home, he promised her, he just had to brave the elements of an unfamiliar area, make sure she is safe from harm, oh, and avoid recapture by a notorious crime family.

He must be crazy, but he couldn't and wouldn't let her down, he looked at her peaceful innocent looking face, he had to get her to safety and that is all that mattered to Darren

Linda looked concerned as she climbed into bed next to her girlfriend Ellen.

"What's wrong." Ellen asked as she put her waist length hair into a ponytail.

"What? Oh," Linda said distractedly "just thinking

of my friend, I've told you about Darren haven't I?" Ellen thought for a minute.

"The redhead who seems to have slept with half of Glasgow? That one?" she said eventually "I would be more worried about the girls he has been with."

"No, that's Jason, Darren is the one who thinks he's in love with that little bitch Blondie and she just uses him." Linda said with surprising venom in her voice as she explained what happened at college and Darren's doomed attempt to ask her out and the fact she has heard nothing since, Darren wasn't even on MSN Messenger tonight.

"Maybe they did hook up Linda, she can't be that bad surely." Ellen said as she put her arm around Linda but Linda shook her head.

"Not Blondie, ever since I was introduced to her there was something off about her, every guy she would be around would be useful to her and no more," Linda looked at Ellen sadly "she knew Darren had a crush on her, and I saw her manipulate him time and again. I would do my best to get him to see sense. He has been a good friend to me and I just wish he would meet a nice girl. I just hope he is okay." Linda cuddled into Ellen.

"You have college on Monday, I can imagine you will walk into class, is he the one that's always early?" Ellen said, Linda nodded and let Ellen continue "you will see him there and no doubt he will have some reasonable explanation for not being in touch."

"You are probably right." Linda said yet if she was honest she wasn't sure she really believed that.

CHAPTER 10

Tegan woke up with a start when she heard the watch alarm go off, she saw Darren sitting on the ground, it was still dark but he was straining his eyes to try and read the map, she didn't know why but the fact he hadn't ran off and left her comforted her more than she thought it would.

"What are you thinking?" She asked yawning.

"Well," he sighed "We need to decide who to contact if and when we get the chance. I don't think phoning the police is the best idea, we don't know what has been told. There's my mother but she doesn't drive, neither does my brother, they have to rely on others and the less involved the less can go wrong." Tegan thought for a second.

"We could contact my parents, both drive, they could pick us up and take us back to the house. Then I suppose we can contact the police and anyone else from there." it made sense.

"That's you sorted, just need…" Darren was about to talk but Tegan cut him off.

"Darren, you will come with me and I'm not taking no for an answer, I will explain to my dad what you did for me. Look, you have saved me from god knows what already and are continuing to protect me out here even now, the least my family can do is help you out with the fallout of all this." she said pointedly. Darren smiled weakly.

"Thank you, that actually means a lot," It was a change to hear a girl wanting to do something for him "I'm not a map reading expert but they clearly marked the house they had us in on this map but there are other little red dots that look like cottages, farmhouses and places like that."

"Maybe head to one of those and use their phone?" Tegan mused.

"We could, there is one quite close," he pointed to the distance and Tegan could see some lights "I say we head there then," he smiled " Have you home soon in no time."

Tegan handed Darren his jacket back but he folded it and put it in the bag after rearranging the food.

"Won't you be cold?" Tegan asked as he put the bag on his back.

"No, trust me this is a warm top and I don't feel as restricted," He gave her a reassuring smile "I'll be fine."

There was a lot of activity at the safehouse as people started to turn up, Andy had called in a lot of favours from associates of the Donnelly family, being careful to select people who wouldn't tell Andy's older brothers what was going on. Andy wanted to keep the whole thing secret from them until it had reached its successful end. Pat walked up to Andy nervously, his head still feeling terrible.

"Andy, I'm sorry. I don't know how but the guy got free.." He tried to explain but Andy didn't want to hear it, besides Pat's fate was sealed, once he did one more thing for Andy.

"Pat, you want to make up for last night?" Pat nodded "when we get that little bitch back, do your worst to her, promise?"

"Oh I promise all right." said Pat smiling.

"I have only one request, I'm the one that kills her, after you have some fun of course." Andy said, but was thinking first he would dispose of her and then dispose of Pat.

Tegan and Darren had just reached the gates of the farmhouse when they saw what looked like a man and wife coming round from the rear, Tegan waved to them and the couple gestured for them to come over.

"Hi I'm Tegan Galloway.." she started when the man said.

"Miss Galloway? Well hello to you too, you are the young showjumper that has been in the papers aren't you? My wife and I have heard all about you young lady" the Man said exchanging a look with the lady who Darren just assumed, correctly, was his wife, both looked middle aged with touches of grey in their brown hair, hers was slightly lighter "I'm Peter and this is Irene." they shook hands with her but didn't offer Darren a handshake.

"Could we use your phone please?" Tegan asked sweetly "it would mean a lot." Irene smiled warmly and took Tegan gently by the arm.

"Come in my girl, you look frozen... " Darren went to follow when Peter put his hand on Darren's shoulder.

"Best staying out here until they are done. You know how women can be," he said in a way that he knew all too well how what his wife was like, the minute the door closed Darren heard a definite sound of a door locking and then Peter just looked at him coldly "How could you?" He said, all pleasantness gone from his voice "your kind sickens me."

Tegan was so busy thanking Irene she didn't notice the door being locked but when she didn't see Darren with her she started to worry.

" Where's Darren?" she asked, suddenly nervous her hands started to tremble "where is he, the guy I came with."

"Oh he is just having a chat with Peter outside, Don't you worry now I need to Check something then I will let you use the phone, okay?" her voice suggested she was trying to sound soothing yet Tegan wasn't comforted, it felt she was being talked down to "Please sit down, you are safe now," then Irene leaned closer " You don't need to fear him now, you're safe here." what was she on about, safe from him, from who. She hadn't mentioned anything to suggest she was in any trouble. Something wasn't right, it felt like they were deliberately keeping them apart. Her feet were starting to hurt a bit too, riding boots were not made for long hikes unless on horseback and were especially not suitable the rough terrain they had already walked through, yet she didn't feel safe taking them off in a stranger's house. Tegan knew how difficult the boots would be to get back on again especially if her feet or ankles swell, it occurred to her maybe that may be why Irene was being so insistent, she looked to see where Irene went and she heard what must be Irene on the telephone.

"Ah Joseph, how are you?... Is Andrew here?.. Hello Andrew.. .yes that poor Galloway girl you told us about... Yes, the girl you warned us about, the one you were put through... What was it... Yes, extreme detox... Yes.. Oh he's outside with my husband... Don't want a drug pusher in my place... Better come quick, the poor girl is shaking... " Tegan didn't need to hear anymore, she ran to the door but there was no key.

Andy was all smiles as he grabbed his jacket

"Frank, Joe, you two come with me. They are at Greenhill Farm." Andy said with manic glee as they headed to the Van.

Peter was in the middle of a full on rant,

"That girl is an Olympic hopeful and here you are ruining her life trying to score her more drugs when she's trying to get off them," Peter said... He was having a full on rant " what is it you have that sweet girl on, huh? You got her injecting herself? I could see a sicko like you getting off on injecting her yourself, your kind sicken me," Darren couldn't believe what he was hearing "She was sent here to get away from the likes of you that's what they said." Darren just stood gobsmacked.

"What the bloody hell are you talking about and who said that? Drug dealer? Me? hell I don't smoke, barely drink and I don't take or sell drugs," Darren said, obviously exasperated, though Peter clearly wasn't listening, just then he could hear the front door attempt to open but was locked "Tegan!" he shouted and ran to the door, he could hear her on the other side panicking.

"Darren! Help! Please!" she was having a full meltdown, her body shaking and all she could hear is Irene, Tegan was resisting the urge to hum even if it would drown out the crazy woman next to her.

"Tegan, dear, you need to calm down. It's a side effect of the drugs leaving your system they said." what the hell was this crazy woman on about, drugs? Tegan never touched the stuff, even refused to take anxiety medication. The constant urging to sit down and relax and she will soon get the help she needs was not what she needed to hear either, they were coming for her.

"Darren!! Please!!" she cried and then in barely a whisper "help me."

On hearing that Darren tried to shoulder the door but Peter interjected himself between Darren and the door.

"She is going nowhere with you, you are a dirty little scumbag, you know that, now get off my property."

"No," said Darren pinching the bridge of his nose in frustration "Not without her. Please listen, If I was a scumbag would I suggest this? Contact her father, tell her you have seen her. Contact Galloway Haulage or Netherfield House, take your pick, listen to her, something is scaring her out of her mind and it's not bloody drugs... You are the one putting her life in danger not me," but Peter started to rant again, Darren looked out the corner of his eye and in the distance he saw the black van coming down the road. Darren just took a breath "This isn't personal but if I can't go through your door.." and he picked up one of the large stone animal statues that adorned either side of the door and went to the nearest window, Peter realised what Darren was going to do and tried to wrestle it out of Darren's grasp, the van was getting closer so Darren, with some effort, yanked the statue out of Peter's hands and threw it at the window.

The smashing of the window startled both ladies inside but Tegan reacted the quicker and ran for the open window, knocking Irene down, as she looked out the broken window she could see the black van get closer.

"Tegan! Hurry!" Darren shouted as Tegan climbed out the window as quickly and safely as she could and he took her hand as they just ran into the nearby trees and kept going out the other side and did not stop until they reached a hedge line to hide behind in case they were followed.

".. He was wearing a grey or silver top of some sort with the number thirty four on it.." Irene was saying to Andy, she seemed quite level headed all things considered. She had given accurate descriptions of both of them but Peter the husband was just angry and ranting

"Never mind that, look at what the hooligan did to my window," Peter said frantically pointing " Am I going to be compensated?"

Andy was livid, he had to control the urge to just kill this couple and be done with it but he calmed down enough to think of a response, Joe and Frank were there too but had wandered off to check the immediate area for the runaways.

"Compensation? No, you didn't wait for us to come to confront him did you?" Andy said, Peter looked like the sanctimonious type who couldn't help himself and go about it mob handed.

"You said yourself, she could be a future Olympian if she kicked the drugs," Peter stated defiantly "we did our best to keep her here until you arrived."

"Okay, I apologise, there will be a check in the post to compensate you, one thousand be enough?" Andy said, lying through his teeth. He saw Peters's eyes light up. Just a pity no such check will actually be posted, Joe came back and shook his head, he couldn't find them.

Frank was starting to wonder if all this effort is worth it. Revenge killing is one thing but this seemed a bit much even for a seasoned guy like him. Not to mention this was like looking for a needle in a haystack so he decided to head back to the van. He found himself rooting for the kid. Hard not to, he was the only thing between her and Pat's lustful thoughts, never mind the ultimate fate Andy has in store for her.

"Anything Frank?" Andy asked when he returned.

"Nothing." He replied as he got back in the van.

"What are you thinking Andy?" Joe asked as he closed the door.

"Well we know roughly what way they are headed and I'm not running through the woods, We will go back to the safe house and I think Malcolm was working out strategic points to send our guys," Andy said, thinking "it's the only way."

They had seen Frank look around at the treeline but thankfully he didn't see them and waited till he was gone before moving a muscle. As Darren tried to get up Tegan hugged him tight and wouldn't let go, she was in floods of tears.

"Please don't leave me like that again, please." she sobbed, all Darren could do was hold her close.

"Tegan, they didn't give us any option but I promise from now on I won't leave you if I can help it, okay?" he said, he could hear the desperation and fear in her voice "I'm here for you." Even just hearing that made her relax a little. He comforted her a while before she was able to compose herself enough but before they moved on Darren made a decision.

"I think we need a new plan," he said, getting the map out "I don't trust these little farms, cottages or even small villages. It sounds like they have told people that you are on some detox to rid yourself of drugs, so if you show up they will phone up Andy and the boys and they come and bring you back and I am the nasty man supplying you the drugs."

"That sounds about right from the way that Irene woman was acting around me and from what she was saying on the telephone, what do we do?" she looked at him expectantly, he shook his head, it was a crazy idea but they had to do it.

"We walk to the nearest town and avoid being seen by everyone until we get there, there are too many variables to control and I'm sure we could use a payphone and reverse the charge if need be," he said patting his pockets, "I think my wallet must have been taken when I was being restrained in the van. it's going to be tricky, until we get there we need to avoid being seen by walkers, cars and also trying to avoid cottages, farmhouses. basically everything and everyone. But you will have to put your total trust in me."

"You have it." she said out loud and then to herself said, "you always had it."

CHAPTER 11

Darren had the map unfolded on the ground in front of him and seemed to be deep in thought, Tegan watched as would make seemingly random measurements with his thumb and forefinger and muttered to himself.

"So," Said Tegan eventually, "Where to?"

"Not much choice, Biggar seems the closest but it's not the most ideal," He said with a sigh "Ironicly it's not the biggest town in the area." he folded the map and then tried to get up, succeeding on his second attempt Tegan had noticed he had been showing signs of sleep deprivation and he was finding it harder to concentrate, he especially looked uneasy on his feet.

"Darren, did you sleep at all last night?" she didn't remember him doing so, he shook his head.

"No, I was trying to think of ways to get out of this. Didn't get much sleep the night before if I'm honest," then added "my first priority is to get you out of here and back home, I will be able to sleep when you are safe." Tegan stood up and looked around and saw there was a small grouping of trees and long grass nearby. It wasn't ideal but it will have to do, all she needed to do was convince him to rest a while.

"Okay, I need you to trust me, can you do that?" she asked.

"Can't think of a reason why I wouldn't, why?" he shrugged with a slight smile.

"Right, Darren before we do anything you need to get some sort of sleep.." she waved away his protests "Darren, trust me please, I'm a nurse... well I will be one day, you really need to rest because right now you are running on empty. Look, It will only be for an hour, okay?"Darren reluctantly nodded

"I suppose you're right, just for an hour though, okay?" Tegan nodded but she planned to let him sleep longer but knew he would not agree even if it was for his own benefit "now let me take your bag for a while." He slipped it off and handed it to her and they made their way to the small grouping of trees.

The best spot she found for them was near the middle of the tree grouping at the base of the largest trunk, there was a dip in between two of the bigger roots.

"Only an hour." Darren stated as he tried to make himself comfortable, using his jacket as a blanket but he couldn't get his head comfortable so Tegan sat on the ground with him and patted her thigh.

"It's okay." she said smiling softly.

"Only if you are sure." and hesitantly rested his

head on her thigh, Tegan stroked his close cropped hair and she started to hum the tune to Loch Lomond, to try and relax him, she wasn't sure why she chose the tune she usually hummed when she was nervous to relax Darren but it was the first song that came to mind, soon he was fast asleep.

She kept an eye on the time, being careful not to stay here too long, but to give Darren more than an hour. Tegan looked down at him and she decided that while he was by his own admission not the best looking guy, he more than made up for it with his heart and if she was honest she found him attractive in his own way.

"Oh Tegan," she said to herself "what is happening to you." she found herself just stroking the back of his neck, he snored but she didn't mind, her mind drifted to what she would have been doing today. That was easy, it's a Sunday, she would have been at mass in the morning with her mum then if she wasn't in the stables she was studying or vice versa. She wished she could somehow let her parents know she was safe, for the time being anyway. She thought back to that horrible moment in that cottage. The fear of being recaptured had reduced her to a nervous wreck. she looked down at the sleeping Darren, if it hadn't been for him... she really didn't want to think about that yet there was something about Darren himself, she didn't know what it was about him but she felt different around Darren and she found it easy to put her trust in him. Tegan continued to stroke his hair absently and looked around her.

RIDE OR DIE

The hills were peaceful and the only noises she could hear were the typical noises of nature. Sometimes when she would take Princess for a nice ride Tegan would just stop somewhere quiet and admire the scenery. It's easy to miss out on the small details. Darren turned over in his sleep, he was still using her left thigh as an impromptu pillow. Tegan drew her right leg was drawn up close to her body as her leg was getting sore, it must have been something she was sitting on.

As she rubbed her sore hamstring muscle as best she could, Tegan noticed her riding boots were getting a bit dirty. They weren't the new Cavallo brand ones she got for Christmas, those were back home still in the box and hadn't been broken in yet. These ones she had on now had been worn in her most recent competitions, she kept her leather riding boots mainly for more formal occasions like showjumping, hunts, though sometimes Tegan would just wore them for when she wanted to look her best going out horse riding in general. However, she had her rubber riding boots for more casual rides and chore work around the stables, in fact, she would be the first to admit she wore her riding boots, especially the rubber ones quite a lot.

The big disadvantage to this particular pair of leather boots was, like most riding boots, they have a thin sole for better contact with the stirrups which was great for riding, however, these had such thin soles that along with other factors like the rough uneven ground made them not so practical for long distance walking, never mind running. Getting them on and off at the best of times is hard and she didn't have her boot pull hooks

98

with her, so she decided that until she is safe and home back at Netherfield she will keep them on and do her best to soldier on through the discomfort.

Just then she heard voices in the distance and she looked round and through the tall grass, she could see over at the farm where they were nearly recaptured there were a few people spread out checking the immediate area.

She dare not move plus she could tell by the rapid eye movements behind the eyelids Darren was deep in sleep, it was not the best time to wake him as he would be groggy and disoriented and she couldn't leave him, not after everything he had done for her. Tegan had to stay and hope she wasn't seen.

Then something emerged from the hedge line, it was a fox of all things and it stared at her and looked like it was ready to run away.

"Oh no," she realised if it ran there was a chance it would give them away "Please don't run, if you do the nasty men will find us, please don't run," the fox just continued to stare at her as if trying to decide what to do "please don't run." she said again pleadingly.

Frank had taken a couple of the guys back to the last known location to search the area properly to see if there was anything, any indication of direction at least, one of the new arrivals, a short redhead called Scott walked up to him.

"Shame about Blondie, She was stunning, which

one did it?"Frank looked at the guy like he was mad.

"What the hell man," he shouted, "don't discuss things like that here." Scott was not the brightest but was useful to Andy, what use was that? Frank was still to find out.

The search was fruitless, Frank had told Andy it was a waste and that couple was asking too many questions too. Something in the small grouping of trees in the distance caught his eye, a black shape. He knew he should go up and check it out. No one else noticed it and if he was honest, this had turned from a simple ransom kidnapping into a manhunt to kill and he didn't sign up for that but only stayed out of loyalty to Andy. Personally, a very real part of him wanted them to escape, all she seemed to have done is live the life Blondie wanted and all he did was be there at the wrong time, this wasn't like the time they took Ricky Campbells boy. Ricky was a rival who needed to be taught a lesson and the kid was returned. Regardless he decided this was the last job he did for Andy.

They got back in the van and Peter and Irene were talking to Frank.

"Hope you find that girl and get her the help she needs." said Irene.

"And string him up from the tallest tree." Peter added, Frank looked at the boarded up window and had to admit if it had been Frank and a girl he liked was needing help he would do the same... And he wasn't even sure that's how that kid saw the girl.

"Don't worry we will do our best." he said eventually and got in the van and drove off, Scott was sitting next to him.

"Frank, me and the lads were wondering, is it just Pat who gets to enjoy the girl or can others.." his head was slammed off the dashboard and Frank spoke loudly so everyone heard.

"If we catch them and anyone here touches her.. I'll put a knife in them myself, got that?" a weary chorus of affirmative followed, Frank looked at the map to see where else was marked out for searching.

"Hold." he said thrusting the map in Scott's hands once they checked out all the probable ways they could have gone the next thing to do was to try and place people along probable routes, they had, excluding Andy, Joe, himself and, for obvious reasons, Pat, about twelve people which didn't sound like much but there were few easy ways to get back to Strathaven. Andy believed that's where they would be heading. Frank believed the smart thing would be to find and follow a road but after today they probably wouldn't try and flag a car down or approach any residences for fear of something similar to what happened earlier occurring again. If he was honest it was getting a bit too complicated for Frank's liking.

Tegan was still silently pleading with the fox not to run when she noticed the people had left the area.

"Thank you." she said quietly and the fox just moved away at a leisurely pace, Tegan just rested her head against the tree and closed her eyes, that was close she thought. She didn't see where the fox went though it was probably safe in the hills, she couldn't imagine a hunt faring well out here, her attentions turned back to Darren as he stirred in his sleep and seemed unsettled, almost instinctively she stroked his hair again and he quickly settled back into a deep sleep.

It had been over two hours before Darren started to stir, Tegan had not moved away from him the entire time. he started to look uneasy then suddenly woke and brought himself up in a sitting position strangely alert, almost frantic before looking round and seeing Tegan and his shoulders sagged a little in relief. Before she could speak he put his arms around her.

"Thank God you are safe." he said.

"What's wrong?" she asked, there had been a few times when he was sleeping she was sure he murmured her name.

"Don't ask," he said sadly, she could see he was troubled "please don't." he repeated, Tegan needed some sort of answer

"Nightmares?" she asked, all he could do was nod but she realised she needed to know more, that look in his eyes when he woke up... Something was haunting him.

"Darren," she started "tell me, please. If we are to get through this you need to be able to tell me things, to trust me." He looked at her and the look he had was one of fear.

"Tegan, I am scared I will somehow fail you and they will catch you again, I'm afraid of what they will do to you." she didn't know what to say, one look at him told her that Darren meant every word he said. People will say they fear failure but Darren literally feared failing and even more so failing her personally. Darren really feared failing her, she could see it in his eyes. Another thing she noticed was that he didn't care what happened to him, it was all about her. Tegan knew she had to say something to reassure him before it consumed him, she sat infront of him and leaned forward, hugging him.

"Darren, please listen to me," she thought about how Blondie used him and how others probably used him. "We are in this together, I know you won't fail me, you haven't before and something tells me you are not about to start now," Tegan then pulled back and took his hand "I have every confidence in you, I trust you more than you will ever know," she looked around, realising it would be for the best if they didn't stay here longer than they had to "I guess we should probably get moving." she said as she stood and helped him up. "Have you been to Biggar yourself?"

"No," he replied "you? "

"No, looks like it's a first for us both then." she said with a shy smile.

CHAPTER 12

The hills were hard going, especially for Tegan who once again had to stop with sore feet, they chose a spot amongst some heather to sit. Darren looked thoughtful.

"I thought I'd miss her, Blondie that is," he said lost in his own mind "but I don't, I carried a torch for her, I idolised her for over a year and a half, why am I not crying my eyes out?.. Why am I not blaming you?" He said looking at her carefully, sadly Tegan felt similar.

"I can't answer that, all I know is when I saw her strangling you I didn't see my cousin, I saw the hate in her eyes. growing up she was the pretty one, she was the confident one. I was this plain, awkward kid who only felt at ease around horses but she always helped me, was kind. The girl you described to me sounds like a different person. At that moment... Seeing you fight for air, I couldn't let her do it... I… " she trailed off and started to softly cry, Darren comforted her.

"It's okay Tegan, no one blames you," he looked her and... There was something about those brown doe eyes of hers that just captured his attention, her hair, the few times he has seen her smile it has been this beautiful understated... No, it's not right he shouldn't be thinking this. What was wrong with him? It wasn't that long ago he was having feelings for Blondie and now here he is thinking about how attractive her cousin is? He averted his gaze just enough to end such thoughts "It feels like I fell for a girl who never really existed I guess."

"I have to ask, just how did she get the nickname Blondie?" Tegan asked curiously.

"It's not the most exciting of stories if I'm honest," he said, remembering it vividly "It's our first day of lectures and I'm sitting next to my friend Jason and the lecturer is trying to explain a few things about what to expect from this class, anyway here's Blondie, talking away to the girl next to her and he's trying to get her to listen and then just shouts 'hey... Blondie' and she reacted then. Whenever anyone wanted her attention they would should 'Hey Blondie' the way he did and it stuck." Tegan nodded absently.

"She loved her hair, saw it as her best feature." she said.

"Tegan, what actually happened with your family and hers, why did she want revenge like this?" Darren asked "I get the feeling her version of events would be slightly skewed a bit."

"Well I can tell you what my mother told me, apparently when the recession started he was affected big time so dad helped, then again and again but the next time tried to help a different way, getting in someone to look at spending and the likes, but no, he just wanted the money, Dad refused and that's what happened." she said honestly.

"Sounds like he didn't want help, just money." Darren said Thoughtfully, Tegan agreed.

"Dad wanted to help him get into a position he didn't need help, maybe he would have got something if he had shown he could get into such a position but I think greed got to him," she thought for a minute "I thought extending an olive branch, inviting her along to the hunt would mend some bridges, how wrong I was." Tegan cuddled into Darren trying to block out what happened that day.

"Tegan you were doing the right thing, if anything it sounds like she has always had a gift for manipulation. You weren't to know she would do anything like this." He put a comforting arm around her. Tegan just sat cuddling into him for a few minutes more then she dried the tears from her eyes and looked around.

"We best get a move on I think." she got up, he noticed she kept the bag on as if she felt she was doing her bit by carrying it, they walked on trying to at least get out of the worst of the hills.

"How much food do we still have?" Darren asked, Tegan opened the bag,

"about three sandwiches which need to be eaten soon, I'm sure neither of us wants food poisoning do we? and a bottle of Lucozade left but I kept the empty one to fill with water and a large bar of aero mint, we need to find a way to resupply, I was never one for living off the land and the only plant I saw that's edible is the nettle so no thanks." Darren looked at her that said she might not like it, mainly because he didn't like it either.

"We will need to steal it somehow," He said with reluctance "a campsite, car, somewhere, neither of us have money so it's the only option." Tegan agreed, as the continued she looked distracted about something in the distance and pointed to something flapping in the heather near the top of the nearest hill.

"What is that?" she said jogging over as best she could with Darren following.

"Some tarpaulin by the looks of it," he guessed as she picked it up it was dark green with a few small holes and tears in it, some rope through the eyelets too Tegan rolled it up as best she could, using the rope to secure it to Darren's bag "could come useful It's not much but could give us some sort of shelter, I wonder what it's doing out here?" she looked up to see Darren just stand up at the top of the hill looking down at the other side. Tegan finished securing the Tarpaulin and then went up to join him "What?" she said turning around, she saw what Darren was looking at.

There was another cottage at the bottom of the hill, a long private road leading to it and a few outbuildings and a few vehicles and trailers.

"Probably came from there," he noted, suddenly he felt both Tegan's hands grab his wrist and pull him back down the hill to the spot where she found the tarpaulin "Tegan! .." he started but as he turned around saw the look of worry on her face "Don't worry, As I said before We will avoid places like this," he took Tegan's hand and looked into her soulful eyes "I'm not going to risk having another incident like this morning, I promise we will find a way around it, okay?" Tegan nodded and Darren decided before they went further to check the map "Well I do have good news, we are going in the right direction, see?" He showed her the map and pointed out where they started, the cottage they were separated at and then the one over the hill behind them. As Darren folded the map up and put it in his jacket pocket, Tegan suddenly had a horrible thought.

"It's probably not a good idea to hang about here too long," she said trying to sound calm "Even if the people down there haven't seen us, what if.. They show up, ask questions, search the area.. " she trailed off and inched closer to Darren, holding on to his arm and resting her head on his shoulder. She didn't need to say anything else.

"Your right," He said "We will need to take a bit of a detour but we should be fine, at least this time no one seen us and we got something useful out of it." he said, gesturing to the tarpaulin that was half folded, half rolled and dangling from his bag. She managed a slight smile then they started the long walk around the hill to avoid the cottage, Tegan holding Darren's hand tight the whole time.

They had been walking for a while when she noticed that Darren looked like he had something on his mind.

"What is it?" she asked.

"Oh Just something that's been on my mind ever since this morning," he said as he gathered his thoughts "when it comes to horse riding are you really, How do I word it, that good? Or was the whole Olympic hopeful thing just something made up as part of the trap to recapture you?" He asked as they stopped halfway up a hill. Tegan looked at him and sighed before sitting down on the hill and he sat beside her, Tegan gave him a shy smile before starting.

"Where to begin?" she said thoughtfully "Well, I have won my share of competitions but its mainly journalists who make me out to be some wonder kid. I will be honest though, it had been suggested by my trainer if I keep up my current level of performance there is a very good chance I could be in the running for the Athens Olympic team in four years. Unfortunately, some papers have hinted I might be in the Sydney team this year." it made sense now, her possibly being part of the Great Britain Olympic team wasn't a total exaggeration by the media, it was when and what Olympics she would probably compete in.

"Is being in the Olympics something you would want to do though?" Darren asked, Tegan gave him a pleasantly surprised look before answering

"You know something? Not one person has ever actually asked me that, they just assume I do. Don't get me wrong, I would love to. But I personally don't think I am ready yet, in the future, yes but not now and when ever I get interviewed I try to tell them Sydney is too soon but they don't listen, they think I'm playing it down. I suppose they can hardly put down in an article that I just love horse riding. I can't be Tegan, the girl doing what she loves can I?" she continued " I apparently have to be Tegan, showjumping champion, Olympic hopeful, Olivia Mackie-Galloways daughter.." Tegan sounded more and more stressed as she recounted the expectation placed on her "My mother used to compete in Dressage, still does occasionally... I have to be the local Lanarkshire hero, an example to little girls up and down the country, I can't just be me." she suddenly noticed Darren had a hand around her, then she looked at her hands and they were shaking.

"Tegan it's okay," he said "how often do you have these panic attacks?"

"Too often," Tegan said as she rested her head on his chest, once again his heartbeat strangely calming her "sometimes I can feel them start, other times I'm not so lucky." She sighed and looked up at Darren "It doesn't help when people hear all that Olympics nonsense and buy into it. It's all I ever hear especially when I go to compete, which adds even more pressure as I feel as if everyone is scrutinizing me more because of it."

"It could be worse," Darren said after thinking "Imagine having no one give a damn, I represented my school in football at under eighteen level, most people would be proud or at least enthusiastic, my father bought me football boots when I made the team but apart from that, nothing from my family. Granted I was usually on the substitutes bench if at all but I was in the team. Surely that counted for something, also I was the only person in that team never to have played at any other level." Tegan looked up at him confused.

"I'm not the most knowledgeable about this but I thought you had to have moved up the age ranges or something." she asked.

"Usually you would be correct, most do, but a lack of naturally left footed players caused them to look elsewhere, my name was put forward... Rest is history."

"Hope you don't take offence were you any good?" she asked not sure how he would answer.

"\well I think it was less a case of ability so much as confidence, I had none, I knew what to do, just wasn't confident enough to just do it, when I would have a kick about with friends or anything like that I could score for fun. Don't get me wrong, there were guys in that team who were very supportive of me but not everyone was, I remember the tryouts for the team that year. I opened the scoring and instead of the others praising what was admittedly a good goal or something like that, some were saying our team needed a better goalkeeper if I could score. But after school, my knees developed an issue and that was that." He shrugged.

"You have a knee problem?" Tegan said, slipping out from under Darren's arm and looking at him concerned "What is it?" He thought for a minute.

"It's got a fancy name, chondro.. chondro.." He searched for the word.

"Chondromalacia patella?" Tegan said remembering that she had read about the condition, basically it affects the knees, most people have smooth cartilage on the underside of the kneecap, however people with chondromalacia patella have rough cartilage which can cause various knee problems and severe pain,

Tegan needed to know how badly if affected him "Darren, how bad is it, be honest please?"

"Yeah that's it and it's pretty bad." Darren nodded, Tegan gave him a stern look.

"Are you in pain now?" she got the feeling she knew the answer, his face suggested he knew she wouldn't like it either.

"Yeah. Quite a bit actually. Sorry, I should have told you sooner I guess" he gave an apologetic smile.

"Darren!" She shouted then put her head in her hands "You really need to listen to me, please. Your body can only take so much, Try to remember what I'm training to be okay? You need to let me help you, we are in this together, understood." he nodded meekly but she walked up, put her hands on his shoulders and waited until he looked back at her "Darren, I wish I knew what I can say to convince you but your mind and body can only take so much, so please trust me, please." her tone turned to pleading.

"Sorry, I guess I just can't fully relax until you are safe." Darren's reply didn't surprise her, yet again he was putting every ouch of strength into getting her home, he literally had no thought for himself. She didn't know what to think about it all but something was telling her that this was not an act to try and impress her, in fact it seemed very much like Darren was this way all the time.

"I won't relax until we are both safe," Tegan countered "we need to work as a team, a cohesive unit. You seem a smart guy, you must have ideas on how to get to Biggar undetected and I trust you to get us there, trust me to make sure you get the in one piece." she then took his hand as they resumed the long walk to Biggar.

They continued on, Darren had a stiffness to his walk, Tegan had noticed it before but didn't pay much attention to it. From what she knew about the condition it can be extremely painful. Tegan had to admit while Darren was being stubborn and possibly a little bit foolish by trying to push himself on through the pain she couldn't see anyone from her university class or any of the guys she would see in the horse riding circles put themselves through half of what he was doing for themselves let alone to help anyone else.

The weather wasn't too bad and under different circumstances, this would be a nice place to go walking. They had walked for some time and realised it would be dark soon and they needed a place to rest but before they did Tegan felt she had to have a word with Darren first.

"Darren, I know you are worried about us being recaptured, I am too but please you need to try to sleep when we stop for the night, promise me." She said, noticing he was starting to look unsteady again. Tegan gave him a look suggesting it was non-negotiable.

"Okay okay I promise," he said, hands up in mock surrender "I find it hard to sleep even at home never mind out here, it was only when you started humming Loch Lomond did I seem to relax enough."

"Really,? Oh, I did it because I couldn't think of anything else to soothe you." she shrugged.

"Big Runrig fan?" He inquired.

"Don't judge, but my parents got me into them but

Donnie Munro's voice kept me there, they haven't been the same since he left," The look she gave him suggested she didn't get much of a chance to talk about her love of the band with others "I only saw them live once but was an amazing experience." Darren smiled.

"I've seen them live three times. Cutter and the Clan tour, Big Wheel Tour and Transmitting live. And I have six of their albums on CD." he said with a smile

"Oh," she said thinking "What concert were you at for the Transmitting live tour?"

"It was Motherwell, why?" He replied, Tegan's eyes went wide.

"No way! I was there too, that was the one time I saw them live, My dad was a guest of Alex McLeish, He was Motherwell's manager at the time. He signed my ticket, I think have it in my room somewhere." Tegan said excitedly.

"I thought I saw him but wasn't sure," Darren admitted "small world, but I agree, after Donnie left the band suffered, what's your favourite song?.. Apart from Loch Lomond obviously." Tegan had a short think.

"Probably City of Lights, yours?"

"It's a toss up," Darren replied " it's either Pride of the Summer or Flower of the West for me." she nodded in approval, eventually They stood on a hilltop, scanning the area for a suitable place to go for the night.

"Hmm, apart from that rock formation down there I can't see anything obvious so far." said Darren

"Come on, lets check it out before it gets too dark." Tegan said, linking arms with him and heading down the hill, hoping to find safe place for the night.

CHAPTER 13

It was all go at the safe house, one of the newer arrivals, Malcolm, an older man with a beard and long curly grey hair in a ponytail, was pointing out the best places to to send people to wait for the two runaway hostages. He was using beer bottle caps as markers on the map. Malcolm was a friend of Andy's late father and a keen hunter.

"Right," said Malcolm "see those markers?"

"Yeah." replied Andy.

"We put two of our guys at each position with radios, camping equipment and supplies myself and Frank will drive between them at regular intervals in his van to get fresh stuff like radio batteries, food, water that sort of thing. My car is too small. Each position has a vantage point for observation and are places known for campers and hill walkers so seeing a tent there won't arouse suspicion and I have had told some guys different cover stories, for example," Malcolm explained pointing to one of the bottle caps on the map " whoever we put there is going to pose as winter fishers. They have all been briefed on how to patrol their assigned areas and if need be we can move people into secondary positions if there are sightings in one area. Don't worry we will find them and if they catch them each team has two off these." he held up a set of police issue style handcuffs.

"Thanks Malcolm," Andy said, taking it all in "This is much better than having us running around on some wild goose chase."

"I still wish you would have let me bring my hunting rifle, I could have hunted them down for you" Andy gave him a look but Malcolm continued "I would have shot to wound but I understand your reasons, its your choice I suppose."

Frank, who had just returned from checking out the residences surrounding the cottage for the runaway duo, came in.

"Andy," he said with a hint of weariness "still no sign of them." but Andy wasn't listening so Frank went over to Joe and tapped him on the shoulder, urging him to follow, once they got outside and a good bit away Frank turned to Joe.

"Joe what were you told about this assignment at first?" there was a cautious tone to his voice, Joe was one of the more intelligent members of the group but was still very loyal to Andy.

"Well, I was the first person Andy spoke to about it and at that point I was told it was a kidnapping, nothing too fancy, other than the hostage will be brought here," Joe seemed disturbed "but as the plan developed I realised this wasn't our usual tactics, no bag over her head or even a blindfold, no masks for us, I told him it sounded very sloppy and she could and probably would identify us. That's when he first mentioned they were going to kill her regardless of payment." Frank wasn't surprised by Joe's concerns.

"Apparently it was Blondie's plan to kill the girl regardless which explains no need to hide our identities I suppose, but killing someone who has done nothing to us isn't my thing, I don't care what her dad may or may not have done to her, it's no reason to outright murder someone." Frank said, he was the youngest in a family where he had four sisters. Three older, one younger and he had two daughters. Any crime against women made him uneasy and usually avoided it, this time Andy guilt tripped him into it by saying someone going to need to watch Pat.

"Yeah, ever since Blondie walked into his life Andy changed. Bringing Pat here was a huge mistake, I can think of a few reasons why he is here and I don't like any of them," Joe said thinking "the longer this goes on the worse it will get for all of us, mark my words."

"Yeah, between us, Blondie brought it on herself, the hero kid, I respect him for not leaving the girl behind so she could spend the last minutes on this planet at the mercy of Pat," Frank shook his head helplessly "What do we do Joe."

"for now? nothing," Joe replied "If he is still obsessed in a few days, we will figure something out and we both keep an eye on Pat."

"Yeah, meanwhile I better get the van ready for our happy campers." Frank said with a sigh.

It was ransom call time, he thought as he came out of the bathroom wiping his nose. Andy realised he probably should have gone to a payphone but he was beyond caring at this point so he decided to use the safe house phone, he dialled the number for Netherfield House, it was ringing.

"Ah mister Galloway so good to hear you." Andy started.

"Where is she can I talk to her, please." came the reply.

"Hey! I make the demands here," Andy said, toying with Quentin "I know the banks aren't open today, it was just a call to let you know I care." Just then Scott who was sitting drinking with the others shouted holding up his can.

"To Blondie." and he downed the can in one. Malcolm clipped him round the ear and told him to be quiet.

"Anyway better feed the poor girl, we have some lovely dog food for her, I think she might like it, being a little bitch." He laughed and hung up, then beaconed Malcolm over.

"Whats on your mind?" Malcolm asked.

"Malcolm, I'm concerned for Scott I'm not sure he

is really suited for this task and you know how it is, accidents happen." he said, Malcolm winked.

"That they do Andy my boy, and the sad thing is no one finds the bodies when they have accidents around me." Malcolm said ominously.

Frank and Joe were still talking outside as Frank got the van ready.

"I think this is going to be my last job Joe," said Frank, "I've saved enough cash to go buy a bar in Spain. Nothing big, just a tapas bar or something, it's been a dream of mine and I'm not getting younger, Andy won't like it but I'm done caring." Joe nodded.

"You're doing the right thing Frank, when your heart is not in the game any more that's how accidents happen, That's how Benny Dempster got himself killed, he was an enforcer for the Harvey's who simply stayed on longer than he should have, ended up knifed saving a young girl from a horny drunk," said Joe "Well that's the rumour but I will tell you something it's going to be a task getting those two back anyway."

"Oh, What makes you think that." Said Frank as he idly played with the locking mechanism on the gate.

"Just a feeling, can't quite put my finger on it but they have evaded us this far." Joe said as he headed back in.

"Bloody hope they continue to evade us." Frank said under his breath as Malcolm came out with the 'campers' ready for deployment.

Quentin sat next to the phone, head in his hands.

"They still refuse to let me speak to her," he told Olivia "I just want to know she is okay." Olivia came over and comforted her husband but ended up crying herself.

"It's going to be hell for her, her anxiety is going to be consuming her, the longer she's there.." She then thought "Poor Lucy, she won't know about Tegan."

"She is fortunate she wasn't taken too, imagine if they found out her mother couldn't afford to pay them." Quentin said thoughtfully.

"I'd like to think you would pay the ransoms for both girls if that happened." Olivia said in a demanding tone.

"You know I would, Lucy has always felt like a second daughter. I lost count of the number of times she was here as a young girl," Quentin looked up at the ceiling lost in thought "I remember when we told Tegan that Lucy wasn't going be able to come round any more, she didn't leave her room for a week."

"Lucy was the only proper friend she had," Olivia said "even when she joined that pony club she always talked about the treks they went on but never anything about who she spoke to." Quentin stood up and went with his wife to the main sitting room.

"Do you remember that boy she went out with." he asked, Olivia rolled her eyes.

"You mean the one who was more interested in you and that Tegan left after only an hour never to see him again?" there was an awkward silence.

"What's on your mind?" Quentin asked her.

"Tegan has never been comfortable around others, has she? Sure she's fine on a horse, or at the football with you and I hear she is coping well with her studies but you should have seen how she was just before the hunt Quentin, she still has a long way to go. This is going to set her back, whatever confidence she has had…" she trailed off, she was concerned that while Tegan may return in a reasonable shape, physically at least, the main worry was what will become of her mentally?

Later on, when Quentin was trying to get some work done, Olivia went into Tegan's room and sat on the bed. Tegan was always a neat girl, posters had to be framed to be on Tegan's wall and it wasn't something her or her father had told their daughter to do, something knocked against her heel under the bed, it was the box Tegan kept her football stuff, Olivia brought it out and looked through the box, it was filled with various match day stuff like programmes, scarves and lots of other little trinkets picked up over the years, it was the one thing Tegan and her dad always did together, there was a photo of Tegan at Celtic Park she must have been sixteen, scarf on, jacket all fastened up, that shy smile of hers, just happy to be there.

"Tegan," Olivia said sadly as she stroked Tegan's face on the picture "I just want you back here, safe and sound. I hope you are okay." and she clutched the photo close and cried.

Frank was returning in his van when Joe came out.

"Frank, Pats done a runner," He said as he leaned against the van, Frank shrugged as he got out, opening the side door to let the guys out, it had been a long day for everyone.

"Didn't see him go past on the way in, probably figured out Andy had something bad planned for him, good riddance though." and he went back to tinkering with the engine but Joe sighed.

"That idiot Scott saw him take one of the maps after he looked at the map Andy and Malcolm have been mulling over and took notes, I think he's going to try and go after them." Frank put his head in his hands.

"That's all we need, we need to tell Andy, I know he wants the two of them killed but not in the bloody open, never mind the state her body might be in.." Frank trailed off and remembered something "Blondie was using that guy for her college work, right? Who's to say we aren't being used too?"

"Who knows," replied Joe "But that thought has crossed my mind. The parts of the plan she came up with just didn't feel right and Andy just agreed with her. Since when have you seen a Donnelly let their girlfriends call any shots?"

"Never," Said Frank "They know better than to interfere."

"Exactly and she's not just interfering, she was going to have an active role," Joe said "I swear it was like she had him under a spell, he would say something, she would stop him and say what she thought we should do and he would agree."

"Odd," said Frank "that doesn't sound like the Andy I know."

"Indeed it doesn't," Agreed Joe "I know it's early days but has anyone found anything yet?" He said to change the subject.

"No, Tam and Derek radioed in about ten minutes after being dropped off as Derek thought he saw one of them but realised she's just in horse riding clothes, she's not actually riding a bloody horse," Frank said with a sigh "They are betting everything on her trying to go straight home aren't they?"

"Yeah, pretty much. You don't agree? Joe asked curiously.

"No," Frank said, rubbing his temples. "I was thinking about what you said earlier about something not being quite right, well, I think I know what it is."

"Oh." said Joe looking interested.

"If it was just her I would agree, she would probably just go straight home if she could," Frank started "but it's not just her, it's him. There is something about the guy I can't just pinpoint, nothing he has done has made sense so what makes you think he is going to change now." Joe nodded in agreement.

"It's a fair point but if not Strathaven, where?" He asked, Frank looked to the sky, feeling the rain fall on him.

"That's the problem, I don't know."

The rock formation initially looked like it was a bust as

far as any sort of shelter and it was going to get dark within the hour, Tegan was exhausted and she suspected Darren was too but she could tell he was trying to hide it from her, funny how she could tell small details like that despite the fact she barely knew him. His walk got stiffer, particularly the left knee, it was obvious now she had seen it. The whole ordeal was taking its toll on the both of them. The fear of being recaptured was constantly at the back of their minds, the terrain was rough and causing problems, They had very few supplies, weren't dressed for such a journey and even simple things like going to the toilet was awkward in such a largely open place like these hills. The truth of the matter was they both needed to get some decent rest soon to stand any chance of getting out of this situation safely.

"There must be something we can do." Tegan said as she saw Darren subconsciously flex his left knee joint, she wanted to sit Darren down and tell him she was worried he was still pushing himself too hard. As Tegan looked around an idea formed. There was a long boulder about the height of Tegan that had a slightly smaller one next to it, if they used them and put the tarpaulin over the gap between the boulders they would have a shelter of sorts. Granted it would be low and neither would be able to stand but it was better than nothing.

"It's worth a try." Darren said after she explained her idea, exhaustion evident in his voice

"Let's try and get it sorted before it gets too dark," Said Tegan looking up at the heavy clouds "and before it rains." she added. The only issue was making sure the tarpaulin didn't blow away in the wind. This was done by getting whatever big rocks and stones at the edges to hold it in place, the fact the tarpaulin 'roof' was at an angle due to the boulders being different heights hopefully would mean the water would just flow off it instead on put so much weight on it that the tarpaulin would cave in. The end result wasn't pretty but it would do.

"Looks secure enough," said Darren, checking out their handy work.

"It's not much but it should do." She said as she admired the shelter they created too, it would be a little cramped but it will shelter them. Tegan looked over at Darren, he was leaning against a rock and was struggling to stand. Exhaustion was about to overcome him as he only had two hours of sleep in two days and it showed, but even now he was trying to hide the full extent from her as looked at her and tried to give her a reassuring smile. She walked over and without a word just hugged him tightly, at first it was obvious he wasn't expecting it but she felt his body relax and felt his arms around her. Then she felt the rain come down.

"We really should get under cover before it gets worse." said Tegan, Darren decided it was best not to argue.

CHAPTER 14

They had just gotten under the tarpaulin before the rain started to come down hard. Tegan did her best to clear a rough bed area and convinced Darren to lay down, she eased the watch off his wrist and put it on hers, setting the alarm for six hours. He lay on his side facing her, eyelids heavy but it was almost like he was still fighting sleep.

"Darren, please try and get some sleep" Tegan said pleadingly and she did the only thing she could, she stroked his cheek and hummed. The soft melody of Loch Lomond did its magic again and he was soon fast asleep. Tegan drew him in closer, telling herself it was for body heat. The reality however she was finding it a comfort being close to him, strangely hearing his heartbeat was something she found quite peaceful and soothing, she just lay with him and watched the rain lash down, a few drips from the holes in the tarpaulin but nothing to worry about and no drips were directly above them.

"Darren," she said in a whisper, knowing he was asleep but not caring "Thank you, for everything, saving my life, never giving up but you need to know something, I don't think I could go on enjoying life if you died for me, I don't want you to die for me... Live for me... Please, I want to know more about this knight in a Warner thirty four shirt who seems to think I am worth putting his life on the line for." she knew he couldn't hear but she had to say it out loud. She lay there looking at him peacefully at sleep.

Tegan's hair was a wild wavy tangled mess and she looked down at her once pristine outfit. Her blouse was drenched in sweat and she would have been tempted to take her blazer off if the weather wasn't as cold as it was. The jodhpurs were dirty and sweaty and then there were her boots which were muddy and hurting her feet. Tegan knew one of the first things she would want to do when she got home was have a long soak in the bath, it was a small thing to look forward to but it was something to motivate her. Darren stirred in his sleep and put a lazy arm over her. If any other man, awake or asleep, had done that she would have gotten them to remove it but somehow because it was Darren she didn't mind, in fact she cuddled in closer and quickly drifted off to sleep.

Quentin went to look to see where Olivia was, she wasn't downstairs or in bed, there she was in Tegan's room, asleep on top of the bed cuddling one of her daughter's bears with an old photo of Tegan at the football beside her. Instead of waking her up, he simply got a blanket from where Tegan kept them below the bed and put one gently over his wife and left, turning the light off.

As he got ready for bed himself Quentin was deep in thought, Tegan wasn't just a daughter, she was like a best friend to her parents. Sometimes he wondered if that was a good thing as she rarely mixed with other girls her age and apart from one bad date boys couldn't be further from her mind. It wasn't like she hasn't had opportunities to meet others,there was the pony club, the competitions, school, university but apart from Lucy, Tegan didn't have anyone she could call a close friend and even then she was family. Tegan's anxiety attacks were a factor but hopefully after this ordeal is over Lucy will help her, she was more outgoing so having her back in Tegan's life could only be a good thing. At least that was the hope

The alarm managed to wake both of them with a fright. Darren looked outside, saw the rain was coming down hard and noted it was was still dark.

"Might as well stay here until it stops." Darren said as he lay on his back, silently grateful for the extra time to rest his knees. Tegan thought for a minute then asked Darren a question she wasn't sure if he even could answer.

"Darren," She started "I know why you rescued me and why you continue to run yourself to the ground but I don't understand why you can't even consider your own survival?" there was silence except for the noise of the rain. Darren sat up.

"Okay, I will be the first to admit I'm very socially awkward, just simply talking to someone,even more so if it is a new person can be a daunting task for me and I can count the number of true friends I have on one hand, I do have acquaintances online and I also have people I am... Useful to, Help with coursework, art, design, access to, whatever other talents or equipment I possess. I freely help in the hope I might be more. Someone to chat to, a friend maybe and if it's a girl maybe more than friends. On top of all that I have dyslexia and dyspraxia and there is talk of a test for autism too," he stopped hung his head and softly said, "I was useful to Blondie."

And at that moment, Tegan understood, Darren was so used to being used by people and hoping it will translate into something beyond just being useful it's become almost a default mode he reverts to and on top of that he is trying his best to cope with a condition few understand. Most people have at least heard of dyslexia, however, dyspraxia is a lesser known condition, luckily for Darren, she had read up on it at university and one of the guys in her class, a guy called Stephen, has it and she remembered him telling people about the condition. The most obvious way it affects someone is balance and hand to eye coordination but it affected the mind in so many different ways, like memory, the short term could be poor but the long term was usually quite vivid and most affected had difficulty moderating their senses, causing misinterpretation of events, sensory overloads and panic attacks, she did wonder how he knew she was struggling with her anxiety earlier. Darren wasn't finished though.

"I worry if I think about us making it through this, us surviving... You're beautiful, I'm useful to you now.."

"Darren don't you dare finish that sentence off!" She shouted with alarming conviction and took his hand and to her surprise tears were welling up in her eyes "Do you think I could just move on and forget about you after all this, it's not like you helped with a school project. You rescued me, saved my life. Darren, you saved my life, you are not some useful tool I intend to toss away once I am finished with you," the tears were rolling freely down her face but she ignored them as she nervously fidgeted with Darren's fingers "You are part of my life now, I honestly don't know exactly how you fit in but I do know I care about you enough not to discard you like you are nothing. I'm not her, I'm not Lucy, I'm not Blondie Darren," she then pulled his arm bringing him close, hugged him tight, "We will get out of this together, I promise you."

When they broke the hug Tegan had a confused look on her face as if just realising something Darren had said.

"Darren? Were you actually saying you find me attractive?" He did basically say he was worried he may end up falling for her after all and the night before had mentioned in an alarmingly offhand manner that she was beautiful, he looked genuinely confused.

"Well... Yes, Tegan, you are very beautiful, why wouldn't I find you attractive?" it was the way he said it that caught her completely off guard, it wasn't the tone of some sleazy guy trying to chat her up, it was the voice of someone stating it as if it was a fact everyone knew. She looked down at herself, at her riding clothes, he had never seen her in anything else.

"Are you saying you think I look good in this?" she gestured to her clothes in a theatrical manner, "The blazer? the jodhpurs? These boots.." she stretched out one for emphasis "aren't exactly sexy." but he shrugged and again it was the way he said it.

"It's an attractive look that really suits you and if I am totally honest, on you they are very sexy. But that is just my humble opinion" she blushed, it was the brutal honesty coming from him that made these compliments mean more to her than if anyone else said it, "Sorry if I'm being too forward but it is true. You really do look amazing."

"Well please don't apologise, okay? You have said nothing wrong, if anything I'm flattered, thank you," she said and she meant it "I'm usually in some sort of riding gear, although not as formal as this, usually I'm wearing my rubber riding boots with different colours of jodhpurs with something more casual on top... But once again, thank you." she hid her face in her hair, going all shy.

"Come on Tegan, you must have guys queuing up for you surely." there was that honest tone again, she gave a cynical laugh.

"No, people barely notice me, I'm not exactly outgoing and definitely have never been a slave to fashion. Take Friday at university. For example, I come to the lecture, hair in a ponytail and no makeup, I'm here to learn after all, my favourite multicoloured Sweater Shop top that I have had for years, a long denim skirt on and knee high boots with a nice block heel... I like my boots by the way, you may have noticed... I am also wearing my big jacket, it was a cold day after all. I walk in and say hi, barely a reaction."

"Really?" He said sounding genuinely surprised.

"In walks Claire Moore, blonde hair highlighted and straightened, makeup caked on. Wearing a tight t-shirt, tartan skirt, ankle boots with a high heel and a trendy biker jacket," she made a face of complete disgust " It was like a shark feeding frenzy, all the guys dying to say hi and complimenting her, and she's not the only one to whom every day is a fashion parade, next to them I might as well be invisible."

"Given the choice between you and the other girls, you would win every time." he said with a smile, she had to change the subject, she wasn't used to hearing someone talk about her like this and she didn't know how to handle it, she knew what to ask him.

"Okay, Darren there is something I have been meaning to ask since we escaped, your shirt." he gave her a perplexed look so she continued, "why Tony Warner's squad number? he only played about three games for us."

"Us?" He sounded amused "Ah, are you a Celtic fan too?" now he hadn't expected her to be a football fan at all, let alone be a Celtic supporter.

"Had a season ticket with my dad every year since ninety five when the stadium was rebuilt," she said with an odd sense of pride "don't think I have missed many home games in years."

"Well okay," He started "you remember the Five-one game then?" He didn't need to state the date, she knew, he could tell by the look she gave him.

"Remember? I was at the game with my dad. I remember his reaction when it was announced Moravcik was going to play up front," she smiled "Dad quickly changed his tune when he scored the first goal."

"Everyone remembers the Moravcik and Larsson goals, Mjallby making a solid debut but everyone seems to forget Warner was in goal, here was a guy on a short term loan. I remember Rangers fans at college before days leading up to the game it was going to be an easy win because we had him on goal. Yet he had the game of his life and then that very night he survived a horrific car crash. It was a real shame he wasn't signed up on a permanent contract though, so when my brother asked what to get me for Christmas... This is what I asked for and it's been something of a lucky top for me since," He noted her cynical look when he mentioned it was lucky but he continued "In a football sense anyway, I usually wear it when I play five a side that is, I still play when I can, usually once a week." she nodded.

"As reasons go, that's not the worst one, I have the current long sleeved home shirt and it has Moravcik and twenty five on the back, that game made me a fan of him." Something else came to Tegans mind "Darren, you mentioned before that you are a Ralf Schumacher fan, why? Just seems an odd choice." she asked, Darren looked at her a moment smiled

"I remember watching the Austrian Grand Prix in ninety eight and saw Ralf keep his brother, who is supposed to be the more talented of the two and who was in a superior car behind him on a track it is easy to overtake on for several laps, plus like me he is younger brother so I kinda have cheer for the guy" Darren replied smiling at Tegan and she found herself smiling back. Tegan couldn't believe it she was sitting under a roof of tarpaulin, her hair a mess and in dirty, sweaty clothes and still in danger for her life with a guy she only met that weekend and he was only even there in the first place to see her cousin yet he had repeatedly risked his life for Tegan and here she was talking with him and enjoying his company. Tegan could hardly believe she was having an enjoyable conversation... With a guy no less.. about stuff she loves to talk about, most people at university were more interested in things like what clubs in town was having a students night. As for other stuff like showjumping? While she loved it and horses in general, it was nice to talk to someone about other things for a change..

"Tegan, are you still with us? You kinda zoned out there," said Darren, snapping Tegan out of her thoughts "Whatever it was it must have been nice, judging by your smile." he added

"Oh, nothing, I was just lost in my thoughts" she said as she listened to the sound of the rain hitting the tarpaulin, Tegan found it oddly calming.

"I better take a quick look outside make sure theres no one around." Darren said as he went to exit the shelter, Tegan put a hand on his shoulder.

"Please be careful," she said softly "and hurry back."

The rain was heavy so Darren had no intention of going too far and besides he reassured Tegan that he would stay within eyesight of her. After a quick look around he concluded that at least for now they were indeed safe, for the time being anyway. If he was honest, Darren doubted the kidnappers would be out searching in such horrible weather anyway, at least he hoped that was the case as neither of them had anything waterproof to wear so it was way too risky to move about in this weather for multiple reasons. He headed back over, giving Tegan a thumbs up to indicate everything looked all clear, for now anyway.

Darren crawled back in and sat down next to Tegan, she inched closer to him and rested her head on his shoulder,

"Is the weather as bad as it looks" she asked as she got herself more comfortable while still using his shoulder as a headrest.

"I would say it's worse than it looks but the good news is that there is no-one within eyesight anyway so we should be safe for here for now, at least until the rain stops anyway. I don't know about you but I don't fancy getting soaked." he said thoughtfully.

"Yeah, we would be drenched in minutes." Tegan agreed as she took a quick look outside herself from the safety of the shelter. Tegan was actually happy at the thought of waiting for the weather to improve while spending a few more hours just talking to and getting to know Darren better didn't seem bad at all in her eyes.

CHAPTER 15

As usual, the ground floor was packed with students waiting for the lifts, despite being soaked by the heavy rain, Linda had been patient as she knew classes didn't start for a while yet, Jason however was getting restless as he always did, refusing to stay still.

"Okay that's it I'm taking the stairs." and ran to the stairwell as Linda rolled her eyes, she knew she would get up there and he will be complaining about his various sores and have the usual argument that he should have just waited. At least Darren will be there to agree that Jason is being an idiot, a theory proved as she managed to get a lift less than a minute later.

"How the.." Jason exclaimed as he turned to walk up the next flight and there was Linda standing, arms crossed.

"A miraculous invention called a lift, you should try it sometime," she said shaking her head at him "It arrived just after you decided to use the stairs, you are a halfwit at times you know that?"

As they walked to class Jason had a thought.

"I'm willing to bet you a fiver Darren went to that protest on Saturday." his smile suggested he believed it to be a safe bet.

"No, Darren would have thought about it though, but it's a little bit extreme even for..." they walked into the computer lab and they were the first there, no Darren at all.

"For all we know he could be running late." said Jason unconvincingly, Linda had a bad feeling, she didn't know what it was but something wasn't right.

"Jason, do you have todays newspaper?" Jason nodded and produced a Daily Record from his bag, she asked if he could check for any news about the hunt.

"Hold on." he flicked through the pages and found a small half page article and photo on the foxhunt.

"Let's see, oh here it is. Strathaven hunt, blah blah blah, peaceful protest blah blah blah Netherfield House blah blah blah no arrests, Quentin Galloway? Is that the Galloway Haulage guy?"

"Think so..." Linda said as she looked him up on the internet "Yes, it is the same guy" she said pointing to the screen. Jason dumped the paper next to his computer as he looked on.

"Oh," he said as he sat down "anyway, surely the fact that there is no news of trouble is a good thing." he said hoping Linda would breathe a little easier but he doubted anything less than Darren walking through the door saying he is running late will do that, that didn't happen.

The lecture today was the subject Graphic Design for Desktop Publishing, another one of the subjects Darren excelled at. Jason dumped two folders between his computer and Linda's, one was his, the other he thought was hers.

"Jason, since when was I called Lucy?" she said picking up the folder, it had the name Lucy Bannatyne in the lecturer's writing but below in more elaborate writing was the name Blondie.

"Sorry," he then looked around to see if Blondie was around "Hey, Blondie isn't here either, you don't think.."

"No, surely not," Linda shook her head but Jason had his hand out and she begrudgingly dumped a crisp blue five pound note in "How? She doesn't like him, you know that." she continued.

"Love works in mysterious ways," Jason smiled, kissing the money "I thought that too, looks like we were both wrong," He picked up Blondie's folder which was full of the work she.. apparently.. done, he shook his head and said "What is the betting most if not all of this work was done by Darren?"

"Knowing Blondie, I'd guess probably most of it"

she replied as he opened it and the first thing he saw was a picture that had been ripped out of a newspaper of someone he assumed was a horse rider of some sort.

"Linda, who is that?" He asked.

"Don't know but she is pretty." she replied.

"Really?" He shrugged "whatever floats your boat I guess."

"Jason, she has a pulse, I thought that made her your type." Linda said mockingly.

"Isn't Anita into horse riding? maybe she knows." he asked, ignoring Linda's comment.

"I think she is," Linda said after some thought "I know she has mentioned something about riding horses before."

"Well, worth a try" Jason said as he got up out his chair and headed over to talk to Anita.

Anita Malik had moved to Scotland from Pakistan when she was only four years old with her parents, now aged twenty, was one of the harder working students in the class and she usually kept to herself most of the time and regularly wore the headscarf, or hijab to use the correct term. Jason sat down as casually as he could on the seat next to her, she stopped what she was doing and shook her head with a sigh.

"Jason, no I'm not interested and not just for the obvious reasons you may think." she gave him a look that suggested if he was had a comeback, to keep it to himself.

"Alright Anita, calm down. Listen, you're a horsey

girl aren't you?" He said flashing a cheeky girl, she rolled her eyes.

"Horsey girl? " she said, looking up to the ceiling and shaking her head "If you mean do I ride a horse yes Jason I am a... Horsey girl, Where's this going?" He dumped the picture on the desk.

"Oh, her, that's Tegan Galloway, she's something of a big name in showjumping, there has been talk of Olympic selection but that's probably paper talk as usual. Why do you ask?... Oh no, you haven't... Jason!"

"What? No!" he said annoyed "not my type."

"Really Jason? she is a female and has a pulse. That is your type," Anita countered "and she is a pretty girl."

Jason snatched the picture and went back to his computer next to Linda.

"It's someone big in the horse riding world apparently, some girl called Tegan Galloway. In line for an Olympic call up apparently" Jason said slumping on the desk as Linda took his paper and read the article herself.

"Oh, this is interesting, the Huntmaster is called Quentin Galloway, maybe they are related..." said Linda when she spotted a familiar sight in the main photo.

"Jason, who is that? There?" and she stabbed her finger at the blonde near the back but just clear enough to see.

"Well," he said slowly "It looks like Blondie."

"Where?" came a voice behind Jason, it was Julia,

Blondie's friend.

"There." Jason pointed to the photo.

"I'll be damned, so it is," she said, "she said she was going to protest it, she never mentioned anything about riding at it. Say Where's Darren?"

"Why?" said Linda in an acidic tone "Need him for help?" she emphasized the word help.

"No," she said shocked "I was just wondering, I've never known him to be off."

"Well, we dunno where he is either" replied Linda when Julia left she turned to Jason "you have Darren's home number don't you? Give it to me," the tone of her voice said no arguing, Jason grumbled and wrote it down on a scrap of paper and handed it to her "back soon." and she left before he could say a thing.

Linda returned a few minutes later, looking quite upset.

"So.." said Jason calmly.

"I spoke to his mother, his family haven't heard from him and they are worried, I told them if we find out anything we will tell them, it's a half day tomorrow... Right?"

"Yeah," said Jason "just a morning lecture."

"Good, if Darren doesn't turn up or found by then I'm going to this guy Galloway's place," she said, her eyes hard and focused "It was the last place we knew he definitely went." Jason shook his head and went to the printer to get his work from it, when he returned he saw Linda looking up bus times on the internet.

"Since when did you become Miss Marple?

Linda, you can't just walk up to some posh guy's house, knock on his door and say, hi I'm Linda, have you seen my pal Darren, he's thin, close shaved brown hair with an obsession for some blonde girl we are sure rode with you guys. Oh and by the way she doesn't like him but he does her coursework for her so she tolerates him." He looked at her as if she was an idiot, Darren was not the most distinctive looking guy out there.

"Your right, I'm not. We are," Linda said "Have you any other prior engagements? Anything in that busy schedule of yours?"

"No," he mumbled sheepishly, then added, "You can be scary sometimes you know that?"

Irene stood looking out the kitchen window of Greenhill farmhouse and was deep in thought, she was worried for that poor girl Tegan. Her reaction to what happened yesterday was haunting. Something about it didn't seem right about what they were told and how the kids acted, her husband Peter was sure the boy was pushing drugs even after the kid did say phone the girl's father, Galloway Haulage or something was mentioned. Of course Peter had no intention of doing so as he believed the boy was just saying that to get to the girl. Irene shook her head and reached for the phone...

The rain lashed down at the safe house.

"You can bet they are holed up somewhere until it eases off." said Malcolm, Andy did note that neither had any waterproof clothes. In all honesty, it allowed everyone to catch a breath after a hectic few days, they were two men down already, Pat went rogue and Scott had an... Accident... Out helping Malcolm as he took another look at the area near that cottage to see if he could spot something the others missed. It looked like they stopped at a small grouping of trees but beyond that nothing. He was tempted to go out and track them down proper but Malcolm was needed here for now.

Frank lay on one of the beds just staring up at the ceiling, his microwave chicken curry going slowly cold, his lager was already flat. He took out his wallet and looked at a picture of him and his sisters at a family gathering, he had his arm around the youngest sister Siobhan, even though he was younger by a year he was so protective of her, that they even share a flat ever since she caught her husband cheating on her, the bond they have drove his ex partner to leave him and take the kids, when he went to Spain he was taking Siobhan, they both needed a new life. Joe walked in.

"Let's hope this weather makes him see sense," Joe said "After Thursday, maybe Friday he can't use the ransom thing anymore, I see this crashing down before then though, just a feeling." Frank admitted the way it was going something was going to have to give.

"We can only hope," he said finally "Andy should have gotten Pat away from all this, the guy was always a liability before but now he suffered a bad concussion, who knows where the guys mind is at."

"Yeah," said Joe "he was brought in apparently because Andy felt his strength would come in handy and he couldn't get a hold of anyone else suitable at short notice after Big Craig was arrested for beating up that cop," Craig would have been a much better option and was Joe's friend whereas Pat even before his convictions was a liability and it wasn't just in regards to women either. Pat was always notorious for being too physical in general, which is fine sometimes in the line of work they were in but not in these sort of situations "But I remember Blondie repeatedly insisting Pat get involved in this regardless and she isn't here now. This time there's no coming back from this for Pat."

The rain was not for relenting and it seemed neither was Linda, instead of going for a break she spent her time looking online for anything in the news about the hunt that may give some clue to Darren's whereabouts. Jason thought she was getting obsessed when she started to look for other reports in that area.

"What next? Phone the nearby hospitals to see if a guy matching Darren's description had been admitted?" He was going to laugh but the look on her face suggested she was already thinking of it "Linda, you are not his mother, why are you doing all this?"

"Jason," Linda said with her head in her hands "You really need to ask that question? You and Darren are two of the few people I know that aren't part of the scene who treat my sexuality as perfectly normal. I'm not seen as the 'lesbian friend', I also know the pain Darren was going through with Blondie and trust me unrequited love can play havoc with your mind. I know, I have been there myself. Also if you went missing I would be doing the same for you and you know Darren would be helping me find you." she stared at Jason intently.

"Linda, I'm not denying your heart is in the right place but what can we do?" He said knowing he would have more joy talking to a brick wall, "Darren is a grown man, for all we know he is taking a few days to sort his head out. Just look at it like this, He goes there expecting to see her there waving a banner or whatever they do at protests and instead she is taking part in the thing...."

"So?" Linda said, staring at him "Jason, he isn't at his place and hasn't been in contact with us. This is not like him and we both know it, are you saying you won't help?"

"Oh no," replied Jason "I'm going, someone has to make sure you don't cause trouble... Or go missing yourself. The thing I don't get is that Julia said Blondie told her she was protesting the hunt so we know that wasn't just an excuse for Darren's sake but what if Julia or someone else was interested in going from this class and what if they saw her riding a horse at this hunt? and Blondie has a newspaper cutting of the daughter of the guy leading it," he shook his head "I've known Blondie for as long as Darren has and this doesn't sound like her," He jabbed the picture Blondie was in with his finger "something is wrong about all this."

"Well," said Linda "Let's find out tomorrow then."

CHAPTER 16

Once he relaxed, Tegan found Darren a charming, and quick-witted, if a bit cynical. She found out a lot about him. Darren had went to school at Saint Ignatius Primary and then Saint Aidans Secondary, both were in Wishaw. He declined to go into too much detail about those days except for what he had told her already like being in the school football team. Tegan also found out that as well as being a fellow Celtic fan, being a Ralf Schumacher fan and liking Runrig, his favourite band was Queen and he was into sci-fi in a big way and he had a talent for art and design. Darren had just finished a tale about an ill-fated bus trip with his dad and brother Charlie organised by a local pub for a tour of Old Trafford stadium in Manchester, where the driver was so lost he ended up at a pub called The Moston which was the other side of the city, Tegan's face hurt from laughing just at all the little crazy stories that happened that day.

Infact, Tegan found herself just smiling a lot just listening to Darren and she was surprised actually just how at ease she was with him. Although the main reason they hadn't moved was due to the heavy rain, they were actually enjoying having the time just to talk. Darren had went out once more just to make sure there was no one nearby, again making sure Tegan could see him the whole time. It was an obviously cold day made worse by the rain so when Darren returned he took his jacket off and draped it over her shoulders as he sat back down next to her. She offered him a shy smile in silent thanks, it was little gestures like this she found charming and endearing about him.

"Tegan, I know I have said this before but I find it hard to believe a lady as beautiful as you is single, what's the deal? There has to have been someone" he asked.

"Well, there was one guy," Tegan started with a sigh, drawing Darren's jacket tighter over her shoulders "Stuart Ramsey, he was a couple of years older than me and seen himself as a bit of a charmer but I doubt he loved anyone more than himself. He asked me out during a competition we were both attending, I think I said yes just because he had asked me just about every time we saw each other for six months and I thought he must have been really into me so I said yes." and she gave Darren a look that suggested it didn't go well.

"go on," he said trying to get into a comfortable position "I'm assuming by your tone it was a disaster." Even though it was technically daylight, was dark, he gazed at her face and not for the last time wondered how someone as obviously beautiful as her, at least in his opinion anyway, did not have guys fighting over her.

"Oh no, it started well enough, he arrived early in his car. I was still getting ready and the zip on my boots had caught my tights so I had to change tights, then I couldn't find my handbag," she let out a sigh " I should have taken that as a sign but I went downstairs. I am in my new knee high boots just bought that afternoon and they had a nice three inch heel, I also made an attempt with my hair and makeup. I'm also wearing a nice sleeveless black dress mum bought for me that day too and what does he say when he sees me? Nothing, he's too busy talking to my dad about some business idea and asking my mum about her dressage career. It took me half an hour to convince him to even take me on the date, we go to this lovely little restaurant and during the whole drive he constantly talked about how amazing he thought my parents were, the subject didn't change once we got there."

"Oh dear." Darren was trying hard not to laugh but was succeeding... barely, anyway, he could see from Tegan's posture that it was only going to get worse as her voice got a little more animated.

"Then he starts paying me weird compliments about stuff like muscle tone, asking how often do I train, work out and all these questions on fitness and then tries to give me tips on keeping my reflexes sharp when I'm riding he was even pointing out what food on the menu would be best for the training regime he believed I should try." she rolled her eyes.

"Quick question, how good was he as a rider?"

Darren felt he had to ask.

"Honestly?" She said "Well, even back then I was getting the whole people seeing the Olympic team in my future thing, Stuart, I think the highest he ever got was one lucky third place and here he is telling me what to do like some silly little stable girl. Then he said I must have good genetics and we were compatible. I couldn't believe what I was hearing, I was being talked about like I was some sort of breeding stock or something…" she stopped when Darren burst out laughing.

"I'm sorry, I'm surprised he didn't check if you had a good set of teeth too," He said holding his hands up in apology "please, continue."

"Well, the only way he mentioned my smile was that I have lovely teeth so you are not totally wrong there... Anyway," she continued, "after the starter, I said I needed the toilet and slipped out, got a taxi home and before my parents can ask anything I go up and changed into old mucking out clothes. You know, my old black jodhpurs along with my rubber riding boots and my old Adidas sweater. I then grabbed my book, I believe it was Watership Down and I was reading it for about the fifth time..."

".. Good choice, I always read it at least once a year... " Darren interjected, "Although the last chapter somehow always makes me cry."

"Really? I thought it was just me, I always cry at that part too. Anyway, I also grabbed my CD player and took it out and spent the rest of the night reading under the lights of the stables reading about rabbits while the voice of Sharleen Spiteri echoes throughout the stable. I think Princess, thats my horse by the way, likes her as I'm convinced she keeps especially quiet when I play Texas CDs. Stuart phoned but my mum answered and told him I came home ill and couldn't come to the phone, now most guys would have just thanked my mum and ended the call, he tried to have a full on chat with my mum until she abruptly hung up on him. She didn't like him anyway, especially how he basically ignored me, she told me later that she was sure he even winked at her as he left with me, so there it is, my one and only date."

"Sounds like his loss then," Darren said "you are a beautiful woman in your own right. Don't get me wrong I am sure your dad is a lovely guy and clearly had a head for business and your mother sounds like a charming lady but if that was me I would have had eyes only for you." Tegan blushed at his comments but continued without responding to what he said

"Well he never did call back and whenever I saw him at events after I was totally ignored. The last time I saw him he was chatting to some new girl competing in showjumping and he was trying to give her exactly the same initial rubbish he gave to me. When he went away I spoke to her, apparently her dad was on the board at Partick Thistle so you can guess what attracted him to her. so I warned her about what he did with me, the girl thanked me and she turned him down, he wasn't happy."

"Well at least you got to that stage," Said Darren "I remember my fifteenth birthday, Her name was Shona McClure and I had decided that I was going to ask her out during Computing studies as we sat together in that class, so I did, she shook her head and that was it." It was Tegan's turn to laugh, though she did try and put her hand over her mouth to try and muffle it to little success.

"I don't mean to laugh, I really don't." she said after she composed herself enough. Once again was something about Darren's bluntness and honesty she found refreshing. She was getting better at spotting the little things she was noticing about him. Right now she could tell he was cold but was trying not to show it. She crawled over and cuddled in, putting the jacket over both of them as best she could.

"It's for body heat." she explained as she lay her head on his chest, she felt him put a tentative arm around her. Body heat was only part of the reason, there was something about him that made her feel safe, well not just safe but she was still trying to work out what exactly her feelings were for him.

"Tegan, what made you choose nursing." Darren asked curiously.

"My mum mainly. She met my dad in the hospital, Dad fell off his horse and fractured his arm. My mum was the young nurse who was attending to his injury, one thing lead to another, gran managed to get her into riding and she developed an aptitude for dressage and would compete regularly. She got a nursing job that was only on weekdays so she could still compete but she never gave up her job. She said it kept her feet firmly on the ground. Grew up seeing my mum the nurse, listening to stories of what went on at work. When it came time to choose a path, I knew I wanted to follow my mum."

"Nothing wrong with that," He said "I always fancied working in a library for some reason," Tegan could see the appeal, a quiet peaceful environment like that would suit him "but I am doing electronic publishing because it interested me and I felt having some college qualifications would be useful" Tegan didn't realise that she had cuddled right into Darren. "You okay?" He asked.

"Yeah," she said, realising what she was doing "just enjoying the quiet I guess." Tegan sighed although not sure what she was feeling, was she falling for Darren? The more time she spent with him and the more she learned about his past, Tegan found herself more and more drawn to him but she didn't want to say anything to him until she was sure one way or another that it was indeed romantic feelings or if it was something else. Too many have played with his emotions before and she refused to do that to him. She couldn't do that to him. All she knew is you can't fall in love with someone that quick, can you?

"I know the feeling," he replied, the rain wasn't letting up. Tegan dished out the last of the food "Next time I make sandwiches for a trip I'm going to come up with more options." he said.

"Don't worry, I'll remind you." Tegan said without thinking, her eyes snapped open in a did I say that or think it look, Darren just put his arm around her and smiled.

"Oh, and what would you want packed." he had a playful tone in his voice.

"Well, it would be wholemeal bread for a start, probably ham and cheese, red Leicester if possible," she looked up at him, her grin widening "if it's not too much trouble."

"Your wish is my command." said Darren, he looked out to the rain and sighed "I'm thinking we get some sleep now and when it eases off, even though it might still be dark we can try to make up lost ground..." he stopped when he seen Tegan give him a stern look."...What?" He said, confused

"Just make sure you actually lie down and sleep this time around, we need you rested and alert." Tegan replied, her features softened a little with a smile.

"Okay, I promise." Darren reassured her.

"Thank you." and without thinking, Tegan kissed his cheek with a smile and then she lay down trying to get comfortable as she would need to be well rested for the journey ahead. Suddenly the thought of going out there, being on the run again hit her like a ton of bricks, she felt short of breath and started to feel her hands shake "Darren.. Hold me.. Please." she managed to say as her voice trembled, she felt him cuddle her close protectively.

"Tegan, what's wrong," He asked softly, the truth was she had been enjoying just talking so much she wasn't thinking about the danger, now they were setting off again, she started thinking of wha had happened and what could happen if they were caught again and it got all too much for her, she explained it as best she could as he held her closer "Don't worry," he sad in a comforting tone, "I promised you I will get you.."

".. Get us.." Tegan tearfully corrected him.

".. Get us out of this alive and well and I'm not about to break that promise. I will not fail you" Once again there was no bravado, just sincere honesty and somehow that honesty filled her with hope, Darren started digging in his bag and pulled out his CD player and handed the headphones to her.

"What are you doing?" she asked.

"Music relaxes me when I'm stressed, allows me to block out the world and be alone in my thoughts, might help you as well. It's worth a try at least," he said pulling out a few CDs "two are just mix CD's I burned on my PC, then there's Runrig Big Wheel and Queen Greatest Hits Two."

"Oh, I'd like Big Wheel, thank you." she replied.

"Sure." he said putting the CD in the portable player, as he set it up Tegan lay down on her side.

"Darren, could you hold me tight, it's really cold." she said, her eyes suggesting that wasn't the only reason, He was curious what other reason she could have but that was a question for another time. Darren lay next to Tegan and held her close, Tegan buried her head in his chest and she cuddled in. He waited until she seemed in a comfortable position he hit play on the CD player.

As the music played in Tegan's ears she smiled and closed her eyes and hoped Darren did the same. Soon she was fast asleep while Darren did stay awake for a while longer before eventually settling down too hoping that with the rain being this heavy it would be unlikely anyone would be crazy enough to be out there looking for them, he kissed her forehead and whispered

"Goodnight Tegan, sweet dreams" and then he pulled her in closer protectively before falling into an awkward sleep himself,

CHAPTER 17

Darren woke up first and seen the rain had stopped but it was still dark. He decided to let Tegan continue sleeping, her panic attack last night must have taken a lot out of her. He looked at her as she slept and not for the first or the last time thought just how beautiful she looked.

If he was honest, it wasn't just her looks that drew him to her now. They both had the same outlook on a lot of things and she was easy to talk to in general, they supported the same football team and both liked Formula One, they also shared a fondness for the same band and so much more, It definitely was more than just looks with Tegan. Darren had fallen for her despite his best efforts to ignore such feelings. He was worried that, just like every other girl he was attracted to, she wouldn't be interested in him in that way. Darren shook his head, this was something they were better waiting to discuss when they were both safe and there wasn't the constant fear of being captured again hanging over them.

Soon after, Tegan woke up and they prepared to leave, taking down and then folding up the tarpaulin first. Tegan took the bag again which made her feel more like she was doing her fair share. The skies were clear and Darren pointed out Orion's Belt again they worked out roughly what way to go and headed that way.

"How does your dad feel about you becoming a nurse?" Darren asked.

"He is very supportive. I don't think he was ever too comfortable in high society either, I think that's what drew him to mum. I remember him saying that very few in his family accepted her at first. He also always hated the big lavish parties and formal occasions, he would blow off a big function for... More important stuff." She replied.

"What like?" Darren said, wondering what would be more important.

"Well last time he didn't attend a family function because.." She then smiled shyly "we were watching Star Trek on video and it was a two part episode."

"You like Star Trek?" He asked curiously, a smile forming on hs lips

"Yeah, Dad prefers Next Generation, I'm more of a Deep Space Nine fan and I love sci-fi in general," she looked at him curiously "You seem surprised."

"I am," he admitted "I didn't take you for a sci-fi fan I guess, though I agree with you Deep Space Nine is the best."

"Dad and I usually have a sci-fi night if there's no

home game at Celtic Park for us to go to. He has always made sure there is at least one day a week we spend time together just the two of us, even when I was growing up," She looked at Darren and asked, "what about your parents?"

"Mine?" He asked. he sighed "here goes, my mother is a practical woman and she does love me in her own way and I do love and appreciate her but she was never someone I believed I could go to for emotional support. My dad left when I was young and we have an odd relationship. I know he loves me but I think he finds it hard to relate to me at times but he does try his best in his own way though. Then there is my brother."

"What's he like?" she asked curiously.

"He has a university degree, confident, outgoing, he's not the worst brother but I think the age gap makes it hard for him to see me as anything other than the 'little brother' which can be frustrating," he looked down at the ground sadly "The guess the one member of my family I was closest to was my grandfather."

"Oh?" Tegan said curiously.

"He died when I was barely a teenager. He was the main male role model in my life after my dad left and I learned quite a lot from him but he died before I fully appreciated what he did for me."

The look on Darren's face seemed to say it all, he didn't have a bad upbringing but it seemed like he had a confusing relationship with most of his family. One thing that seemed obvious to her now was that his grandfather was a massively positive influence on Darren's life. She wasn't sure why but Tegan took his hand as they walked and gave him a reassuring smile.

They marched on, careful to avoid anywhere too muddy. Tegan made sure Darren paced himself and when they got to a small rock formation just as the sky was getting light she told Darren to rest as She had noticed he was starting to walk stiffly again, a sure sign his knees were troubling him.

"Okay, Now you will need to trust me here, can you please pull your jeans down." she said quietly but firmly.

"Excuse me?" He sounded shocked.

"Darren, I know your knees are hurting you and massaging them may reduce the pain and help blood circulation. It's worth a try," she insisted "so, can you at least pull your jeans down?"

"Would rather not." he said sheepishly and she just gave him a look.

"I'm a nurse... Well I will be, so I will be seeing a lot of naked people so don't be shy, I just need you to trust me on this." he relented, pulling down his trousers and Tegan started to massage Darren's knees, starting with the left one and then the right, being very careful and deliberate

"How does that feel." she asked as he pulled his jeans back up

"Much better actually, thank you." he leaned over and kissed her cheek, luckily he was too busy with his belt he see her blush, they stayed a short while to rest up and give Tegan's feet a chance to recover, while they rested she took the opportunity to check Darrens wrist bandage, the wound didn't look as raw but she kept it bandages anyway. Now they had daylight they could see roughly where they were going, the idea was to get out of the featureless hills and to somewhere they can reference on the map.

It had been an hour and Tegan could see what looked like a road and trees on the other side, trees would make it easier to move without being seen but they had to be careful not to be seen getting over there but Darren had an idea, there was a low point in the hills so they made their way to it intending to cross that section of road.

"It's too risky crossing any other way," He said as Tegan followed close, clutching his hand tightly "if the wrong people driving past happen to see us come down those hills…" he didn't need to or even want to finish the sentence off for Tegan's sake, he could see it in her eyes, the longer they were in open ground the more vulnerable she felt.

As they were walking up one of the hills they heard what sounded like people talking, Darren dropped down and Tegan belatedly followed suit and crawled up the crest of the hill. They saw four people, two looked like a couple out hillwalking judging by their attire, the others not so much and the second pair looked like they were asking questions and were showing what looked like a newspaper clipping.

"Darren, what are we going to do?" said Tegan, "They must be looking for us." it was obvious to her that the clipping was something with her photo on it.

"We go the long way round." He replied softly, crawling back down the hill a little before standing and heading around the hill. As they came round the hill they spotted an empty camp with a tent.

"Do you think this belongs to the walkers or.." she couldn't complete the sentence, Darren put his hands on her shoulders and looked at her intently.

"Either way I have an idea. Tegan, please trust me on this okay?" he said.

"Of course I trust you, what are you going to do?" she asked

"I'm going to have a look inside that tent and see what supplies I can get my hands on. Regardless of who it belongs to I think we need it more than them, keep an eye out" he replied as crept close to the camp.

"Darren!" Tegan whispered as she felt her anxiety levels rising "Please be careful, they could return at any time".Tegan stayed were she was keeping lookout and trying to stay calm.

Darren went over and carefully opened the zip of the tent and looked inside and he pulled out a set of handcuffs to show Tegan.

"Well I think that answers one question..." Darren started to say but Tegan interrupted.

"Darren, please hurry" She said shakily, Darren turned round and saw she was noticeably shaking with fear so he quickly grabbed a shopping bag that had some cans of things like beans and soup with a few smaller items and took what looked like a single burner gas stove along with spoons, putting them in the shopping bag before getting back to Tegan just as they they heard some voices some closer from around the hill so Darren grabbed Tegan's arm and they ran for the nearest cover that came on the form of a ditch. Tegan nearly fell into her haste to get away.

Darren peered over and could see the two men, he was right, it wasn't the hillwalkers' camp. One was looking like he was searching in the tent while the other was looking around and had a radio in hand. Darren ducked down before he could be seen.

"It's okay, I don't think they didn't actually seen us but we probably should get away from here quickly." he said, she nodded in agreement but he could still see the fear in her eyes. No point telling her about the radio, she was terrified enough, he took her hand, being careful to be quiet and keep low, they followed the ditch towards the road.

Luckily the cover of the ditch took them out of sight of the camp but Tegan was still nervous, gripping onto Darren's arm tightly. They both managed to reach the road with no sign they were being pursued, Darren was sure it was because they were probably waiting for backup or whoever they were planning to contact on the radio.

"Tegan, it's okay they didn't see us," he had tried to reassure her, though he could see she was in full panic mode, that had been way too close for her liking "look, once we reach the trees we should be okay, just trust me, okay?" Tegan nodded, the road was quiet so they started to cross but they only got a third of the way across when they heard an engine in the distance, Tegan bolted across the road.

"Tegan! Wait!" Darren shouted and did his best to keep up. Good job for him that her riding boots aren't suitable for running and despite his bad knees, he caught up to her just as she got past the treeline though that was only because she stumbled over a tree root and fell to her knees, Darren looked behind him briefly to see a Volvo estate drive past with no intention of stopping and dropped to his knees in front of Tegan.

"Tegan, Tegan! It's okay.." he looked at her and saw she was wide eyed, shaking, she was beyond terrified. He had also noted she was frantically trying to hum Loch Lomond to herself. Darren took her head in his hands and touched his forehead to hers "Tegan, please. I am here okay? You are safe, I am not going to let anything happen to you, I promise." he kept repeating himself until he just decided instead to hold Tegan close until she stopped shaking.

"I'm sorry." was all Tegan could say in between the tears, she hadn't had an anxiety attack this bad in years, she gripped onto Darren tight.

"Tegan, they won't get you, not as long as I draw breath." Darren said with honest confidence "I had to investigate that camp for supplies"

"I know" Tegan said tearfully, her voice trembling "Sorry, I guess I let it all get to me..."

"I understand, I'm here for you." Darren reassured her "We probably should get moving, the further away the better" he added as he helped her to her feet and they continued on their way, Tegan holding onto Darren's arm, giving her some measure of comfort.

Andy was studying the map as usual when Frank came in.

"I'm going for supplies, you want anything?" He asked, Andy, looked at him intently.

"Yeah, two runaways so I can slit their bloody throats," then his shoulders sagged "Sorry Frank, still upset over Blondie, She was the one, you know? I could have seen myself spending the rest of my days with her. I know you didn't like her but she wasn't as bad as you may think, you know we hadn't even had sex yet? She was saving herself for a special moment, like when we got the ransom," Andy's eyes had a faraway look "plane to Ibiza, a villa had been rented, ride out the aftermath then return with a good tan, it was a good plan." he slumped in his chair, head in hands.

"Oh, Okay," Frank said " I'll just see what I can get you." Malcolm was heading inside as Frank headed out.

"Still lovesick?" the older man asked.

"Yeah," Frank replied "Never seen him like this before." Malcolm agreed.

"I have known the Donnelly boys a long time, he was always the quietest, I'm surprised he even came up with this whole plan." So even Malcolm had noticed.

"Something tells me it was his girlfriend's idea, apparently she was constantly making suggestions about what to do on this job." Frank confessed.

"That little blonde tart? I figured there was something about her," Malcolm said "I never trusted her, always trying to manipulate everything to suit her..." suddenly the Radio inside came to life.

"Camp five to base," was the voice of Sandy. One of the more level headed Donnelly henchmen, "I was questioning hill walkers to see if they had seen our two... Fugitives I guess... But when Greg and I got back to our camp someone stole our food, it was either them or Pat, either way better to let you know, we are going to search the surrounding area." Greg was another reliable guy, Malcolm picked up the radio and spoke into it.

"Base to Camp five, will be out as soon as we can to help," Malcolm said and turned to Andy "Let's hope it's them." Andy nodded.

"Go, Frank, you can pick up supplies later on." he ordered and Frank and Malcolm left.

"Personally I'd be surprised if it is them, Camp five is a bit off the road to Strathaven. Only put it there on the off chance," said Malcolm getting in the van "Seems more like Pat to me, he would be more brazen."

"Yeah, well we will find out when we get there." Frank said starting up the engine.

After a short walk into the woods Tegan started to relax a little and they decided to have a quick break. She sat crosslegged close to Darren as she took the opportunity to look at the stuff he managed to take from that camp, it was four tins of beans with a tomato soup tin and a few grain bars and bottled water. Tegan carefully repacked them in Darren's bag. After packing away the tin opener and spoons, Tegan held the stove up examining it, this was something she was glad to have, as especially in this cold weather as having something hot to eat would be more than helpful.

"Ever used one of those?" Darren asked.

"Seen dad use one a few times whenever we went camping," she said, as she examined it a little more, eyes lighting up as if reliving a happy memory "We always went camping in the summer, even if we went elsewhere too, to be honest, I preferred camping to going abroad," Tegan smiled putting the burner in the bag with the rest "so yeah I think I could work one," and they made to go with Tegan standing up ready to move, she leaned over to help Darren up, "I think next time we stop we should use this stuff to have a warm meal for a change," and she gave him that shy smile "I'll cook, it's the least I can do."

"Sounds good to me." He replied, Darren just stood a moment to once again admire Tegan, most guys probably would see her as some silly horse daft rich girl, others would likely see her as the plain one in the group but she wasn't. She was a beautiful young lady with so much to like about her and she had so much to give, he saw her sling the bag over her shoulder… Suddenly he felt something strike his head and it all went black...

"We should get a move on before it gets too dark." she said thoughtfully.

"You're not going anywhere.. My pretty little thing." said a familiar voice from behind and it certainly wasn't Darren.

CHAPTER 18

Tegan knew that voice, it was the tall bald kidnapper, Pat was it? She turned to see Darren on the ground, the thug dropped the lump of wood he must have used on him, the kidnappers had found them she thought, her anxiety levels rising again.

"Playtime." He sneered and made a grab for her, she ran but with a combination of her feet hurting and her boots not suited for running she didn't get far and he caught up with her and tossed Tegan to the ground.

"Now, now my pretty girl, I won't hurt you... Much I just want some fun, so be a good girl and.." Tegan swung her leg back between his legs landing a blow to his crotch "You little bitch." he said after doing his best to block out the pain. Tegan scrambled to her feet and instead of running further away, she ran back to Darren.

"Darren! Wake up!.. Please!" she pleaded, Darren made moaning noises as if starting to wake but she felt her hair being grabbed as she was pulled backwards and dumped on the ground, Pat standing over her.

"I tried to be nice.." he had a sadistic look in his "but looks like I have to teach you a lesson" and he took off his belt... Tegan did the only thing she could do, scream.

"Darren!!!"

Darren opened his eyes, his head felt like it was being used as part of a drum kit. He tried to get up but was struggling but he heard Tegan and it sounded like she was in trouble he looked in the direction of the shouting to see the big guy from Blondies merry band of kidnappers standing over Tegan lashing out at her with a belt, Darren looked over and saw lump of wood the guy must have used to knock him out and grabbed it, Darren had one thing on his mind, saving Tegan…

Pat threw away the belt and started to undo the top button of his jeans.

"Now my pretty little thing, time for.." he let out a scream and arched his back as something struck his back, he turned to see Darren, staring at him almost vacantly but the rest of his body was in a loose fighting stance.

"Should have stayed down hero, now I'm going to have to kill you first" Tegan went to get up and Pat slapped her hard.

"Stay down bitch." and he kicked her in the ribs, when he turned back round Darren punched him in the jaw but Pat just looked at him menacingly.

"That hurt, but not as much as what I will do to you." Pat said smiling coldly and started to land a few body blows on Darren as he aimlessly fought back.

Tegan's hands were shaking, tears welling up and she felt helpless, curled up in the fetal position she could just see in Darren's eyes that he was concussed and that made him vulnerable and there was nothing she could do to help as Pat kicked the legs out from under Darren, it was hard to see from her angle if he hit his head again.

Pat went to land a kick on the side of Darren's head only for Darren to roll out the way and from a crouching position, launch himself at Pat in a shoulder tackle but Pat just pushed him on his ass and grabbed the younger man by the throat.

"Once I finish you off I'm going to have so much fun with your pretty little friend here." Pat said as Darren tried pitifully to fight back.

She lay there still paralysed with fear, the last time she got involved in a fight she killed someone and Tegan was scared she would have to do the same again. She was watching as Darren, who was in no fit state to fight once again rushed to her aid, she needed to act. Darren needed her and he had time and again been there for her,

Tegan couldn't let him die like this, not Darren, anxiety attack or not she had to do something…

Darren had one hand on Pat's cheek trying to push the big man away while trying to throw weaker and weaker punches when all both of them heard was.

"Hey! Leave him alone" shouted someone. It was Tegan who was standing defiantly, her hands were trembling as she held Darren's bag by the straps like some crude weapon ready to swing it at Pat and her voice shaking but she stood her ground "leave him alone now!" Pat laughed and said.

"Or what you little.." as Pat turned his head to face her, Darren's thumb, which was pressed against his face slipped between Pat's eye socket and eyeball, the weird feeling made Darren instinctively withdraw his thumb… and the eye popped right out.

Pat howled in severe agony and let Darren go, clutching his hands over the affected eye, Tegan rushed in and started beating on him with the bag on his back to drive him off, Pat ran off screaming in sheer agony, the discarded shopping bag handle got tangled up in Pat's foot as he stumbled around. She went to Darren, tears in her eyes, he repeatedly tried to get up but was having great difficulty.

"No, Darren you have a concussion, we need to get you somewhere safe before others come to find us," she slipped Darren's bag back over her shoulder, they had to get away from the immediate vicinity and from what she saw on the map going deeper into the woods was the best way and she dare not go too far with Darren the way he was right now. Tegans first priority was to find somewhere to rest for Darren "Darren I'm going to help you get up okay? listen to me, we are going to find somewhere to rest."

"No, we must go on... Get you..."he tried to say, even after sustaining such an injury the fact that his only instinct was saving her.

"No, listen to me Darren, I know what I'm doing." she briefly checked to see if there were any other major injuries then lead him by the arm away, her own body aching from being tossed about and then whipped by Pat's belt, even through clothes they stung, suddenly she heard a noise like something big being hit by a moving vehicle and screeching tyres.

Pat was in a world of pain and just wanted to get away, he staggered out past the tree line... onto the road, still clutching his face and eye in agony.

Malcolm was deep in thought as he sat in the passenger seat of the van

"So.. " said Malcolm "You think its our young friends or big Pat?" Frank had to think before answering.

"More likely to be Pat, as you said there are more likely routes for the others and we know where they are roughly going or we hope we do."

"It's a tricky one.. Look out!!" someone wandered onto the road and Frank didn't get to slam his brakes in time and they hit the guy hard.

Malcolm was there first.

"Bloody hell it's Pat," he shouted as Frank came over to see the body, the blood was freely flowing from the back of his head.

"Oh god, look at the eye," Frank's stomach nearly emptied itself on the spot "He must have stolen from that camp and was following the road and... Hell I dunno, it's one less worry I guess." Sandy came down from the hill to the roadside.

"Greg is back at the camp," he said then looked at Pat's body and seen the bag at his feet "That's our bag... It's bloody empty, were is our stuff?"

"Best not get bogged down with small details, I will get that sheet from the back of the van, Frank get his carcass out of here and we will dispose of him later," Malcolm was always the practical one "Sandy, we will bring you guys more supplies on the road back, okay?" Sandy nodded and headed back to his camp.

Frank looked down and noticed no belt and the top button of Pat's jeans was off, oh.. he had an idea what he may have been doing, or at the least tried to do. He looked over to the woods where Pat probably came from.

"Well done kid," he said softly and smiled "Don't worry they won't find out." and he redid Pat's top button.

Tegan lead Darren away deeper into the woods, she was

being very careful with Darren's head as they went on until she saw a spot that would be ideal, it was deep enough in she couldn't be seen from the road and the cars didn't sound as close or anything. She set Darren down, being careful with his head, Tegan knew by stopping she ran the risk of recapture but it would be an even bigger risk to Darren's health if they kept going.

"Darren, stay there, please." She said to him as if he was a patient on a ward and she was his nurse, which right now she effectively was, her need to care for and protect him seemingly overriding her own fears of being captured again she had to help him. He nodded.

"Okay," he said almost in a daze "did we get him? I could not let him hurt you Tegan, I just couldn't.." he kept on repeating himself as tears absently rolled down his cheeks until Tegan held him close.

"Yes, we got him, I doubt he will bother us any more." she said reassuringly. As Tegan looked at him she thought he did not deserve this, any of it, he was just in the wrong place at the wrong time. She knew he needed rest. She stood up after repeatedly reassuring him she would be back, a nearby tree had quite a low branch so Tegan tested it and it was quite sturdy. She had an idea, getting the tarpaulin out of the bag and unfurling it she threw it over the branch and evened out the amounts on either side and even though there would be a gap between the tarpaulin and the ground it would still at least shelter them from the worst of the weather. She found some thick twigs and pushed them into the soft ground and used the rope on the tarpaulin to tie the corners to the twigs. What she ended up making was a rudimentary tent.

She checked on Darren who was just staring into space, when he saw her he said.

"My head... It really hurts." Tegan squatted down and looked into his eyes.

"Darren as I have said, you have a concussion and you need to rest, just give me a minute and we will get you rested okay." he nodded blankly, she went inside the makeshift tent and cleared debris from the floor of it and took her blazer off rolling it up for a pillow, Tegan would be cold but she could cope. She went back to the tree Darren had been propped up on and took him in and eased him down and laid his head gently on her blazer, covering him with his jacket and sat crosslegged next to him as she looked through the bag.

"I'm sorry, I... I failed you... Should have seen him coming," Darren said "Maybe... For the best... You go on without me... I'm not useful." Tegan turned to him and took his hand in her hand.

"Darren you didn't, if anything you saved me... Again," she said fighting back fresh tears, she knew he wasn't thinking straight but it was still painful to hear him talk about failing her "I won't leave you, not now, not ever. I'm only alive now because of you and stop with that useful nonsense and you know I don't see you that way," she had to stop herself from saying anything more and took a deep breath "now just lay and rest please." Tegan made sure he was okay and then she took out the little stove burner, wondering how much gas it had left, her priority was getting Darren fit enough to continue, so she selected the tomato soup as Tegan could have him drink it. Tegan opened the tin carefully and placed it on the burner, being careful putting it on, the little lighter that was taped to the side helped light the flame.

"Darren, are you okay?" she asked she knew he wasn't but still felt the need to ask even if all it did was keep him talking.

"Head hurts, closing my eyes helps a little." he said, he sounded in a bad way, Tegan was ignoring her own pain because the truth was he needed her right now and she did not want to let him down.

"Darren don't sleep, not yet, did I ever tell you about my eighteenth birthday?"

"No," he replied vacantly "why?"

"Well," she began, she had to say something, she didn't want him falling asleep before he at least had something in his system "You see, most girls I went to school wanted and generally got a huge party, not me. My big landmark birthday was spent on the grounds of the house, I had my tent up, sharing it with my mum, dad had gotten out of a business meeting in Edinburgh just to be there and he had his own tent pitched next to ours, anyway,there I was happy as can be, wearing my rubber riding boots, black jodhpurs, the Celtic bumblebee away shirt and my ski jacket, it was January so was quite cold but it didn't bother me at all. We had some snacks and a bottle of wine with some plastic wine glasses. I spent my birthday staring up at the stars in a tent with my mum and dad, listening to him as he told us all these various things about the stars, I guess this got me thinking about that night, sad I know... Darren... Darren.. "she checked him" Darren, you okay? "He opened his eyes.

"It sounded lovely actually." he said softly, Tegan checked on the soup, it was hot enough, she had to be careful about picking it up and laying it to cool a little, tin and contents both, she checked on Darren again, he was sleepy but she couldn't let him sleep quite yet she told him little tales of her riding adventures, if he was bored of them he never let on if anything he urged her to keep talking.

"... Anyway, where was I? Ah yes, there was my mum on Lolita, riding along the field behind me and we get to a gate and I just know Princess is feeling feisty and itching to jump and we are far enough away that she can jump it with a run up and she had been a good girl so I go for it," she paused to check Darren was still awake, he was... Barely "I make the jump but my mum thinks better of it, gets off Lolita and then opens the gate to walk Lolita through," she smiled at the memory "I swear Lolita sulked the rest of the trip. I think she wanted to jump too, I have never saw a horse look so disappointed before." Darren gave a weak smile as she went to check the soup.

When the tin had finally sufficiently cooled down to touch, Tegan helped Darren sit up and held him for support.

"Use both hands if you need to," she instructed "and take it easy okay," as he shakily raised the tin to his lips "there you go." she said as he drank two thirds of the soup before he had to stop, Tegan finished it off for him.

"I am really tired Tegan." She knew the there was a danger in letting him fall asleep in case it was a severe enough concussion but she also knew sleep can also help with the healing. It was a fine line she was walking with this sort of decision but the sad fact was she had no idea what was going to be best for him in this exact situation.

"Darren, promise me you will wake up." it was a silly and irrational thing to say but what else could she say? It was risky plus It wasn't just his head, Pat had done a real number on him, fortunately, he suffered no broken bones that she could tell but he was still in a bad way. He nodded blankly.

"I promise." he said sleepily and tried to get up to hug her but Tegan put a hand on his chest to stop him and instead she leaned over and kissed his cheek.

"Get some rest Darren and don't worry, I'll be here for you" she said forcing a smile for his sake.

Tegan made difficult choice to let Darren sleep mainly because there was nothing else she really could do for him but she was going to watch over him, she owed him that much and he was soon asleep, soon thereafter Tegan lay next to him, arm and leg over him, as much as to keep the body still as for her comfort and she started to drift off slowly to sleep. The pain she was suffering from Pat's physical assault, belt whipping and the emotional distress all caught up with her.

CHAPTER 19

Yet another day and neither Darren nor Blondie were at College and Jason could tell Linda was not happy.

"I can't focus," she said putting her head in her hands, if the mouse wasn't attached to the computer she would have launched it across the room in frustration "I can't stop worrying about Darren."

"Linda, please tell me you're not going to go through with this stupid idea of going to that foxhunt place." said Jason, Linda gave him a stern look.

"You don't need to come if you don't want to you know." she told him, he had been trying to talk her out of it all morning to no avail.

"No," he relented "I need to go to keep you from going nuts on them, I assume his mother has not heard any word either?" she shook her head.

"No," said Linda "in fact, the most he told any of

his family was that he was going out to meet a girl. No name or location, nothing"

Just then Jason felt a tap on his shoulder, when he turned around it was Anita.

"You two still interested in Tegan Galloway?" she said in a deadpan voice, Linda looked over and said.

"Well, he was, why?" Anita shrugged and looked at Linda.

"A friend of mine at the stables was involved in that hunt on Saturday," she said "And that Tegan was there, of course she would be," she saw Jason's blank face "Her father was leading the hunt before you ask. Now what she said was first she was with a blonde girl that no one else had seen before but was apparently her cousin," at that point, Jason smirked "What? oh please clue us both in why don't you?"she said and she slapped him on the head.

"Well, first for your information we had sort of figured she would be related to that Quentin Galloway guy, anyway, there's a good chance the blonde girl is actually Blondie, are you saying she could be some rich girl's cousin?" and he burst out laughing, Anita stared at him like he was a moron then turned to Linda.

"What's with Captain Redbeard? Is he always like this?" she asked pointedly, Linda just shrugged so she continued.

"Anyway," She said giving Jason a withering stare "The last my friend heard they were still searching for Tegan." that got their attention.

"She went missing?" Linda said slightly confused.

"Apparently from what I was told she was thrown

from her horse after just a few jumps but I don't believe it myself. You just need to read about the sheer amount of awards she has won from showjumping to know she's better than that," Anita said then smiled at Linda "If you ever need better company than laughing boy here, you know where I am, ever ride yourself?"

"No," admitted Linda "Had wanted to try though."

"Might show you sometime if you wanted." she smiled and went back to her computer.

"She is weird," Jason said with a shudder when she left "and this is getting stranger, Darren and Blondie are missing and Blondie might be this Tegan's cousin and she is missing too? What is going on here?"

Later on, they were on a bus to Strathaven and had just arrived outside Netherfield House.

"I'm mad for letting you talk me into this," Jason said as they walked up, "how do we know if anyone's in?" just then a lady with dark brown hair and wearing riding boots, black jodhpurs and a green quilted jacket came into view leading a horse. Jason, before Linda was able to react, ran up to her.

"Hi, I'm Jason Gallagher and this is Linda McKay, are you the owner of the house?" Linda shook her head, she looked too young.

"Oh no," the girl said in a distinct German accent "Allow me to introduce myself, I am Astrid Dietrich, I work at the stables during the week, they are in if you wish to see them." She smiled warmly at Jason.

"She is," he pointed at Linda "Now, am I right in

saying you are from Germany? You have a very lovely accent." Jason said, smiling. Astrid nodded.

"That is correct yes." she replied.

"Interesting," said Jason now in full flirting mode "what part of Germany.." Linda sighed as she walked up the path leaving Jason to it.

Linda rang the doorbell and stood back, it was a lovely big house she admitted that, Quentin came to the door looking slightly confused.

"Hi, listen, this may be a long shot but I'm Linda McKay and I'm wondering, my friend was here Saturday and has since gone missing, he may have been amongst the protestors… " Quentin held up a hand.

"Look... Linda is it... No offence but if he was a protestor I doubt I would know, is there anything else." Linda noted he looked tired and strung out.

"Well, have you heard of someone who goes by the name of Blondie?" Linda said thinking then turned in Jason's direction "Hey Jason hurry up!" Jason was writing something down and it looked like he kissed Astrid on the cheek and ran over punching the air as he did.

"You called?" He said smiling.

"What's Blondies real name?" She asked, as Jason stopped for breath and pointed to Astrid.

"Just got her number, we are meeting up at the weekend... Blondies name? I think its Lucy," He said, "Lucy Bannatyne, why?" Linda saw Quentin's reaction.

"That's my niece and she was here on Saturday but had to leave early due to illness" something about the name Blondie somehow seemed to ring a bell "you know her?" Linda nodded.

"Yeah we all go to the same college, my friend kinda had a crush on her and turned up to impress her." she told him.

"By protesting?" Quentin looked unconvinced.

"To be fair," Jason butted in "She told him she was protesting the hunt and Darren thought if he turned up and joined in the protest, well, you know..." Quentin looked less than impressed with the story he was hearing and the way Jason was wording it.

"So you are looking for a friend who came to protest against the hunt to impress my niece because she told him she was protesting too when she was in reality the guest of my daughter? That's what you are trying to tell me?"

"Yeah, though when you put it that way it does sound stupid but that's pretty much what I'm trying to tell you, if you met Darren you would understand why that doesn't sound that far fetched," Jason said as Linda facepalmed in embarrassment "Oh, by the way, where is your daughter? Is she okay?" Jason asked with very little Tact.

"Please leave now." Quentin said quietly but with authority and he headed back inside.

"Real smooth Jason," Linda said shaking her head as she headed back down the path, "you are a halfwit at times you know that?"

Olivia was on the phone when Quentin came back in.

"Quentin, it's the office, they have a message to

pass on."

Linda was busy berating Jason for his lack of tact when suddenly from the house they heard.

"Excuse me.." It was Quentin "Could you come back a moment? Please."

Soon they were seated inside the house in the main sitting room though Jason was fidgeting in the leather wingback chair, a sharp look from Linda made him stop.

"What I am about to say can not go any further okay?" Quentin said, both Jason and Linda nodded "On Saturday my daughter was abducted and is being held for ransom, or so I thought."

"What do you mean." Linda asked curiously.

"Well, I just received a phone call from the office, a message was left by an Irene Lawson, they left no contact number, the message simply read. I saw your daughter, she describes her and it matches her description, she was with a young man, tall, thin with very short brown hair and wearing a top with the number Thirty four on the back and it looked like they were trying to flee somewhere." Linda and Jason turned to each other.

"Darren," they both said "It has to be Darren but if that's true what's he doing out wherever the hell this Irene woman saw him... And with your daughter?" Linda asked, shock evident in her voice.

"I don't know, it sounds like what your saying is

your friend and my daughter are potentially somewhere out there somewhere."

"Unless recaptured." Jason said unhelpfully.

"Why is your friend Darren involved in this? Why is he with my Tegan?" Quentin asked, confusion evident in his voice

"I don't know, I wish I could tell you but I can't," she looked at her watch "we really should be going, May I leave you my number so you could keep me updated?" Linda asked hopefully, Quentin nodded.

"If she has escaped them and it is with him, will he take care of her." he asked in a hopeful tone.

"Darren will look after her yes, it's the way he is, he wants to help others, gets him in more trouble than anything else," she sighed taking out some scrap paper from her pocket and writing her number on it, passing it to Quentin "Let me know if you find anything, I promise not to tell anyone what's going on."

Later on, the phone rang, Quentin knew who it was.

"Hello." he said as casual as he could.

"Have you the money?" said Andy "One more day to go." Quentin decided to test them.

"I know you won't let me talk to her but how is she holding up." if they really had her she would be in full panic mode.

"She has been very well behaved," Andy said with confidence "She probably knows you will pay up."

"No nerves or panic?" He asked.

"Well she is getting on our nerves a bit, expect a

call tomorrow." and the line went dead, he seemed quick to finish the call, It wasn't conclusive and he would have to play it by ear, can't let them know he knows, what if they do recapture her? What then? but for now, it seems she is out of their hands and with this Darren, he held the note with Linda's number.

"I hope you're right and he keeps her safe." he said with a sigh, this was getting complicated.

When Tegan woke it was dark, Darren was still asleep and his jacket had slid off him. she got up and decided to put it on for now while she did a few things, they seemed safe for now as it looked like no one else had followed them into the woods. Tegan still checked on him, making sure there was no bleeding from his head or anything, she needed to keep herself busy so decided to rearrange the bag and the food to keep herself occupied. She looked over at Darren and smiled sadly.

"Darren, you can't hear me right now," she said softly " but never think for a minute you have ever failed me. From the moment we met you have shown yourself to be brave, kind, warm, gentle and caring. I can't bear to think what might have happened to me if you weren't there. You have never quit on me before so don't start now, you can do this." the truth was it was increasingly hard for her to imagine a future without him in her life. Tegan couldn't quite pinpoint when exactly but she had started to fall for him in a big way.

Looking at him now and seeing how peaceful he looked, hard to believe this pale, thin guy could have endured a kidnapping, multiple assaults, travelling over hills for days, now a concussion and yet he still managed to save her life multiple times.

"I won't leave you, I promise." Tegan said softly as she tried to settle again. Suddenly she heard some noises and decided to investigate.

Tegan exited the tarpaulin tent and for whatever reason grabbed a fallen branch, kicking the branch to break it down into a basic weapon, gripping it like it was a baseball bat she checked the area around the camp when of all things, a fox came out the bushes.

"Don't panic, I won't hurt you," she said seeing it stare at her, Tegan lowered her makeshift weapon and gave a sigh of relief "I thought you were some very nasty people," she squatted down and stared at the fox, who was just as transfixed, it's markings looked very similar to the one she saw near that cottage "Your quite a lovely creature aren't you? You need a name but I think but Mister Fox seems a bit lame," she looked at it intently "Reynard, that's it, that's your name. I don't know how much you can understand me but in that tent there I have someone I really care about and he is needing my help so as much I'd love to stay and admire you, I have someone who needs me and I need them, so please try to stay out of there, please. For me?" great, she thought, I'm not just talking to foxes, I'm naming them and being friendly. What next? The fox looked into the tent briefly but then ran back into the undergrowth "Thank you Reynard." she whispered.

Tegan headed back into the tarpaulin tent, Darren hadn't moved, she took the jacket off and laid it back on him, Tegan then sat crosslegged next to Darren and as she watched him sleep a thought occurred to her.

"I don't know why I'm telling you this now but I'm going to tell you anyway," she said softly "because I don't know what else to do and you will be sick of horse stories. When I was just eleven, my dad and I watched the movie Aliens together. I had seen the first movie a few months before and it gave me nightmares for a week, mum wasn't happy with Dad for it. Anyway, there was this one character, Corporal Hicks, soft spoken, kind, yet would put his life on the line to save others and step up when he needed to. He was my first movie crush. Couldn't get any posters of him so cut a picture of him out of an old magazine my dad had and framed it, that picture still sits next to my bed.. " she stopped to wipe away tears and lay down, cuddling into him protectively.

".. Anyway I found out the same actor was in Terminator, I mean I found out he was in other movies but he was his best in Aliens and who wouldn't want a man who who was willing to go through everything his character in Terminator went through to protect Sarah Connor? I watched both movies religiously almost every night for a long time, well watch one of them one night and the other the next anyway. Then as I grew up I realised most guys are selfish, narcissistic pricks who if they showed interest in me it was for what I was and not who I was. I had given up hope of finding someone.." she couldn't continue, she felt stupid talking about all this and she was starting to cry again. she rested her head on his chest, letting his heartbeat calm her down enough to sleep.

CHAPTER 20

Tegan didn't remember when she drifted off to sleep only that according to the watch when she woke up a few hours had passed. It was a restless sleep as she had nightmares about the fact that they could be found at any moment. The first thing she did was check on Darren who still hadn't woken up, he was breathing steady but she didn't want to try and forcibly wake him however she did feel if he didn't soon she would have no idea what to do, she didn't want to leave him but he would need help, more than she can give out here. She got out of the makeshift tent and looked up, she could see through the trees. it was still dark but thankfully just looked cloudy with no hint of rain, she looked back and saw he still hadn't moved.

She went back and sat crosslegged next to him and ran her hands lightly over his short hair and sighed.

"This is all my fault, I'm sorry. I got you into all of this," she started "Darren, please wake up, I never wanted anyone to be part of my life as much as I want you, I don't know exactly how I feel about you... Well, that's a lie. I do know, how could I not? I'm just scared to tell you and when to say it, I'm worried about how you will react. damn, why can't I have the courage to tell you to your face when you are awake, Darren I don't just want you, I need you," she took his hand and held it close to her and she thought for a moment "I mean it Darren, I have never felt like this before about anyone, I need you not just as an acquaintance, not as just a friend but as something more, something special," she started to fidget with his fingers "Darren, I need you. Please wake up," and she fell forward burying her head in his chest, sobbing away " Please wake up Darren, please."

She didn't know how long she lay there listening to his heartbeat as she cried, willing him to wake up but it was long enough that she noticed when she looked outside the makeshift tent it was daylight.

"Did you see it?" came a familiar, comforting voice, Tegan looked up and seen Darren trying to prop himself up on his elbows,Tegan was so overcome with emotion she hugged him, gave him a quick kiss on the lips and buried her head in his shoulder.

"Well," he repeated "did you see it?" Tegan broke the hug and looked at him.

"See what?" she asked slowly, unsure of what he was trying to ask.

"On your eighteenth, you said you looked up at the stars, did you see Orions Belt?"

"Oh," she said realising what he was referring to and now she thought about it she did remember her dad pointing it out to her "yeah, amongst other things, how are you feeling?"

"Like someone's used my head as a drum kit but apart from that I feel as fine as I can be, what happened anyway?" what Tegan had to remember was, as someone with dyspraxia, Darren's short term memory wasn't the best even when he was in full health, who knows how a concussion would compound such a condition.

"Darren, what do you remember happening?" she thought it best to ask that first, easier to fill in the blanks that way, Darren paused to think.

"I remember the big guy from the van, standing over you, I tried to get him away from you. I remember getting choked and suddenly he ran away howling in pain and you taking me away to here, a story about you stargazing for your eighteenth birthday... Have a strange tomato soup taste in my mouth, oh and your mum's horse being disappointed," he recounted slowly, Tegan sighed he seemed to remember more than she thought he would, she took the time to fill in the few blanks as best she could, like the accidental eye gouge "Oh okay, so that's why my thumb feels weird." he joked.

Tegan started to look into his eyes, his focus was back and it wasn't a vacant look any more, she grabbed a twig from the ground.

"Darren, follow the top with your eyes, just the eyes. Keep your head still please," Darren stared at her for a minute as if she was mad then did as instructed "just your eyes, keep your head still," she repeated then felt around his head, checking for blood, she knew there wouldn't be but just checked anyway "Darren," Tegan said, in serious nurse mode now "You had a concussion and you're not fully recovered yet, but you're well enough to move. Just try and take things easy and avoid hitting your head, I will look after you, okay?" She smiled sadly "I was worried you would never wake up." and hugged him again.

They took down the makeshift tent and Tegan put her blazer back on and took the bag before Darren tried to pick it up himself.

"I will take it, at least for today," he knew better than to argue so they headed deeper into the woods and they made some decent time, there were a few clearings but nothing too much, they stopped after a few hours as Tegan's feet were starting to hurt again and she took the opportunity to check up on Darren,

"Tegan," he said "I know I took a nasty blow to the head but why am I suddenly thinking of the actor Michael Biehn?" she gave him a confused look then it clicked, oh no, she thought, Did Darren really hear her confess that was her first big crush,

"From Terminator?" she tried to be casual about it " the guy who played Kyle Reese?" Darren smiled, she knew her sci-fi.

"I guess, though I did admittedly prefer him as Corporal Hicks myself, from Aliens." he said and Tegan laughed nervously and shook her head, it was obvious he had picked up some of what she had said but, thankfully not everything.

Darren noticed something about her reaction, a

little glint in her eyes when he said Corporal Hicks was curious.

"Maybe I have seen that movie too many times, the special edition is one of the few DVDs I have," he smiled and hugged her "Thank you." he said softly.

"What for?" She asked.

"Taking care of me, I know you are training to be a nurse but you didn't need to do what you did, any of it." he explained, Tegan looked up at him with that shy smile of hers, she hoped that maybe he would now start realising she doesn't see him as just useful to her.

"Darren, I did tell you we will get through this together no matter what," She said, then looked down and asked, "How're your knees?"

"Left ones a little sore though I think the pain in my head is cancelling it out and if you're going to give it a massage can you do it through the jeans, don't want my butt cheeks flapping in the wind again." she burst out laughing and nodded.

"Okay, I think I can manage that." and she got him to sit down and started to massage his left knee. Darren couldn't help but admire her, she meant what she said about not being like any others. There was no doubt in his mind if that had been Blondie with him she would have deserted him before now but Tegan was different. She really did seem to care for him, he was still trying to tell himself don't fall for her, it's too soon and it will only lead to hurt but if he was honest. He was falling for her but it felt... Different, he wasn't sure how, just different.

"Better?" she asked, he flexed the knee to check.

"Yeah thanks." he said with a smile.

"We better get going from what I saw on the map looks like it might take another night or two to get to Biggar, I don't know about you but I don't wanna be out here any longer than we really need to be." Tegan was also worried Darren might get injured again or worse but she was even more afraid to try flag down a car or go to a cottage or something after what happened last time and they might not be so lucky this time around, no the original plan will have to do, once again she took it upon herself to carry the bag.

They made it to the edge of the treeline and now could see fields and general farmland before them. Darren turned to Tegan couldn't help but be once again in awe of her, he still couldn't get over that this lovely gorgeous, intelligent and caring lady was still single, he shook his head and followed, Darren could also see that Tegan wasn't just worried about the kidnappers any more, but she was concerned about his well being, it was the little things he noticed. Suddenly there was a car engine noise, it was a beat up Land Rover Defender, probably owned by a local farmer, they both dropped down and hid in the long grass near the trees.

"Tegan, be honest, are you okay?" Darren asked, he worried how she would react after the previous times they were nearly discovered.

"I think so," she said eventually in a low whisper, gripping Darren's arm tight "Who is it anyway?"

"Hold on" Darren said and raised himself to a crouch, it was just as he suspected, the local farmer and it looked like he was checking his gate for damage."Its just a farmer," he told Tegan but as he looked into her eyes he saw her fear slowly return "Tegan it will be okay." he reassured her as the Farmer got back into his Land Rover and drove away, it did seem he was unhappy at something. Darren helped Tegan to her feet and she hugged him tight.

"I don't know how much more of this I can cope with." she said, her voice quivering slightly

"Tegan, you are doing better than you think, trust me" Darren replied "But might be an idea to move on in case he returns." as they heading over to the gate Darren saw why the Farmer wasn't happy, once of it's hinges had broken clean off.

"What caused that?" Tegan asked as she looked around,

"No idea," replied Darren "and I don't intend on staying to find out." They ran as best they could to the other side of the field, using the other gate and carefully shutting it over, but as they turned round Tegan lost her footing and fell into a shallow ditch that ran alongside the hedge line, but not before she grabbed Darren's arm, taking him with her and he fell on top of her. They both lay there and initially started to laugh but then fell silent and stared deep into each others eyes, their heads leaned closer, lips were about to touch... But the noise of the returning Land Rover broke the silence, they could hear it from the other side of the field. Darren peered over the edge of the ditch and could just make out between the gaps in the hedge that it looked like the farmer had returned with someone else and it looked like they were going to make an attempt at mending the gate.

For the next hour they said out of sight in the ditch waiting for the farmer to leave, they couldn't risk him seeing them even at a distance and stayed as quiet as possible. Tegan sat quietly cuddling into Darren tightly, using his chest as a very convenient head rest, listening to Darren's heartbeat while his arm was draped over her protectively, even after everything he had been through her safety was still his first priority. Tegan realised she would have to tell Darren her true feelings for him and soon but it was a matter of when was a good time to say to him. She was shaken out of her thoughts by the Land Rover engine, it sounded like it was driving away, Darren went up to check.

"That's them away for now. We might as well get going in case they come back again." he said stepping out the ditch and helped Tegan up on to her feet. She gripped his hand tight as they continued on their way.

Frank stopped at the road junction and got out, two guys dressed in black emerged from the bushes.

"Radio battery is flat." one of them said but Frank wasn't interested in that.

"So.. any sightings at all Rob?" He asked the one holding the now useless radio.

"No, had a few people on horseback but two were guys and none of the girls had dark hair and just before you arrived Barry here was sure he saw two people on bikes but it wasn't them. This is a wild goose chase, I have gear sitting at home waiting to be sold and what am I doing... " Rob looked like he was going to rant.

"I know, I know, isn't your cousin helping while you are away?" Frank asked, Rob shook his head.

"Yeah, that's why I'm a bit worried," Rob retorted "What if the Harvey's or the Lyle's or anyone else gets wind of this? Never mind that, what if Andy's brothers find out he has pulled in a lot of favours for this? He does know if he doesn't at least get the ransom money they won't be happy and that's putting it nicely." Frank was starting to question this tactic too, These guys were all just drug dealers, brawlers and other undesirables, they weren't a big cohesive unit, just a strange alliance of career criminals loyal to a particular crime family, no wonder they weren't having luck.

"At least you did better than Mick, he radioed in a sighting of a fox" Frank said shaking his head "will pick you guys up later." he added as he headed back to the van and drove back to see Andy

Frank got back to the safe house and went to see if Andy was okay but stopped short as he saw Andy still in the bathroom and it looked like he was snorting cocaine, as Andy left the bathroom, rubbing the bottom of his nose, Frank confronted him.

"Okay, how long have you been on that crap?" he demanded.

"What?" Andy said innocently "Oh.. That," and he made an exaggerated sniff for emphasis "So? Blondie got me into it. Look, it's kept me going and it's just a bit of coke." Frank couldn't believe what he was hearing.

"None of your brothers has ever touched the stuff yet you meet up with that blonde bitch and you think your scarface or something, I knew something was up." Frank said not caring if he offended Andy at this point, Andy got up in his face.

"It was a good plan, still is, you see? We get them, kill them and collect the ransom, or we collect ransom, get out of the country with it before the two surface. It's a win no matter what. It's only you and I that need to flee, she never really got a close look at Joe and Pat is dead, you use Blondies ticket, It's foolproof, but I want them to die, Frank, I want them to suffer, we got one more day to find them," Andy brushed past Frank "Malcolm, get on the radios, find out if they have been spotted." Andy looked crazed and Frank realised there was going to be no reasoning with him.

Linda had decided not to go to college for at least the rest of the week, she told Jason her nerves couldn't cope but that she had phoned Darren's mother to update her as best Linda could. While everyone else was busy working away. Jason took a moment to look out the window and thought of Darren out there somewhere with that rich guy's daughter and shook his head and said to himself.

"Mate when I said go find another girl, I meant one of the protestors, stay safe wherever you are."

CHAPTER 21

The going was generally easier once they left the trees and on to the rolling fields, fences, hedges and ground that Tegan found much more familiar.

"Princess could probably make that sort of jump." She pointed out a particularly high hedge.

"Really?" said Darren suitably impressed.

"Yeah," she nodded "Of course, she couldn't at first but after a few hunts she really shone, I think it's the fact that in a pursuit, you have the speed and adrenaline pumping through rider and horse and eventually your horse can almost glide over such obstacles. In fact, after a few hunts, the jumps in showjumping get easier." Darren smiled silently, it was the first she ever really went in depth about her riding since they started. You could see the passion she had for it in her eyes, he let her go on for a while explaining various aspects of horse riding.

"You make it sound elegant." he said eventually. Tegan figured that if they roughly followed the road to Biggar and tried to stay out of sight they should be okay. Ever since Darren's concussion Tegan had stepped up and even taking charge when she had to. She found a nice overgrown hedge that would hide them from the road and offered some protection from the elements for the to rest up a while, she got the burner stove on and Darren opened the tin of beans to heat.

"We don't have any plates." He pointed out but she had thought of that and produced the empty tomato soup can she had washed out in a puddle, not the most hygienic but it was better than nothing.

"Just put half in that." she said matter-of-factly, as they waited Tegan took the opportunity to see if Darren was okay, doing the same checks as before though she changed it up this time by holding up three fingers.

"How many fingers am I holding up?" she asked.

"Three," he replied but then looked at her, "Tegan, I know your trained and I am thankful but don't you think this is overkill?" but her stern look told him otherwise, as they sat and waited for the beans to heat Tegan looked deep in thought.

"Darren, what would you have been doing today if Saturday didn't happen?" she asked, he had to think before he answered.

"Probably in a lecture I think, listening to Jason's wise words of wisdom about women or his views on the Rangers team while Linda cracks up at us because we are distracting her. Yeah that sounds just about right, you?" he replied.

"In university, either at a lecture or maybe sitting somewhere reading a book, I don't socialise much even if I wanted to," she said with a hint of sadness "Darren, What do you see when you look at me?" she asked.

"Tegan, we kinda been through this before.. " but she held up a hand.

"No, I'm not talking about attraction or noticing me in that sort of way. You see, because I'm not the most talkative person, I live in a big country house and I ride horses competitively, others do see me as a little bit... Stuck up," Darren laughed "What?" she said confused.

"You are anything but stuck up," he answered once he composed himself "from what you have told me it seems you are quiet and keep to yourself in general, nothing wrong with that. In regards to what you wear going to university, you don't dress typical upper class or anything, I seriously doubt sweater shop jumpers are what the supermodels are wearing these days," he had to word the next part carefully "I do admit when I saw you with your full clean riding gear you did look kind of like the stereotypical image of a rich girl with a horse but as you said yourself that's only for hunts and competitions, I know you have mentioned that at home your usually in some form of riding gear but that's a comfort thing, right?" Tegan nodded and gave a sad smile, her eyes suggesting she was reliving a painful memory.

"Unfortunately the majority don't think so, one time when I was still at school and I invite a classmate to come round for a study session for biology thinking it will be a good opportunity to make friends, so Andrea turns up at my door she's got the jeans, converse and a t-shirt on, I answer the door, Celtic top, black jodhpurs and my rubber riding boots, it's Sunday and I'm dressed for comfort. The next day she told everyone dressed like that to show off and I was labelled a poser." she looked at Darren sadly.

"Why?" He asked putting an arm around her, she rolled her eyes and sighed as if she still hadn't quite worked that one out fully either.

"Apparently I missed the school memo stating you must only wear riding gear when in a stable or on a horse. Rumours went around that I didn't horse ride as much as I said I did, I just dressed like someone who did. Never mind I was in the stables before she arrived and went for a ride after she left. The fact I was in riding gear the whole time she was there, was enough to label me a stuck up poser for dressing like that for Andrea coming over."

"Tegan, high school can be very cruel, trust me I know.. " he started to say.

"Yeah I know but Darren this was Saint Aloysius. Ad majora natus sum and all that" she gave him a knowing look "Apparently it means I am born for greater things" she shook her head.

"I prefer the Saint Ignatius motto myself. Ad majorem dei gloriam, for the greater glory" Darren said and then he realised, "Hey, isn't Saint Aloysius the big posh Catholic School in Glasgow? Where you... Pay to get in?" He asked, she nodded sadly.

"Yeah, but even then I was labelled as a poser and

up myself, never mind the ones who actually were like that, no, they somehow always got a free pass. Andrea herself had not one but two horses at the time. In Fact that's why I invited her, I hoped we could be friends with a common love of horses. I remember sitting on my bed crying, now I could have given up riding and gotten rid of all my stuff. Been like the other girls and the endless weekend fashion parades but no, if I did that then the bullies won. So I doubled down on my riding.." she noticed Darren had taken her hand.

"Tegan, you definately made the right choice. You didn't change who you are and you are stronger than you think." he said with that honest tone that got her every time, she relented with a smile.

"Yeah, sorry, it's just the prospect of being amongst people again who if they aren't ignoring me, girls see me as a stuck up poser and guys see me as a chance to enhance their standing in high society or I am breeding stock," she leaned against him "and my parents wonder why I spend more time with horses than people." she said softly, Darren nodded.

"Could be worse," he said and gave her a strange look "You might need a flowchart here. In high school, a guy I knew told me this girl liked me and maybe I should ask her out, I know I should have sensed it wasn't true but when your lonely... You take the chance," Tegan instinctively cuddled in, she sensed this was not going to end well "well I ask her and she politely says no as she has a boyfriend. These things happen right? So on the way home is a Library and I go in to see what sci-fi they have in and a couple of Star Wars books later I'm leaving and see that same girl waiting at the bus stop outside.. "

"With her boyfriend?" Tegan asked.

".. No just herself but I felt terrible for earlier and went up and said I was sorry for earlier but I wasn't told she even had a boyfriend, she accepted my apology and even admitted she had just started dating the guy so it wasn't like I would have known she had someone. I thought that was that," He gave her a look suggesting it wasn't "Oh no, her boyfriend was telling people I pestered her for a date then stalked her to the bus stop, guess who the boyfriend was? The guy who told me to ask her out in the bloody first place."

"You are kidding surely? Would you have looked at her if he hadn't mentioned she liked you?" she asked as she gripped Darren tighter.

"She was attractive but not my first choice, but it was one of a long line of incidents in which people would say, hey that girl likes you or it was a case of me telling the wrong people I think a girl looks nice and being urged, more like goaded into doing something about it, leads to me asking them out or otherwise letting my intentions be known only for them to have zero interest and then I'm made out to be a creep and the poor girls are embarrassed, sometimes I'd accept it won't happen other times I'd either be confused about why they say no, especially if I have been told they did like me, or just desperate for a chance I would stupidly keep asking in the bizarre hope there would be a change of heart, some don't even say no outright and that causes its own problems. People either laughed or vilified me, of course no one wanted to hear let alone believe my side of events, plus I had no one I felt could really talk to about it all."

He was so lost in his memory he didn't see the look on Tegan's face, she was horrified about just how calmly he accepted it all. His dyspraxia would have made things like that all the more difficult for him, even worse if he was undiagnosed at the time.

"Darren, how the hell are you so normal, I'm sorry but it's true. It just seems that it doesn't matter if it's at school, college or wherever if you are not the butt of someone's joke they are using you because you are useful to them. It's not right." she was starting to cry about it.

"Tegan, calm down," He said taking her hand "it's crazy I know and it was horrible but look at me now, I learned some vital lessons. I know how most people see me, I'm socially awkward, my mental conditions affect my interactions with people and how I talk. I know to a lot of people I usually come across as at least weird and misjudge me as a result. It's a horrible situation, Trust me I know but here I am, I just do my best to try to learn from past mistakes. I'm not totally blameless though and I am prone to making stupid judgement calls. Case in point, remember I'm only here because I thought if I turned up to a protest I would get the girl I thought might be the one," then he looked deep into Tegan's eyes "I know you blame yourself for me being caught up in all this but please don't. I chose to stop that van, I chose to confront them over the noises you were making and I chose not to escape without you, the thing is I do not regret doing any of it? Not in the slightest and I if I had to do it all over again I would do exactly the same thing. I wouldn't have met you if I didn't would I? You are.." he stopped and he got up quickly "Beans!"

"What? " she said quizzically.

"beans!" he ran over and used his jacket sleeves like oven gloves to take them off the stove as she turned the burner off, as they waited for it to cool a little Darren crouched next to Tegan and took her hand.

"Tegan, you are a wonderful, beautiful person, if people can't see that they are not worth knowing..." he looked like he was going to say something but changed his mind "I'll get the food ready." and he kissed her head before getting up and preparing the food for them. Tegan blushed shyly and hid her face in her hair, grateful he wasn't looking.

They had a meal of half a tin of beans each, one using the tomato soup tin before packing up and heading out on a long trek through the fields.

Quentin was still trying to focus on his work at home but failing, he went for a stroll out to the horses, he saw Astrid who was busy grooming Princess.

"Astrid," he asked, "Where is my wife, have you seen her." Astrid pointed to Lolita's stable.

"I think she is tending to Lolita." she replied and continued with her duties.

He went up and saw his wife wearing her casual riding gear, Tegan and her mother were so alike it was daunting sometimes. Quentin stood quietly and watched Olivia tend to the horse, he knew it kept her mind occupied which was probably for the best all things considered. She stopped once she noticed him.

"What is it Quentin? Any news?" Olivia said with concern and she came over to him.

"I can't concentrate on anything. Even if Tegan is with this Darren, I know that Linda woman said he could be trusted but still my mind is racing and I can't help but worry," he braced himself against the stable wall for support "What if he tried to take advantage of her or something?"

Olivia shook her head and leaned against the wall next to him

"From what I understood about him, he does seem, if anything, almost a little too nice to the point of being a pushover. Oh, while I remember, have you heard from Lucy at all?" she asked, Quentin shook his head.

"To be honest there was something I meant to say. During one of the ransom calls, I'm sure I heard someone mention the name Blondie, I didn't think anything of it at the time until I heard that Linda tell us Lucy's nickname was Blondie." Quentin gave Olivia a knowing look.

"No," she said, shocked "You can't mean.."

"The first time they meet in years is the one time Tegan, a champion showjumper and a natural on a horse in general, is thrown from her horse..."

"Of course she wasn't just on any old horse, it was Princess." Interjected Olivia.

"...Exactly, so we are told Tegan was apparently thrown so badly she couldn't get back up? Then we get a kidnap demand, which now that I think on it, was for the exact amount her father pestered me for months to loan him apparently just one more time now that I come to think on it. Maybe she convinced this Darren fellow to get in on it and he changed his mind, maybe he went to find Lucy and found them, who knows but some of it is starting to make sense now." Quentin was seeing clearly now, it made too much sense.

"It would explain why Lucy was wanting to get away quickly, I thought it was just nerves. Lucy played us all by the sounds of it." Olivia mused, things were falling into place for her too and she didn't like the way things were playing out.

"I going to try and get some work done," Quentin said after a brief silence, he hugged Olivia close then headed back into the house.

Olivia waited until Quentin had headed back inside to his office again and made her way out of the stables and into the kitchen pick up the phone, she dialled quickly.

"Hello, Police.." she said, voice trembling "I'd like to report a crime.."

CHAPTER 22

It was ransom call time again and Andy was wiping the underside of his nose with his hand, he felt more than ready for this, he picked up the phone and dialled, and Quentin answered.

"Got the money?" He said directly.

"Yes." Quentin lied.

"Good, tomorrow at midday, go to the payphones at Queen Street Station, one will ring and reveal the location of your daughter, you leave the money in a bag and go get your spoiled little bitch." Malcolm would be heading back into Glasgow tonight for the pickup.

"Can I.." Quentin started.

"Oh no, you know the rules." Andy said smugly but Quentin wasn't done.

"I hope that Blondie girl is looking after her." He wondered what the reply would be.

"Oh she is, you can trust me on that" there was a slight but noticeable strain in Andy's voice "Good care of her." and the phone went dead.

Andy sat brooding, the mention of Blondie which should have sent warning bells off in his head instead made him think of her all the more, he went out to clear his head. Frank looked on, Joe came up behind.

"Joe in all your time doing this, has there ever been a ransom hand-off where the kidnappers don't even have a bloody body?" He looked back at Joe "I mean we have sent people out to every possible place they would go to from here to Strathaven, nothing," He massaged his temples, "We have found doggers, pony trekkers, hill walkers, foxes, badgers and bloody mice.. everything but them." ever since they found Pat, Frank hadn't been as convinced that was where they were going but he had no idea what the real destination was and had no real desire to find out.

"The closest was that time we did that fake kidnap of that Latif girl but she was willing". Frank remembered that, Nathan Kelly, a cousin of the Donnelly boys and a nice guy had fallen for a girl called Shazia Latif, who came from a strict Muslim family and she was arranged to be married but Nathan and Shazia really wanted to be together so the Donnellys, well at least the oldest brother Michael, liked Nathan enough to help so they staged a kidnapping and sent the couple to family in Ireland and that was that, no ransom, no demands, nothing. Shazia got a whole bunch of fake documents, that didn't come cheap, new passport, a driving license. everything. They still live there in the city of Cork, last Frank heard they got married and expecting their first kid.

"I remember that one," said Frank "I mean from what I know of arranged marriages, its not all that bad usually but if I remember right her dad was pretty much making her go through with it all and she would have had to leave the country to go and live with this arranged husband. I remember Nathan telling me all that. Oh, the look on her dad's face when we came out in balaclavas and all in black and grabbed her, she could act scared a little too well." he remembered fondly, Joe nodded.

"Yeah, when she started pretending to beg her dad for his help in whatever language that was she spoke he really got aggressive." Joe said.

"Was that when you punched him?" Frank asked as he tried to remember.

"Yeah," Joe replied "broke his nose too. Then I jump into the back of the van and there they are, Nathan has his balaclava off, she has ditched her headscarf thing and there they are kissing and cuddling and you standing there pretending your shouting at her to stop crying."

"I actually enjoyed that one, this one, however? It's all gone to hell." Frank said looking down.

Quentin just sat there in his home office, That all but confirmed it in his mind, Lucy was part of the plan. He looked at a picture of both of them, how happy they both were in it. Maybe he should have done more for her when her father died but Lucy's mother blocked his attempts to help. He tried but he had his daughter to look after. If only Lucy had come and spoken to them. He couldn't change the past but he could have helped them going forward or at least help Lucy if her mother was still bitter, he could have done something and all this, the fear and the worry could all have been avoided.

It was something he knew haunted Olivia too, she was close to Sandra, Lucy's mother and was the one who encouraged them to be as close. At one point people did think they were sisters which made it all the worse.

All this was because he refused to simply bail his brother out once more, Quentin thumped his desk in despair.

The light was starting to fade as Tegan and Darren were continuing to hike across the fields, they were going along a hedge when Tegan looked over to the road and stopped, dropping to her knees, Darren looked over and saw a Police car on the side of the road and two officers were in the field next to the road, he felt Tegan grab him and pull him down.

"Tegan, what is it?" he tried to ask Tegan "It's just the police..." he was going to tell her at least if they went to the police they would be alive and safe but the fear in her eyes told him she wouldn't see it that way.

"What if they are looking for us? What if they had reported Lucy's death? Who knows what story they have told." she said franticly, she held onto Darren tight.

"Okay, we'll stick to the original plan and contact your parents first, it's okay Tegan." he relented on the issue, he didn't realise just how worried she was about it until now.

"What are they looking for?" Tegan asked, they peered through the gaps in the hedge and saw one officer run in their general direction, "Oh no.." Tegan said and was about to get up and run away until something caught Darren's eye and he had to pretty much tackle her down before she could be seen.

"Darren?" she asked in a harsh whisper "what are you doing?" as he felt her body shake.

"Look." he pointed as he saw the officer grab a man who had a shirt on unbuttoned and what looked like suit trousers who had been running towards their general direction, he only came into Darren's field of vision at the last moment.

"What the.." She said softly then saw the other officer further down with a redheaded girl who looked only half dressed, it was only then did they notice the black sports car stopped in front of the police car "They weren't, were they?" Darren looked at her as if she was naive.

"Oh they were... it's the old let's go do something spontaneous thing. Couples want to have sex in strange and sometimes public places in the heat of the moment. Never got the big fuss though." he said as they watched the couple get quizzed by the police.

After a while, the police drove off and it was safe to move on but it was getting darker and they needed somewhere safe to camp for the night. It was then they came to a small farmhouse.

"We will need to go round it I suppose." Tegan said as she felt herself tense up but her feet were hurting and she knew they would need to stop soon for the night, as they went round Tegan noticed a small grouping of trees in the next field and what caught their eyes was that, in the middle, it looked like someone set up some sort of camp "What about there? The trees will hide us from the house, who do you think made it?" she asked.

"Probably the farmer or local kids by the looks of things, I can imagine when there are leaves on the trees and stuff that it makes for quite the hangout," Darren mused, there was an old rear car seat that had been taken out whatever car it had once belonged to and put in this little clearing as a makeshift sofa, it looked like the middle, with the ring of stones, was meant to be a campfire pit and there were a few other makeshift seats, a plastic crate, a plastic garden chair that had seen better days and an old wooden box, Darren looked over to the house, it was far enough away and obscured by a hedge to make it worth the risk making camp there "Looks like it's been there a while. We could stay here tonight, as long as we are up early enough to get away before being seen." he said. Tegan looked around and agreed with Darren and she was looking at the car seat craving the chance to sit on something soft for a change.

"Okay, let's do that," she smiled as she let herself fall onto the car seat "This feels better than it has any right to be." she said eyes closed and smiling, she wasn't going to move any time soon.

"Well it's settled then," Darren said picking up the

bag Tegan unceremoniously dropped and started to get dinner ready "For tonight's dinner we have a few options beans, beans or for a change we have beans." Tegan sat forward in mock indecision.

"I think," she said slowly "I will have the beans, baked ones of course." Darren smiled and was about to say something but they locked eyes, it looked like she was going to say something too but they just laughed instead.

Frank was cleaning the back of his van with a hose, it had been dirty from bringing back all the merry campers and then dropping them off near a nearby train station with train fare given to them out of Andy's own pocket and a promise of a cut of the ransom. Washing the van gave him something to do before the big day, Joe came over with something in his hand.

"Is that Malcolm away?" Joe asked.

"Yeah, he's away, the others are away too talking about going drinking and thinking of a big payday," Frank said with a hint of sarcasm "we haven't found them and if they surface before everything goes down.." but he saw Joe shake his head.

"No, if you ask me something went wrong with them, trust me there's no way some city kid and a rich daddy's girl could evade us that long, Malcolm has been tracking and hunting for years and we had people in the right areas and nothing. One or both could be severely injured, could be dead... Remember we don't know if Pat got to them and the way he was, he would have killed both," Joe looked out to the hills "Some hill walker is going to discover their bodies in there someday and I plan to be long gone by then." Frank had never thought of it that way, a part of him hoped it wasn't true though and he felt Joe sold the young hero short but something caught his eye in Joe's hand.

"What's that in your hand." Frank asked, Joe lifted it, it was Blondie's bag.

"Found this cleaning the place up." he gestured for Frank to follow him to the front of the van where he emptied the contents onto the passenger seat. There were some little bags of cocaine, a purse, some college papers, a passport, a pair of denim shorts and dirty beige Jodhpurs along with a few other items, Joe retrieved the purse and something that looked like a printout.

"Have a Look." Joe handed Frank the printout it was a confirmation email for flight tickets... For one.

"You will like it even less when I show you this," Joe pulled a card out of Blondie's purse, a Glasgow College of Building and Printing card "How much of the plan were you told about?"

"Well to be honest," Frank said, "only that we abduct the girl and take her to here and the ransom was half a million, why?" Frank had a horrible feeling "I think Andy mainly wanted my van."

"The original plan was the girl is kidnapped and brought here but on Monday, Blondie would go back to college like nothing happened and maybe play the concerned relative if need be. Malcolm wasn't the original person to pick up the ransom, she was. You see her college is right next to Queen Street Station, so she could retrieve it then get in a taxi and meet up with us afterwards," Frank could tell Joe didn't like that part of the original plan either "money is shared out, they get on the plane and we do whatever."

"You think she would have grabbed it and got on that flight, which I notice is earlier than the one Andy has mentioned, leaving us to deal with the aftermath." Frank said, the realisation hitting him.

"Actually," Joe said mournfully "It wouldn't really surprise me if on the way out she planned to phone and tip off the cops about the whole abduction plot, leaving her involvement out of it of course."

"In all honesty that sounds exactly the sort of stunt she would pull, Told lover boy yet?" Frank asked.

"No, better wait till the morning or at least until after the ransom drop off if we tell him at all, see how it goes. If it all works out might be no real need to tell him to be honest. Let him think she was his perfect partner. It's a big day tomorrow one way or another." sighed Joe.

CHAPTER 23

After a dinner of baked beans, Darren was packing the gas burner back in the bag and looked at Tegan, she had a rather worried look.

"Tegan, what's wrong?" He asked, she looked at him with that shy smile, though her eyes gave away the sadness inside.

"Darren, I have been doing some thinking about this and maybe when we get to Biggar it might be better you go into town yourself as you can blend in easier." Tegan had a point, walking down the main road dressed in full riding regalia, Regardless of how dirty it looked the attire would be way too distinctive, if the kidnappers or anyone else were still looking for them she would be too easy to spot and they both knew it but Darren shook his head.

"No, I have a better idea," Darren said as he took

his jacket off and then took off his lucky top, revealing his Marvin the Martian t-shirt underneath, handing the goalkeeper top to her he said "Here, put this on and we can put your stuff in the bag." she took it hesitantly.

"Are you sure?" she asked, Darren nodded.

"I'm not leaving you, not now. What if they found you while I'm away phoning your parents? No, we go in together," there was something she saw in his eyes when he spoke, it was that fear of failing her she saw after the incident that first day at that cottage with the couple who tried to keep them apart, he then added "And if anyone.. Especially the police asks anything about what happened to Blondie… I will tell them was self defence." that was unexpected, back when they first spoke about it all those nights ago he was adamant it was not, something has to have changed his mind.

"Why," she said, surprised "why would you lie for me?" He had not brought that subject up in a while but has been clearly on his mind, all he did was look at her, and said

"Please don't ask," then he sighed "I can't risk you going to prison, especially not for saving me, I just can't risk anything like that happening to you." There he was, once again doing everything to protect her, no matter the cost to him. She sat for a few seconds then stood and went behind the old car seat then she started to undo her blazer eventually Darren took the hint and turned his back, she laid the top out over the seat, She looked at it and remembered when the kit came out she did like it and nearly bought one herself. The number Thirty Four was still mostly clean and white despite what they had been through and she traced the outline of the numbers with her finger, Tegan wondered if this was his way of passing on his luck to her, she admitted it was a really sweet gesture regardless. Smart too as people will see and probably remember a girl wearing a football shirt before they see anything else about her.

Tegan removed her blouse and then eased the goalkeeper shirt on, it was a baggy fit, and the sleeves were slightly long but Darren was right it was warm. As she adjusted the sleeves, she looked at Darren who still had his back turned and realised she couldn't hide how she felt about him any more, here was a guy who a few days ago didn't know her, had no reason to help her at all yet repeatedly did everything he could to protect her. It didn't matter if he was brave or foolish, it didn't matter to him whether he was in pain or suffering injury. He genuinely cared about what happened to her, not her the showjumping champion and not Quentin Galloway's daughter... Just her... Just Tegan. She needed him in her life, it wasn't a case of wanting him, it was a need, pure and simple. He deserved to know how much he meant to her and what her feelings towards him were and she had to do it now.

"I'm ready. You can turn around now, what do you think?" she said eventually as she rounded the car seat. as he turned around she stepped forward grabbed his shoulders, stared deep into his eyes and for a moment it looked like she was going to say something but instead she simply pulled Darren close and kissed him and did not let go, time seemed to stand still.

Darren was initially surprised but put his arms tight around her, feeling her do the same to him. Despite his tired body aching all over and despite the danger they were still in, he didn't want this moment to end. It felt like little electrical pulses up and down his body and it was intoxicating as it seemed the more they kissed the more intense the feeling got. Only the desperate need to breathe broke the kiss, Tegan looked at him intently with a glint in her eye. Despite the strange appearance of her wearing a Metallic grey Celtic shirt, beige Jodhpurs and tall leather riding boots with spurs on, to Darren she was a beautiful sight.

"Regardless of anything else that happens, I need us to be together, I need you, not as an acquaintance, not just as a friend, you mean more to me than you can ever know... I.. I.." Tegan said but was struggling to continue, tears welling up. She knew what she wanted to tell him but couldn't get it out.

"I know... Somehow I know. I have been wanting to tell you the same thing, just didn't know what to say or even when to say it," And he held her hands, looked deep into her eyes "Are you really sure about this, it's not just because of all that's happened these past few days or anything? You really want... us?" she simply nodded and said.

"Darren, I promise you I have never been more sure about anything before in my life and it's not just a want, its a need, a need for you." with that they kissed again, a long deep loving kiss.

Quentin heard the doorbell and was ready to answer the door when Olivia said she would get it, if he was honest it was probably a good thing as his legs were like jelly, the stress of what may or may not happen tomorrow was getting to him. There were some voices at the door then footsteps, at the doorway stood a blonde woman aged roughly in her forties in a dark grey suit and a black coat, a male in a dark blue suit and two uniformed officers and a very sheepish looking Olivia.

"Mister Galloway I am detective sergeant Turner from Strathclyde Police, this is my colleague detective inspector Marriott. Now your wife phoned us about an abduction involving your daughter.." the blonde officer said, Olivia looked at Quentin almost pleading.

"I'm sorry Quentin but I had to, it's gone on far enough." Olivia blurted out.

".. Anyway Mister Galloway, you really should have come to us long before now, your wife told us a lot already but we need to know everything from the start including any and all possible involvement of one Lucy Bannatyne. I was informed she is your niece, would this be true?" Turner asked sternly as Quentin offered her a seat.

"She is indeed and you better sit down, this may take a while." he said slightly flustered.

Tegan sat with her sore boot encased feet up on the car seat and cuddled into Darren, holding his hand as well.

"Can't wait till Jason hears about this" Darren said smiling as he stroked Tegan's hair.

"And whys that," Tegan asked, her voice one of contentment.

"Well one of the last pieces of advice, before we left college last Friday, I was told to go to the protest in the hope I would meet a nice young protestor. Instead, I end up finding you." he told her as she laughed.

"Instead you ended up with one of the people you were protesting against," she admired the irony there "Does he try to dispense advice often?" Darren sighed.

"Not really, he just tells me all his exploits and conquests. Though for every one there are about five he has rumoured to have been with which aren't true so it's hard to keep up these days. He is a nice guy, just has a bit of a reputation that's all."

Tegan cuddled into him a little closer, ever since admitting her feelings for him she had seemed more relaxed.

"It's strange," she said softly "I thought the hunt would go as usual. Dad and his friends go hunt the foxes while I follow near the back, then go home and spend the night in my room reading or watching videos.."

"I would have been doing the same, but playing games on my PC too, think we had an event scheduled, some big squad versus squad battle. They can be quite fun." Darren interjected.

"... But then Lucy accepted my invitation to come over and be part of the hunt so I thought we would have a chat and catch up. After all, it has been four years since I even saw her in person, but then all this happened. I don't want to think about what would have happened if you hadn't been there," she looked up "Darren you mean more to me than you will ever know, I keep thinking about if anyone else have done half of what you did and the answer is always no." Darren smiled, looked down and stroked her cheek.

"Tegan, I know I've said this before but you really don't realise how beautiful you actually are do you? yes, you have the looks but you are also very kind, smart and amazing company. Oh and you have impeccable fashion sense too.." he started to say but Tegan gave him a look.

"Really? This is what you like this? jodhpurs? tall riding boots? Baggy football tops that don't show much off?" she looked and sounded amused "This is what gets you going?" she gave him a playful look.

"Yes really, I've told you before you do suit riding gear," he kissed her forehead "And yes it actually does if I'm honest." he admitted and she smiled shyly.

"Glad to hear it, because you are gonna see a lot of me like this, the few times I'm not in some type of riding gear are when I'm going to university or if I'm out somewhere that doesn't have anything to do with horses, but you probably figured that out already," she said in a tone that suggested she was grateful he understood "so get used to it." She added cheekily with a playful grin,

"Oh I think I could get used to it" he said before asking "Tegan? Can I ask? What's the deal with you and boots anyway? You mentioned before you like them and I get that you need them for riding.." he trailed off, not sure where he was going with the conversation.

"Well," she started "I guess it started when I took

up riding and helping out at the stables from an early age. I was in them more often than not and I suppose it got to a point I don't feel right without some kind of knee high boot on. Just a comfort thing I guess," she thought for a minute "The thing is most others I know in riding circles tend to put on the boots as late as they can and take them off the minute they don't need them on any more. I get strange looks from the others when I turn up and walking around in them the whole time," gave him a look that suggested this happened a lot "I do understand some people do want to keep them looking good for the actual competition. Looking their best and all that but I just give them a clean and polish while I'm wearing them before I start," she then looked at him oddly "why do you ask?"

"A few reasons I guess, you did make a point of telling me you liked them before which suggested it was something you wanted to get out there in the open," he replied "I also think it is a good for look in general and sexy too."

"Oh really?," Tegan said with a sly smile and a playful wink "most people I know just rudely ask don't I wear anything else? Others just try and suggest ways I could change my look in general. Well, that's if they say anything at all."

"Tegan, trust me when I say this. You are perfect as you are, I wouldn't change you for anything" Darren said smiling at her, without warning Tegan pushed him onto his back, kissing him deeply.

"Thank you." she whispered in his ear and smiled down at him and went in for another kiss.

"What for?" He said a little confused after they broke the kiss.

"For wanting me," she said just looking intently at him again "not some idea of me, not the successful showjumper, not the rich daddy's girl, you want me, you want Tegan Galloway, the girl who will wear her riding gear all day most days, spending quite a lot of time at the stables and more likely to smell of horses than Chanel number five, Eternity or anything like that. The girl who loves wearing boots, especially riding ones in general. The girl more at home going to Parkhead to watch Celtic play football than get all dressed up to go out shopping with the girls and where a night of sci-fi beats going clubbing," she rested her head on his chest, listening to that heartbeat that gave her so much comfort these past few days, a tear rolled down her cheek "You want... Me." she said just loud enough for him to hear, she felt him put his arms around her tight.

"Tegan," Darren started to say "You are..." but he heard a sound, it was of Tegan snoring "Sweet dreams." he said and tried to get comfortable himself without disturbing her as they both had a long day tomorrow, he managed to get his jacket that was on the ground and loosely put it over them both for extra heat. But as he settled, Darren couldn't be sure but he could swear he saw a fox nearby just standing around and was still there when Darren drifted off to sleep.

CHAPTER 24

"So Mister Galloway, let's start from the beginning shall we?" Detective sergeant Turner said, detective Marriott had a notebook in his hand.

"Okay," said Quentin "Last Saturday Netherfield House was host to a Foxhunt, you may have read about it in the papers. My daughter Tegan was taking a break from university studies to take part, she is studying to be a nurse you see, between that and her showjumping she doesn't get much time to do much else." Turner pointed at one of the larger pictures on the office wall of Tegan with her awards.

"Is this your daughter there?" She said as Marriott went up to look closer.

"Yes it is, that picture there was taken last year I believe. Anyway she had invited her cousin over to take part in the hunt." he said with a sigh as Turner consulted her notebook.

"This would be Lucy Bannatyne correct?" Turner asked, Quentin nodded.

"Yes, Well she used to be Lucy Galloway but you are correct. They had been estranged for a few years now after a family dispute. Before that, they were close, like sisters in fact and when the dispute between myself and my brother happened, it devastated her. When she got back in touch with Lucy it was the happiest I had seen her in a long time."

"What was the nature of the dispute? It must have been a big deal to cause such a divide." Turner looked thoughtful.

"Long story," Quentin sighed deeply "We ran the family business but my brother Ronald wanted to strike out on his own so I bought out his shares, at first he done well but when the recession hit he kept coming to me to bail him out and even after that he was still wanting handouts. This one time I decided instead of just giving him money, I offered to give Ronald contact details of people I knew could help look at his business and give the best advice.. "

"I take it he wasn't too happy with that." Marriott, who had an English accent, sounded as if he came from the Cheshire area.

"No," said Quentin shaking his head "he lost everything not long after, rumors were he was making increasingly desperate attempts to turn things around. A few years later he committed suicide, the funeral was the last time any of us had seen Lucy until she turned up on Saturday."

"How did she seem?" Turner asked "did she show any sign of awkwardness? Maybe some hint of residual resentment?" Olivia, who was standing in the doorway answered.

"No, if anything it was as if all those years not seeing her had never even happened, she was delighted to see us, especially with Tegan. Our daughter suffers from anxiety issues and has done so for years, Lucy is one of the few she has fully felt comfortable around."

"She seemed apologetic for not getting in contact all this time, you see it was Tegan that reached out to her," Quentin said agreeing with Olivia "I didn't have that much direct contact with her as I was busy with the hunt but when we did talk, she seemed fine, seemed to want to put all the bad blood behind us."

"Okay," Turner said, making her notes" So, the hunt itself, what happened... In regards to your daughter, that is." Quentin took a minute to think but Olivia answered.

"After a while, they weren't away that long, Lucy returned saying her horse threw her and she hurt her knee, but I couldn't see or feel anything wrong."

"As a nurse, do you think she may have been faking it?" Marriott asked out of curiosity.

"At the time no, I did have a look at it and if anything I thought she had simply sprained her knee," Olivia said after thinking about it "she then claimed not to feel too good to the point of being physically sick and just wanted to go home, I called her a taxi and she left." Quentin picked up the rest of the story.

"Not long after she left we returned with Tegan's

horse in tow, sometimes if a rider is thrown the horse will continue with the rest. I assumed Tegan would be here waiting for us but she wasn't and neither was Lucy, it was only then once Olivia had told me what happened to Lucy and I had time to think that something wasn't right".

"Why was that?" Turner asked curiously.

"You see," said Quentin standing up, and after a few moments walked to a map of the area he had on his wall "Lucy claimed she fell here," pointing to one point "and said Tegan was still on her horse at that point," he then pointed to another area further along "This was the first anyone saw Princess, that's Tegan's horse," he pointed to the Grey horse in one of the photos "was first noticed without a rider, we also found her helmet here," he pointed at another point in the general area he previously highlighted "There is no way she simply fell, its simply not possible."

"Why do you say that Mister Galloway?" Turner asked.

"Just look around you, look at the awards for showjumping. I have seen Tegan and Princess too many times to mention and the fences in that area would be no match for them even on a bad day, I know my daughter's abilities Detective Sergeant, it had to have been an outside influence," he took a deep breath "I apologise, You are only doing your job. Anyway, we looked for hours and no sign of her, then they phoned."

"The kidnappers?" Marriott said.

"Yes, they didn't identify themselves, but the one I spoke to had a strong Glaswegian accent, they demanded half a million pounds by Thursday and then more details would follow, he quite strongly suggested we not get the police involved."

"Then what happened?" Turner asked.

"I was fully prepared to pay the ransom and was making arrangements for the money when two things happened, first was two college classmates of Lucy's showed up looking for their friend." Quentin replied.

"Ah, your wife mentioned this, Linda McKay and Jason Gallagher arrived at the house and were apparently looking for Darren Douglas, they allegedly told you he was part of the protest against the hunt, am I correct?" Turner said Reading her notes.

"That is correct," He confirmed "we then received a phone call at my office at work with a short message stating my daughter had been seen, with a man matching Darren's description, part of me wondered if it was him who made the call, made me doubt this woman Linda's story as time went on.."

".. Very unlikely it was him," interjected Marriott checking his notes "Darren Douglas, aged nineteen was born and raised in the town of Wishaw, lives with his mother, no previous convictions. At the very least the accent wouldn't match up."

".. Anyway something made me suspect Lucy was involved in all this, you see on one of the phone calls the kidnappers made I heard someone say the name Blondie in the background, this is a nickname that I later found out Lucy has through her classmates, then I dropped the name in a later phone call and the kidnapper I spoke to didn't seem to react to it." Quentin concluded.

"So, the ransom drop is tomorrow is that correct?" Turner asked while also thinking about preparing for the drop off.

"Tomorrow at noon the drop off is at Queen Street Station, A payphone will ring and tell me where to go and get my daughter, I leave the bag and go retrieve her, well that's what they said anyway." he answered, Turner looked deep in thought.

"Okay Mister Galloway, this is what will happen, Detective Marriott will drive you to the station and you will make that drop with counterfeit money that will pass casual inspection that we will supply, we will have a plainclothes officer near to see and possibly arrest whoever makes the pickup. You come back to the car and tell Detective Marriott the location, he will take you there after informing us. Now here is the difficult part, we do not know what to expect, so we will send in officers first. If she is there and she is okay, we will allow you to see her," she looked at him, a mix of anger and disappointment evident in her features "I do hope she is okay Mister Galloway, you should have come to us sooner," she said with a hint of sadness then added, "We will be back in touch in the morning, We will find her one way or another."

"Do you have any ideas or leads on who did this?" Quentin asked hopefully.

"A few Mister Galloway but it's all speculation at this point." Turner answered as she started to head out, Olivia leading the Police to the door.

As they left, Detective sergeant Turner rubbed her temples as if bothered by something "There is one thing I still don't understand." Marriott looked confused.

"What would that be?" He asked.

"Darren Douglas's involvement, from what we were told he had romantic feelings for Lucy but also they were not shared by her. By all accounts he believed her to be there to be part of the protest .."

"Lets see, several arrests at various protests and rallies confirm that it would be would be a reasonable assumption to make." Marriott added thoughtfully.

".. From his background, it is unlikely he was in on the abduction, one theory we do have is he may have seen it and has tried to stop it. The fact is no matter how we look at it, his involvement in any of it makes little sense."

"Why?" Marriott asked.

"Well," she started "If he had such strong feelings for Lucy, why was he seen running around with Tegan?"

"As opposed to helping out Lucy, the one he had a crush on?" Marriott mused "He was obsessed enough with her to turn up to the protest to find her after all."

"Well that is the dilemma?" Turner said "he's a wildcard, hard to tell what impact his involvement will have had," she raked her hands through her hair "I know I have not heard of anything like that happening in any ransoms I've had the misfortune to deal with."

"So, who could have done this? " Marriott asked outright, Turner leaned on the car.

"There are only three gangs that are crazy enough to pull this off," she counted them off in her fingers

"Lets see, here's the Harvey's but kidnapping isn't their usual thing. The Lyle's? Possible but most of them are in prison," she saw Marriott look at her as if he felt he was missing vital information, he had only transferred up a year ago so was new to the Glasgow crime scene "Its all for separate crimes... Now the Donnellys, they are so unpredictable it could be them, I worked on the Latif girl case and I was sure they were involved but proving was near impossible."

"Oh, what happened there," Marriott asked with interest.

"A young lady from a very well respected Muslim family in the Queens Park area was walking home with her father when a van pulls up next to them and a group of men all in black and in balaclavas come out and grab her straight off the street," she shook her head "and that's the last we hear of her, no demands no threats, nothing."

"So she just vanished?" He didn't sound convinced.

"Exactly, but I suspected the Donnellys and if I'm honest I am thinking this could be them too." She sighed.

"That's if it's a gang at all." Marriott shrugged and got in the driver's side of the car.

"Well there is that," Turner got in too and put her seat belt on "this is what I hate about cases like this. Of course, the bloody criminal is going to tell them not to contact us. Then they think they can handle things themselves and it's only when one of them sees sense do we get any wind of it and then we are running about trying to do a day's upon days worth of work in a few hours," a thought occurred to her "has anyone spoke to

The Bannatyne girls mother?" Marriott checked.

"No, not yet." he said.

"We will that first thing on the morning,"Turner suddenly looked deep in thought "just a hunch, I was thinking, two of the Lyle boys are in their early twenties, Ewan Harvey just turned twenty and Andy Donnelly is twenty four." she said thinking out loud.

"You think one of them may know the Bannatyne girl?" Marriott asked "maybe she was the one to suggest that they abduct the Galloway girl in the first place. She possibly tells them of this great opportunity to make a lot of money on one job.." he shrugged.

"It would make some sense," Turner said, "after all how else would she be involved?"

"If we are right who knows what will happen to the poor girl?" said Marriott as he sat in the driver's seat.

"Maybe Miss Bannatyne's mother can shed some light on all this." Turner concluded.

"We can only hope." Marriott countered, starting the car and driving down the path.

CHAPTER 25

It was still dark when Tegan and Darren set off again, determined to get to Biggar that night at least. There seemed to be a slight bounce in Tegan's step, telling Darren her feelings seemed to have taken a lot off her mind, she was still worried about what may still happen but she had one less concern to think about.

"Darren," she asked playfully "ever thought about growing your hair out a little?" Darren smiled at her.

"Oh,trying to change me already? Unfortunately, when I do try I end up looking like Harald Brattbakk." he shrugged. Tegan laughed.

"Sorry, I can't help it, Harald Brattbakk? Really?" she managed to say eventually.

"At least I kinda looked like him unlike the recent nicknames I get sometimes at five a sides where I play with my brother and his mates, I would sometimes get called Dimitri despite wearing that." He pointed to the top Tegan now wore, she looked at him quizzically.

"As in Kharine? Why?" she eventually asked.

"Well," he replied, "You see I never wear shorts, always tracksuit bottoms." Dimitri Kharine was a russian goalkeeper who usually wore long trousers while playing in goal.

"Strange, was it once he signed for Celtic?" Tegan said after some thought

"Yeah," he admitted, "I wouldn't mind if I at least kinda looked like the guy." Tegan shook her head and continued talking.

"Thankfully you look nothing like him. Anyway... I don't mean that long, I just mean grow it out just at the top just a little, you know? The Corporal Hicks look." she continued as she walked past Darren with a cheeky, almost flirty smile on her lips as he stood thinking, as if trying to remember something he thought he may have heard, he definitely remembered how her eyes had lit up last time she spoke about the actor and the character of Hicks in particular.

"Oh, now I get it... Michael Biehn? Really? You had a crush on him?" He realised Tegan turned around looking innocently.

"Pretty much, let's put it this way I think I wore out my dad's copies of Terminator and Aliens" she hid her face in her hair, blushing "I liked him in both roles but I always preferred him as Hicks. I know Michael Biehn isn't exactly a typical teen girls heartthrob is he?" she gave her shy smile, Darren walked up and kissed her forehead.

"So what your saying is, you like the soft spoken take charge type? And that I better hide my Aliens special edition DVD?" she gave an innocent smile and took his hand, they walked far enough from their camp from last night and decided it would be safe to have something to eat, so they sat and had some grain bars.

"I am so looking forward to simple things like a proper hot meal," Tegan said, leaning on a fence post "a bed too, I feel could sleep for a week."

"Same here, it feels like these past few days are starting to catch up with me." Darren admitted.

"How's your head." she asked suddenly aware that while Darren seemed fine he wasn't out of the woods yet.

"It's just a dull pain now, barely noticing it if I'm honest. I know you're still worried but I feel my brains so haphazardly wired as it is any further damage won't affect me that much." Darren said cuddling her side on, but Tegan looked up and shook her head.

"Darren, I can't lie to you. I still feel bad that you even got involved in all of this," she turned to look at him "But if you hadn't, I might not be alive... And I definitely wouldn't have met you."

"Well the way I look at it, everything happens for a reason. How else would we meet? Me being treated by you in a hospital a few years down the line for a bruised finger from online gaming?" Darren said to lighten the mood.

"Really? Can you honestly get an injury like that from gaming?" She said, half curious, half appreciating his attempt to take her mind off things.

"Oh yes," Darren said with mock seriousness "It's

mainly thumbs though if they use a gamepad. You do get other injuries though, Craig nearly broke his finger on his keyboard although he was drunk and his seat broke."

"Is drinking while gaming common? Is it wise to play and drink?" she asked genuinely interested.

"Can make it more interesting. Though if you are someone like Gareth who drank some out of date beer cans, it can produce interesting results," he looked at her "Don't ask, You should try it, gaming online that is, you would like it I think,"

"You know something?" she said taking his hand with a smile "I think I would" and kissed his cheek

They continued on their way and after a while, he asked "What's it like at competitions? I'm assuming you would want me there with you."

"Of course I would want you there," She replied as if it was a silly question "It depends on the level of competition but be warned there will be a lot of spoiled rich mummy's boys and daddy's girls, and that's just the riders. I do my best to try to avoid them and Princess is much better company."

"Are there any notable people for me to keep an eye on?" He asked.

"Well there is Stuart Ramsey of course, imagine his face when you turn up with me," her smile went from a cute shy one to a playful one at the thought "Oh there's Charlotte Rothman, she is one of those girls who has to use the brand names for stuff, for example, it's not look at my new riding boots, it's look at my new Aigle boots," she rolled her eyes "the ones I have on now are Regents and very expensive but I don't go about telling everyone. There's Angela Blacklaw, who if she's not talking about herself, it's about her arrogant rugby playing fiance. I should mention Gregory Sanderson, thinks he is God's gift to women," she gave Darren a look that suggested he wasn't "And how could I forget Ruby McKinnon? Her dad is a Minister and acts holier than thou but in reality, she is probably the bitchiest girl around." She noted a sly smile on his face when she told him that "What?"

"Ministers daughter you say? I think I could have fun there, I did convince a Jehovah's witness I didn't think the Devil is evil, amongst other things," he noted Tegan's shocked yet amused expression "I'm sure she wouldn't be a challenge." At that point, Tegan aimed a playful slap on his arm.

"You wouldn't dare," she said, Darren just smiled "Darren, you wouldn't," she stared at him, trying to be angry and failing then giggled What am I going to do with you." she said resting her head on his chest

"I have a few suggestions." he said playfully.

"I bet you have." she replied, kissing him.

The sky was getting lighter and despite Tegan's feet and Darren's knees hurting both were pushing through the pain. Neither wanted to spend another night roughing it, Tegan nearly slipped into the mud as they were opening a gate, luckily Darren caught her.

"Okay, I think I will pass on camping this year." then they burst out laughing.

"I think your dad will understand." Darren mused, they decided to take the opportunity for a short rest. There was a tree with thick roots that created a seat of sorts so they weren't sitting in the mud, it was nice and peaceful as Tegan cuddled into Darren closely as they sat under the tree.

"I can see why you chose to wear this top," Tegan said as she adjusted the goalkeeper shirts sleeves again. "It's warm and surprisingly comfortable, I could do with something like this for riding."

"You can keep it if you want." Darren smiled at her.

"But it's your lucky shirt... are you sure?" Tegan asked, completely taken off guard "You really want to just give it to me? Why?" She didn't know what to say or how best to react but Darren just kissed her and said.

"Meeting you is the luckiest thing that will ever happen to me. I think it's already done its job don't you?" Tegan didn't answer, she just pulled him close and kissed him lovingly instead.

As they left the Knightswood flats where Blondie and her mother lived, Detective Sergeant Turner looked at Detective Marriott and shook her head.

"So, Lucy hasn't been in contact with her mother since Saturday and even before then was barely around the house these past few months, and last she heard Lucy told her about a guy called Andy?" She asked as Marriott looked at his notes carefully.

"Yeah, no mention of a second name though," he

flipped the notebook shut "it also seems that while her mother just wanted to get on with her life, Lucy did seem to carry a grudge."

Turner nodded and they made their way to the car, once inside she put her head in her hands and let out a groan.

"Unfortunately that can happen, the kids carrying over feuds long after the parents have moved on, I will say from the sounds of things, It looks like the two main suspects are either Andy Donnelly or Andy Lyle," She turned to Marriott "Andy Donnelly is the insecure baby of the Donnelly family and he might do something like this to show his worth to the others," Marriott nodded in understanding "Andy Lyle is an unhinged maniac, he killed his own aunt for rejecting his advances another time robbed a corner shop and burned it down with the owner inside, his cruelty knows no bounds, he was once arrested for possession and spent the entire time saying what nasty things he would do to the arresting WPC"

Detective Marriott thought for a few seconds and pinched the bridge of his nose.

"So," he said carefully "one option is someone who may kill her to prove he is as ruthless as the rest of his family and the other sounds like he is going to kill her if he hasn't already," he rested his head on the car seat headrest "regardless of who it is, it sounds like the poor girl can't count on Miss Bannatyne to come to her defence. We can only hope it is Donnelly in case he decides getting a good amount in a ransom might be enough to prove to the others."

It was going to be a long hard day.

CHAPTER 26

Final preparations were going on at Netherfield House, Quentin was understandably nervous about the whole thing and his imagination went into overdrive. what if they had recaptured her? What if all this is putting his daughter's life at risk? Was it too late to get the real money?

"I'm not sure what would be worse, not finding her or.." he started to say but couldn't bear to finish the sentence, Olivia sat next to him and put a comforting hand on him and said.

"I couldn't sleep last night thinking the same," she admitted "My gut feeling is she is alive. I don't know what it is but something is telling me she is out there somewhere, alive and with that other kid, Darren." Quentin looked at her and smiled sadly.

"You know, I just hope she is alive and this whole

mess hasn't affected her as much as I fear it might." he replied. That was a big concern with her parents, Tegan was always prone to anxiety issues and who knows what effect something as traumatic as this could have on her There was a knock on the sitting room door frame, it was Detective Inspector Marriott.

"It's time Mister Galloway." he said politely.

Quentin got up and grabbed the bag that had the fake ransom money in it and kissed Olivia's cheek, she was about to say something but they caught each other's eye and decided against it, he left with a simple.

"I'll do my best to bring her home."

Darren and Tegan were continuing to follow the road to Biggar when suddenly a car had pulled up next to the field they were crossing. fortunately they managed find some some large bushes to hide in before they were seen and sat huddled together and tried to stay out of sight. Darren peered through the branches and seen a couple get out of the car.

"Wonder why they have stopped?" he wondered out loud "Hold up, they are going to the back of the car." suddenly a brown and white King Charles spaniel came running into the field, the couple, who must be its owners close behind.

"Dog walkers?" Tegan said "Either that or they are on a long car trip and want to let the dog run around a while." she squeezed Darren's hand.

"Well, lets hope they don't stay too long" Darren sighed as they watched the couple throw a tennis ball for the dog to fetch, after a while Tegan started to worry.

"What if the dog finds us? what if it alerts its owners? What do we do?" she said shakily, and fought the urge to just get up and run, instead she held onto Darren tight, her head resting on his chest listening to his heartbeat to calm herself down somewhat.

"Tegan, it's going to be okay, trust me" he tried to reassure her. Fortunately luck was on their side as the couple, along with the dog got back in the car and drove off. Tegan just sat, still cuddled into Darren listening to his heart as he held her close as they watched the car disappear into the distance, he could tell that the constant stress of it all was really getting to her so he just sat and stroked her hair.

"I guess the constant tension must be getting to me." she said softly.

" I know how you feel, I keep worrying that you'll be recaptured." he said with a hint of fear in his voice she hadn't heard before. She looked up at him and held on to him tighter. It was typical of Darren's thought process that his biggest fear wasn't him being caught again, it was her recapture that haunted him.

"That night," she started "the one you were out with your concussion,I realised my biggest fear was you not waking up, I couldn't do this alone and I didn't want to leave you," she looked up again deep into his eyes "That was when I realised just how much you meant to me." He stroked her hair and kissed her.

"When woke up and saw you still there, I thought it was a dream at first," he explained "I wouldn't have blamed you if you had just up and left. The fact you

didn't leave means more to me than you will ever know."
Tegan stood up and held out her had to help Darren up
too, once he was she pulled him in close and kissed him
deep and tenderly, when she broke the kiss she looked
into his eyes with a slight smile

"Darren, how could I leave someone as special to
me as you?" she said and kissed him again then she took
his hand in hers "The sooner we get to Biggar the better,
for both of us." and they continued on to the next field.

The safe house was a busy place to be as well with final
preparations in place.

"Do we tell him?" said Frank to Joe, who was
cleaning up the place of all the gang's mess.

"In his state of mind might not be the best idea, if
we do get the ransom money, just get last minute flights
and say something like you can't find the tickets Blondie
bought." Joe said as he dropped a can of lager in the bag
bag he was holding.

"And if it isn't?" sighed Frank "there are so many
ways it still could go wrong. Her father could figure out
we don't have the girl anymore even if she isn't found
yet, he's not an idiot."

"We will have to work out what to do if and when
it happens I suppose," Joe shrugged "If all else fails, he
will need to hide out in Spain at one of their properties
for a while."

"Where was the... Body..." Frank forced himself
to ask this question "...going to be located for the parents
to find?" Joe put the bag down and leaned on a nearby

countertop.

"Well, apparently they would have," even Joe, who never was squeamish found it hard to say what he needed to say "done whatever they planned to the girl the night before and first thing in the morning they would have been taken to Strathclyde Park. In one of the car parks would be a car dropped off by... You know Colin Edwards, right?"

"Yeah, has the broken nose and the scar on his forehead, yeah we did a few jobs together. Surprised he wasn't involved more in this." Frank remembered.

"Colin was in court this week, his ex girlfriend is demanding child support, anyway he was going to meet them there with that old royal mail van he has in his lock up, put her in there and tape the key to the underside and just leave it there." Joe continued.

"seems risky." Frank noted.

" If she was alive, yes," Joe said mournfully "Colin is still taking the van there and setting up, Malcolm will be driving him back and I think Colin will be waiting outside for Malcolm at the station later to drive off the minute Malcolm gets in the car. At least that's the new plan."

"Why not have Colin make the pickup, he's less.. Distinctive than Malcolm?" Frank asked, already seeing how the plan could go wrong "Malcolm is a tall guy with a white beard and long hair, he's quite noticeable, despite his nose and scar Colin blends in a lot better."

"You are assuming Andy is thinking rationally, remember he's drug addled and mourning the girlfriend who was probably going to have him take the fall and had the idea of murdering the poor girl to begin with," Joe took a deep breath "His brothers are not going to be happy, they don't know anything about this, he told them he was taking Blondie away for a week."

"Andy better bloody hope he gets that ransom money or they will tear him a new one." Frank admitted, they heard movement in the next room as Andy made his way to the toilet, still groggy. They heard a few long sniffs and Andy came in suddenly acting invigorated.

"Payday boys," Andy said, flecks of white powder still on his nose "Let's get this show on the road. Only a few hours until showtime."

"See! Look, there it is again," Tegan said as she pointed into the distance "I've seen it a few times now and I know I'm not going crazy." Darren was sceptical.

"What is it," Darren asked when a fox emerged from the hedge in the next field "Oh, it's the countryside, you hunt them in the countryside what's so surprising? I saw one last night before I fell asleep." Tegan watched as it ran off again and looked at Darren as if he didn't understand.

"For all we know it is the same fox I saw after the cottage incident and that night you were recovering, the markings are familiar," she said in a tone that suggested she knew how crazy she sounded "he is following us, he has to be." she could tell he wasn't all that convinced and trudged on. The majority of the route looked like fields and general grassland with the odd trees from this point on which made it easy going, the sound of cars passing in the distance helping with bearings. Tegan stopped and rubbed her temples.

"Tegan, are you okay?" He asked all concerned. she went up and hugged Darren and sighed.

"I must be going crazy." She said as Darren held her protectively. Tegan looked deep in thought.

"Tegan?" Darren said carefully "What's on your mind? I know that look."

"Oh, just thinking about what people will say." she replied.

"About the kidnapping?" Darren shrugged as she nodded in reply "Well I do get the feeling that the media will jump on the story like a pack of wolves, the whole Olympic hopeful kidnap plot thing, you know what the they are like, especially the papers." he said after some thought.

"I guess you are right," she said with a sigh "They will sensationalise everything, the abduction, you and I becoming a couple... Oh God I just had a really horrible thought." she buried her head in Darren's chest letting out a groan.

"What?" He said, a little confused.

"I can see it now oh so clearly, we get out of this and it all becomes public knowledge what happened, you know some newspaper will start an ill advised campaign to get me on the Sydney Olympic team, all the feel good story crap. You know the type, if I go there and win something its a wonderful British comeback story and if I don't, I'm the brave wee Scottish girl who gave it her all despite recent trauma." she gave a deep sigh. Darren just smiled and hugged her.

"Unfortunately I can see that actually, either the Daily Record or The Sun probably, one of the ones that wouldn't have cared if you made the team before all this.." he went silent, then said "If I'm honest, I never really thought that much about what will happen after this, the whole courts, media.. All that sort of thing." he felt Tegan hold him closer.

"I hadn't thought about it much either until now, but we will get through it together." she said looking up, Darren could see she was scared but there was a hint of determination he hadn't seen before as he held her close.

The thought of dealing with the aftermath terrified Tegan, she hated dealing with the press at the best of times, court would be worse still and their relationship will be scrutinised by the media too but ever since she and Darren started this journey, and even more so since they admitted their feelings for each other, she knew he would be there to support her no matter what and she would certainly be there for him.

"Come on." Darren said, smiling softly as he took her hand.

"What's got you in such a happy mood?" She said looking a little confused.

"You, everything about you." he pulled her close and kissed her.

Jason was waiting in the computer lab, it felt so eerie just him there as it was just him left out of the trio of early birds to the lectures. He wasn't alone long as the door opened and Anita walked in.

"You still here?" she said rolling her eyes, Jason

looked around.

"Yeah, and?" He said pointedly.

"Nothing," she said with an insincere smile "just glad to see no one else has mysteriously vanished into the night." just then Julia walked in.

"I see we are still down a few classmates" she said shrugging her leather coat off

"It looks like it," Anita sighed, rolling her eyes."if only Captain Redbeard here would go missing"

"We all know I come here for your good looks and charm." Jason joked, Anita's answer was, using the swivel chair for momentum, driving her handbag into Jason's crotch.

"What the hell!" Jason said after a few minutes bent over on the floor, as more classmates came in, Jason just shook his head and started on his assignment in the hope it would take his mind off it all, Jason sighed as he looked up at the ceiling.

"Darren mate, where the hell are you?" he said to himself.

CHAPTER 27

Malcolm sat down at a vantage point near the payphones in Queen Street Station, feeling his bones creak he wondered if he was getting too old for this but he had known the Donnelly boys' dad and promised to keep an eye on them after he died, Andy was the one he expected to break the mould and not get involved in crime. Malcolm even advised him against this whole plan from the start but the kid had his heart set on it, wouldn't be long now before he would see if it works out in the end.

Detective Marriott stopped his car just outside the Queen Street Station entrance at George Square.

"Good luck Mister Galloway, just try and remain calm okay, we have some plainclothes officers in there so nothing is going to happen to you." Quentin nodded.

"Thank you and I hope luck is on our side, for Tegan's sake." and he got out and headed to the station. His nerves were getting the better of him. Maybe this is where Tegan's anxiety came from he thought as he tried to look casual around the phones.

It was midday, Andy picked up the phone and dialled, it rang for a little too long.

"Y... Yes." Quentin's voice sounded shaky even through the phone.

"Hello, I would love to stay and chat but let's get to business, on the far end of Strathclyde Park in one of the car parks there is a red van. There is a set of keys taped to the bottom of the bumper, your daughter is there, remember to leave the bag behind." Andy said, all business.

"Is she okay?... Is she hurt?…is she... " Quentin asked but Andy hung up.

Quentin hurried out, almost forgetting to drop the bag and got in the car.

"Red van in Strathclyde Park." Quentin said with urgency, Marriott radioed through and then started his car heading for the motorway.

Malcolm walked up casually to the payphone, phoned the safe house and simply said.

"Got it." and lifted the bag as if he had been the

one who put it there and casually went to head out the side entrance, as he did two men approached.
"Detective inspector Nevans.." started one...

"Hey," said Anita, "look, there's a lot of police at the station" the lecture had ended and they were getting ready to leave but that made them run to the windows.
"Yeah, looks like someone's getting arrested." Julia pointed out, as everyone looked out the window and watched the whole thing as it all unfolded before eventually leaving the class for lunch.

Andy was about to leave the safe house for the last time when the phone rang, he shrugged and thought and answered.
"Andy... " It was Colin's voice "Malcolm has been arrested, it's all gone to hell." and he hung up. He just stood, hands on the table for a few seconds then in a rage picked the phone up and launched it at the wall and started smashing up anything he could see, Joe and Frank ran in and it took both of them to get him seated and calm again and he explained what Colin said, Frank had enough.
"Brilliant, just brilliant. Why did I let you talk me into this? No girl, no money, nothing. You let that blonde bitch convince you that stupid scheme would work, you told us to pick up out have a go hero then to continue the charade even when they escaped and now we have nothing to look forward to except jail time, the worst

part is that wee bitch was planning to run out with the money from the start, one plane ticket Andy, one... " He ranted, Andy started to rise off the seat "Hey, it's the truth, she used you, she used everyone."

"She wouldn't do that.." he started to say but Joe pushed him back down.

"It's true, Andy, it's true. One good thing is Malcolm won't talk, so we have that but we better act, I'll go to Glasgow and talk to your brothers to see how they can help but you two need to get out of here and not to Glasgow," he went over to the map and looked for the nearest town "wait for me... At Biggar."

"She told me she loved me," Andy said to himself "she loved me," Joe and Frank exchanged glances.

"Just get him to Biggar," Joe written a number down "phone me here at four o'clock, hopefully, I will have an update by then, find somewhere, a pub or something and sit tight," he looked at Andy "Get him dressed and cleaned up first, he has to look like a respectable young guy out and about," he lowered his voice, "not some heartbroken drug addled wreck." Frank looked over at Andy who was still muttering to himself how much Blondie loved him.

"I'll do my best." then walked over to Andy as Joe left.

"Good luck." Joe said.

"You too," Frank replied then turned to Andy "Come on, let's get you dressed and ready." Andy looked at him, a desolate look in his eyes.

"She promised me this would work, where did it all go wrong?" He said pitifully.

"Who knows," Frank said, he really wanted to say several things went wrong, agreeing to Blondie's plan, stopping for and snatching the have a go hero... The list was endless, but now was not the right time for such repercussions, they needed to get out of here and soon.

Jason was in the college canteen with some of the others from the class, despite not everyone getting on they did tend to eat at the same table when Julia came up and sat the other side of the table with her choice of lunch, she had just been to the McDonalds at Queen Street Station, judging by the bag she dumped on the table.

"I see the diet is off." said Mark, the class know it all in a sarcastic tone, Julia rolled her eyes.

"And who are you? The diet police? Anyway, The word at the station is the police arrested someone as part of some ransom attempt, but that is all I heard."

"Any more details? Who was involved? Who was being ransomed? Anything?" Jason asked with intensity, suddenly having a bad feeling about it all.

"No, why?" she replied as she took her lunch out the bag "Though someone did mention that guy who owns Galloway Haulage was there just before the police swarmed the place.." she didn't get to finish before Jason stood at headed quickly to the nearest payphone, Anita stabbed at her salad with a fork and shook her head.

"What is Captain Redbeard's problem now?" she said with disgust.

"I have no idea." Julia as she watched Jason run out the door..

Jason reached the payphone and fumbled with change, he had to call Linda. The chaos at the station had to be about the thing Darren got caught up in, it had to be...

The police had found the red van and no one was inside. Detective Sergeant Turner walked over to Quentin, not sure what to make of it herself.

"I am sorry Mister Galloway, there is nothing to suggest she was even here, we have people looking over the CCTV as we speak but no telling what if anything that will reveal, this was the right van, the keys were taped to the underside of the bumper. We do have someone in custody but it's early days. You may want to consider going public with an appeal for information. But let's see if we get anything out of our suspect first, Detective Marriott will drive you home, once again I am sorry." she said, wishing she could say something to give the man comfort but couldn't. Quentin looked like a broken man but managed to say.

"At least she's not dead... right? That's got to be something surely?" she said almost pleadingly.

"There is that," she replied, "but there are still too many unanswered questions Mister Galloway."

"I'm going back there." Linda said over the phone.

"What? Linda, we can't just go charging into the guy's house, can we? Maybe he hasn't contacted you yet because he is busy." Jason tried to reason with her.

"You aren't going to convince me otherwise, I haven't heard anything from them and keep in mind that Darren's mother is relying on me to get any information about him too so I'm going, what about you?" she barked back, there was a pause and then Linda said in a soft voice "I bet Astrid will be there."

"We are already going out on Saturday night." He replied.

"But you can see her tonight too, plus she will think you are such a sweet and caring man for being so concerned about your friend." Linda almost sounded seductive on the phone and admittedly Jason couldn't come back with a counterargument.

"Okay, Fine, I'll meet you in Strathaven at three." Jason sighed and hung up.

The worst part of the fields was the gates, most of the time the ground on either side had been churned into slippery mud and Tegan's riding boots had no grip on the soles and Darren's tread on his trainers had been so worn down as to be useless so there were a lot of near misses, Tegan had noticed Darren started slightly limping again.

"Darren? How are your knees?" She asked

"Fine,well, okay the left knee is a bit sore" he said as he tried to flex his left knee, the pain in his face showed her he was really hurting "I'll be fine, honestly." But Tegan disagreed and walked over and put her hands on his shoulders and looked up into his eyes.

"Darren, please listen to me okay? Once we find a

suitable spot we are going to take a short break for at least fifteen minutes, okay? You need to rest your knees" she said in a tone that suggested he shouldn't argue "I'm just looking out for you, it's what couples do, right? Look out for each other?" couple, they were a couple, she took a minute to soak the word in and smiled "You know, I like the sound of that" Tegan admitted "Couple." she repeated as she took his hand and found a good spot to stop under an overgrown hedge and sat down.

"It does sound good doesn't it? Being called a couple" Darren admitted as Tegan kissed him lovingly and then cuddled in as they listened to the traffic go past. After a while Tegan sat up and looked in the bag.

"Oh, Just had an idea." she said and pulled out the the gas burner and get the flame burning. She then looked around and took a rather slender stick and broke it down to roughly the length of a pencil then took the shortened stick and put it over the gas flame to scorch it, Darren sat mesmerised by what she was doing and was unsure what she had in mind.

"What are you doing?" He said curiously as she turned the stick and looked at him playfully.

"You'll see," she said with a smile "Its something I remember hearing a girl at school saying she did this once," her expression then slowly changed to one of slight uncertainty "or did she say she heard of someone try it." after few moments Tegan just shrugged and continued. After half an hour she started tentatively touching the burned part of the stick.

"Okay it will do," she started to rub her fingertips on the burned areas till they got dirty and closed her eyes, rubbing it on her eyelids and round the eye socket area and repeated a few times until she was satisfied, the finished effect was like black eye shadow, not too vivid but just enough to change her look a little "What do you think?" Darren just stared.

"You look amazing," he eventually said, she looked a bit gothic, a good look for her he admitted "was this girl a goth by any chance?"

"Yeah, she was," Tegan smiled "I figured might be an idea to change as much as I can about my appearance and some gothic looking girl wearing a Celtic top is not going to be what anyone is looking for." she said.

"Depends on how you define looking for." He gave her a kiss on the cheek, she playfully slapped his arm and gave him a stern look but her gaze lingered, softened and they kissed deeply.

"You know what I mean." she said in mock anger.

"I know," he replied and kissed her again "Come on, not long to go now." and they continued to Biggar.

CHAPTER 28

Detective sergeant Turner stepped out of the interview room feeling the need to hit her head on a brick wall.

"If he even thinks about saying no comment one more time.." she started, Detective Marriott looked over his notes.

"We do have something, that is Malcolm Devlin in there and he has had strong links with the Donnelly boys." He was right but it wasn't much to go on.

"Best we can do is have officers watch the houses and known hangouts of the Donnelly clan for now and see if Andy Donnelly shows up, it's not ideal but it's all we have," she sighed as she leaned against the wall "there is one good thing I guess is it wasn't Andy Lyle, Devlin would never work for them."

"Do I want to know why?" Marriott said, curiosity getting the better of him.

"Devlin's best friend was the infamous Fergus Donnelly, patriarch of the Donnelly clan, Alistair Lyle killed Fergus about eighteen years ago. You could say he has reason to hate them," she said "I need a coffee, then back to dealing with Mister Devlin."

There was a wailing cry from the trees, Tegan ran over, half dragging Darren behind.

"Tegan, what has gotten into you?" he said a little confused.

"You don't hear that?" she said not even slowing down, when they got there she saw what was making the noise, it was a fox and Tegan was pretty sure it was her fox and he was looking like he was struggling. She squatted down.

"Hey Reynard.." she started.

"You named it? Why Reynard?" Darren asked as he squatted down too.

"Old medieval tales, Reynard was a trickster fox, think the cartoon version of Robin Hood where he's a fox, similar idea." she said Darren just looked at her.

"Well I had to call him something," Tegan said as she inched closer "and what's wrong with you Reynard you crafty fox?" He started to try and lash out, like any cornered animal but she didn't relent, she turned to Darren, "could you use your jacket? Better yet my blazer to trap him?" Darren knew better than to argue and took her blazer out of the bag and with some effort was able to hold Reynard down in a safe way.

"He's a bit feisty." Darren said as he tried to keep

hold, Tegan soon found the problem, a shard of glass from a beer bottle in its front paw.

"We will have that out soon and you could go back to your vixen, she will be missing you, can't be following us," as she spoke she eased the glass out, the fox tried to kick out a few times but she kept talking in soft tones, reassuring it until. ".. okay, there we are." and gestured for Darren to let go, the fox limped off into the undergrowth.

"Think he will be okay?" Darren asked.

"Should be," Tegan said looking distracted "He will be away licking his wound clean," she started to laugh "who would have thought it, me, a girl who just a few days ago was going on a foxhunt and the daughter of the local Huntmaster no less, goes and helps a wounded fox, don't hear that happen every day do you?." they both laughed, probably a little too much but it was the release of emotion both were needing. Darren got up and helped Tegan to her feet.

"We don't have far to go, should be in Biggar by nightfall hopefully." Tegan gripped Darren's arm as they walked, keeping trees between them and the road, she noticed Darren always positioned himself between her and the road. It seemed every little thing he did, didn't matter if he was even aware of it or not was protecting her. She kissed his cheek, then drew him in close for a full kiss.

"What was that for?" He asked when they broke the kiss.

"Do I need a reason?" she replied smiling softly.

"No," admitted Darren "I guess I'm still getting

used to all this." That was something else about Darren she kept forgetting. While Darren had repeatedly told her he found it hard to believe she was not only single but almost always had been, it equally hard for Tegan to believe that even with his mental conditions, quirks and past issues he had never even been on a date. She just hugged him too for good measure.

"I guess we are both new to the whole dating thing. I hardly count that date with Stuart, he didn't kiss me or even hold my hand and if I'm honest I didn't want him to but with you it's different, everything is," and she kissed him again "that one was for you just being you, for always being here. For refusing to leave me behind... Everything." she said and gave Darren another deep kiss.

He had barely explained to Olivia what happened with the ransom drop off when Quentin heard the doorbell, when he answered the door he was greeted by angry Linda.

"You were supposed to let me know if there were any updates, I'm guessing that fiasco at Queen Street Station was to do with you!" she shouted, Quentin half-heartedly invited her in as she was already in any way, Jason followed somewhat sheepishly.

"I'm sorry, everything moved so quickly with the police involved," Quentin told her "no sign of Tegan.. Or your friend and tomorrow they want me to attend a press conference to appeal for any information and they have someone in custody but I haven't heard anything more," Quentin said as Olivia gave Linda a drink "if she's with your friend, what do you think is going on in his mind, why haven't they shown up somewhere?" Linda thought for a minute or two.

"Darren is, different. He does things that you can't account for, which might explain why no one's found them. He will look after her, probably to his detriment too." She shook her head and Jason continued.

"If anyone can keep her safe Darren can. But yes he is... How to say it?" He tried to think "Ever played anything involving strategy?" He asked finally.

"Chess, plus a few other things in my time, why?" Quentin asked, confused by the question.

"Never play against Darren, just don't," Jason explained "It's not that he's particularly great at strategy or anything, but he will frustrate the hell out of you. He doesn't use regular logic." the more Linda thought about it, Jason was right.

"Even our lecturers have to tell him not to help others because he has such an unusual way of doing a lot things and it would be so obvious he did it" she added. Quentin processed this information, he wasn't sure if it brought him any comfort. Darren's unpredictability could be a good thing as it may have kept her alive but the issue would be that no one can guess what the bloody hell he's doing or going with her.

"Why didn't you tell me this before?" He asked, Linda shook her head and looked at Quentin.

"We didn't say because believe it or not you get oddly used to Darren's unusual ways, you come to see it as... Normal for him I guess." she replied

"I just wish I knew where she.. I mean they were."

he said eventually.

"You and me both." Linda said with a sigh

The drive to Biggar was awkward, Andy just sat quietly in the passenger seat while Frank drove.

"Don't worry, you know Joe will come through for us," he tried to reassure Andy "It was a bad deal, best just put it behind us," Frank pulled off into a side street to park the car "Look l, we will find a place to sit for a few hours than before we know it we will probably be on a beach in nice sunny Spain."

They found a high street pub, the Crown Inn, to sit and lay low, the pub wasn't too busy so Andy went to the bar and ordered a pint for himself and bought Frank a fresh orange and lemonade.

"I'm sorry Frank," Andy spoke for the first time since getting in the van "I let it all get to me. I wanted to show the others I could be as ruthless and cunning as them, that I could take the lead on a job. Blondie offered me a way to do that, I was a tempting score. Rich girl, middle of the country, wouldn't be noticed straight away. It sounded foolproof the way she described it, or it would have been but that guy, the hero. She mentioned his name but I forgot it.."

"Me too, I can't remember either so don't worry." Frank admitted.

".. Suddenly he's there and we are wondering who the hell he is and it turns out he knows Blondie.." Andy continued. It did seem to have gone wrong the moment Darren got involved.

"Andy, did you want to kill the girl as well as get the ransom or was that her idea." Frank asked tactfully.

"Her idea, my idea, was a initially going to be a typical kidnapping and ransom but she believed killing her was necessary but wouldn't elaborate too much other than to say it was more of a risk to let her live. Blondie suggested no masks for us and no blindfold for the girl, saying making her see everything will play on some panic issues she has a little more or something. She was really adamant the girl has to be ransomed and die, in her eyes there was no other way. She played me, didn't she?" Andy answered, Frank just nodded.

"She did, she played us all." he added.

"Apparently the girl had emailed her after not talking for years and she hatched this plan. Dropping hints about always wishing to go on a hunt as they talked about when they were younger," Andy started to explain "grabbing her at university wouldn't work, it would be too open, she couldn't risk having the girl go missing on a night out Blondie arranged... Apparently, she never got out much. The hunt was the only logical place, the girl took the bait and that's how it started," he sighed "I admit I did think that part was pretty good, grabbing someone in the chaos, after they won't immediately assume she was abducted and by the time they did it would be too late and no one taking part in it would be a suspect." Frank admitted that part of the plan was good and quite simple too, Andy seemed at least partially back to his old self.

"Who wanted Pat there?" Frank felt the need to ask.

"Her idea, once she found out why he had been in prison she kept saying he should be involved. Like you I had my doubts but the truth was in the end, we needed to bring him into it." Andy replied.

"Well what's done is done I guess," Frank said, "we all make mistakes, the best thing we can do is learn from them."

Frank saw the clock in the Pub and realised it was time to call Joe so he went to the payphone in the pub and rang the number.

"Hello." Said Joe as he picked up.

"It's Frank, how are things going?"

"The boys aren't happy about it but they have made arrangements for you two to go to Spain, which means driving from Amsterdam.."

"Newcastle ferry?" Asked Frank.

"Yeah, I have some credit cards and other stuff you will need to get there." Joe replied.

"Joe, I'll need my passport, Andy already has his, mine is at my place. Tell my sister I'll bring her over when I'm settled and.. Look after her till I do. I trust you Joe." Frank added.

"Will do, you can count on me. You guys are in Biggar I assume?" Joe asked.

"Yeah, the Crown Inn." Frank confirmed.

"Will be down as soon as I can, just try and stay out of trouble." Joe then hung up and Frank went back to his seat.

"Joe will be here as soon as he can, it's all sorted.

Going to be quite a road trip." Frank said smiling trying to raise Andy's spirits.

Tegan practically ran to the sign that said Biggar and hugged the pole and turned to Darren, smiling broadly.

"Told you I'd get us here." He said smiling back.

"I never doubted you for a single minute." she said before kissing him. They tried to clean up as best as they could, Tegan used some water from a puddle to wash the dirt off her boots as best she could and wiped them with her blouse that she took out the bag to use as a sort of towel. The Jodhpurs were another story however.

"Any ideas?" she asked, Darren took his jacket off, turned it inside out to its grey lining and wrapped the arms around her waist, using the main body as a sort of skirt around her upper legs. Tegan's whole profile was different and there was no way anyone looking for her would immediately look at her, for a final touch she brushed some hair in front of her face.

"Still beautiful to me." He said and meant it, Tegan looked beautiful regardless of how she looked to him, After a quick kiss he took her hand and walked up Biggar high street...

CHAPTER 29

It felt odd, walking along an actual normal path together, Tegan had her arm linked in tight with Darren's and was leaning her head on his shoulder, her feet were sore but at least the terrain was solid, smooth and even. Tegan was looking at the ground to avoid eye contact with anyone in case... well she would rather not think, that time at the cottage still scared her just thinking of it.

"There should be a phone box in the town centre," Darren said casually "and hopefully it's not vandalised."

"I'm worried dad won't accept a reverse charge call, he has always been wary of them. Even under these circumstances." as she was talking, Darren bent down and picked up something, a ten pence coin.

"A few more of these and we won't need to." walking along what is a more or less straight road looking for and discarded coins took Tegan's mind off things for a while, forty seven pence in total by the time they had hit the start of the town centre and things looked to be winding down, people moving around to get home. Tegan started to panic so Darren just pulled her aside under the shelter of a closed storefront and held her protectively.

"This was a really bad idea, me coming along that is," Tegan said, she on the verge of a full blown anxiety attack "just look at me, I'm a nervous wreck." but Darren knew just what to say

"It's okay, Tegan, you know I won't let any harm come to you and we have been through this, If we had separated like you suggested last night I would have been too worried about you to think straight. What if you had a panic attack? What if they found you? No, we have done the right thing, okay?" she looked up and nodded slowly. He was right, she also knew she would panic without him nearby and worry about being recaptured herself.

"I'm okay, I'm okay, I guess it's all those days with just the two of us, seeing all those people.." she trailed off.

"I understand, it's kinda strange for me too," he said holding her and stroking her hair as Tegan buried her head in his chest ear clamped to his sternum listening for his heartbeat. It always seemed to calm her down and she wasn't sure exactly why. Darren said then spotted something "hold on.."

A couple were getting into a taxi when Darren saw something flutter down as the guy got in and was messing around getting his wallet in his pocket. Darren stamped on the item and made out as if he was tying his shoelace until the taxi pulled away, he returned smiling holding a five pound note.

"Darren!" she slapped his arm "That's stealing!" though her facial features weren't as serious as her voice suggested, "At least I think it is."

"Maybe so but we haven't stopped for food at all and I think we both can agree that we need something to eat, other than beans. There has bound to be a chip shop around here," he shrugged then continued "we could do with more change for the phone." he made a convincing argument, or so her stomach was telling her.

"Okay, you do the talking though," Tegan's hunger overruling her morals on this occasion, "I think I'd be too nervous to say anything."

"That's okay." he reassured her and they continued walking up the high street, Tegan was still holding onto his arm as they did.

Andy had gone to the toilet and Frank was sitting at their seat near the window he glanced out and saw, from the back, the young couple but as the last time he saw Tegan, she had her hair up and in full clean riding attire. A girl with long wavy black hair, a football top and a jacket around her waist didn't register with him and Darren from the back in a t-shirt and jeans definitely didn't stand out, though why did the number thirty four something to him, he shook his head and sipped his fresh orange and lemonade. It did make him think about what his sister used to say that he should try to settle down again with someone, he had been separated from his ex partner long enough. maybe she was right.

"Hey, what's with you?" Andy asked as he sat back down.

"Oh sorry, nothing just watching the world go by," He said distractedly "lots of young lovers, has got me thinking." Andy nodded, He had been a lot calmer since they arrived here and had been talking honestly about things, Frank was glad to have the old Andy back.

"Frank, for as long as I have known you there's only one girl for you and she has been in your life from day one, you know it and I know it, your sister Siobhan, your bond with her even drove your ex partner away and took your girls away with her, what is it with you two anyway?" Frank looked down, it was true, while it is a pure sibling love they have for each other it was a close enough bond that, if he was being honest, Frank only needed other women for... Intimate pleasure so to speak.

"Well, she's not just my sister, she's my best friend. I also hate to break it to you but the minute we are settled she is coming over." he said in a tone suggesting there would be no arguments to the contrary, Andy had already figured that was the case.

"Most of the properties we have over there are big enough anyway, I hope it's the one in Murcia they tell us to go to." Andy's eyes had the old flicker of life back in them.

"That's the one near all the golf courses isn't it?" Frank asked.

"Think so, either the courses are recently built or will soon be, can't remember which it was, so I know what I will be doing," Andy said as he drained his glass and pointed to Frank's "Want another?"

"Sure, Joe won't be here for at least an hour." Frank replied and he returned to looking out the window. He had to admit, the job itself was a total disaster but hiding out in a nice area of Spain, in the beautiful weather, all in all not the worst way to end a job all things considered.

After some discussion they had decided to order a sausage supper (two sausages in batter with chips) as it was a cheaper option and gave them a sausage each, that was Tegan's argument anyway, they entered the chip shop and there was a short queue, Tegan's anxiety was troubling her as she cuddled in close to Darren, he could feel her tremor in fear. Luckily the other people just seemed to assume she was just cuddling in for other reasons. Soon it was Darren's turn.

"A sausage supper please?" He said as calm as he could "Oh and a can of cola and a diet cola too." The girl behind the counter took note.

"Salt and vinegar? Brown sauce?" she asked with a tone that suggested she had asked this question too often already tonight, Darren turned to Tegan.

"What would you like on it." he asked.

"Just salt." but something about her voice, she put on a slight nasal whine to her voice but then gave Darren a look that suggested she wasn't entirely sure why she did that. It didn't take long and the brown paper wrapped supper was handed to Darren and he paid using the five pound note, he handed Tegan the supper and they left as he put the cans in his pockets with difficulty.

"Tegan?" Darren asked looking confused "what was with your voice in there?" She looked embarrassed.

"I don't know," she replied in her normal tone "I realised if I didn't speak it would look odd but was worried... You know.."

"you were worried you sound too distinctive?" He asked, she nodded in return, "Oh Tegan, what am I going to do with you?" He said hugging her "it's going to be fine," Darren took her hand and pointed to a phone box "Let's phone your parents."

They crossed the road and made their way to it, both of them got in the box, neither quite prepared to be fully out of sight or touch of each other, Tegan put a full pound in and dialled her parents' number, her free hand holding on to Darren…

Quentin and Olivia were just seeing off Linda and Jason, Astrid had finished for the day and was going home and kindly offered them a lift into Glasgow. Linda made Quentin promise to ring her the moment anything new happens and asked Olivia to keep him right about it. Jason was just happy to be able to chat more with Astrid. As they drove off in her Volkswagon Polo, Quentin rubbed his temples.

"I'm tempted to offer that woman a job, I need someone with that sort of determination to keep some of the drivers in check." he half joked, as the phone rang.

"Expecting a call?" Olivia asked.

"Police with news possibly?" He said as he looked down the driveway, unfortunately the Polo was too far away to call them back, Quentin rushed in.

"Hello?" said Quentin as he answered the phone.

"Dad?" it was Tegan... Quentin was... He wasn't sure what to feel...

"Tegan, where are you? Are you okay?" He asked, mind racing, Olivia must have heard as she was standing in shock.

"Yes dad, we are okay... " She started, Tegan was crying, overcome with emotion.

"We? who is with you?" he asked even though he kind of figured out who, he didn't want to get bogged down explaining how he knew.

"Darren... I will explain later... He saved me more than once dad… He's the reason I'm even still alive" she replied.

"Where are you?" Quentin was curious to know Darren's exact involvement but that would come later.

"Biggar," she said, an odd place to be he thought, there sounded like a discussion for another time "We will be at the top entrance into town." Quentin realised what she meant, the main road ran right through the middle of town, she was meaning come in from the north of the town.

"I will be there in just under an hour. Tegan... Your mother and I love you, see you soon." he put the phone down and went to get his car keys, Olivia decided she was going too.

"She will need both of us there Quentin." She said defiantly, no matter what Quentin said she was not going to be persuaded otherwise, they got into his Range Rover and headed off to Biggar but not before Olivia phoned Linda's house and told Ellen about the phone call from Biggar and their intentions to go get them and to tell Linda when she gets home what is happening.

"It wouldn't be right to keep them in the dark a second time" she explained as she put her seatbelt on

Tegan burst into floods of tears the minute the phone went down but thankfully they were tears of joy. Darren just held her as best he could within the confines of the phone box before exiting.

"See Tegan, it's all going to be over soon." he said still holding her.

"I couldn't have done it, any of it, without you." she said stroking his face, looking into his eyes and she kissed him deeply.

"get a bloody room." someone said walking past and heading to the pub but they didn't care, and the fact they had a little chuckle about it, suddenly Tegan looked worried for a moment, ran back into the phone box and came back out, they had nearly left the sausage supper behind.

As they walked Darren opened the bag enough to get at the contents inside and handed it to Tegan insisting she could do with the residual heat, despite him looking cold in just a t-shirt on top. Tegan handed him a sausage as she ate hers. It had just occurred to Darren that to others they probably look like any young couple out on a date or just returning home from one. Tegan was walking close to him ravenously eating away and Darren trying to get what chips he could with one arm around her.

The same thought occurred to her too, a few people and cars had passed and she realised that people weren't seeing two runaways trying to avoid recapture but instead saw a young couple. A smile formed on her lips thinking about that.

"Darren," she said rolling up the empty wrapper as they were reaching the edge of town, putting the wrapper in the bin as they passed it "where would I be without you?"

"I'm sure you would have figured something out." he offered but she shook her head.

"No, I wouldn't have," she said looking at him intently "There are no two ways about it, I'm alive because of you." and she kissed him again and just held him close under the Biggar sign, soon they will be home and safe.

CHAPTER 30

Andy drained his fourth pint of the day.

"Want another?" He said pointing to Frank's glass, Frank nodded. Joe should be here soon so one for the road Andy thought, the bar was kind of quiet, there were a few people Andy assumed must be the regulars, as he waited to get served he heard the conversation between one of the barmen and a regular who seemed annoyed about a couple in one of the phone booths kissing.

"I'm telling you Stevie, I get it they are in love but people like them need to keep that sort of thing private," Stevie the barman rolled his eyes, but the guy continued "It's worse when they do it outside, when I was coming in I saw a couple and they were all cuddles and kisses, she was dressed weird too."

"Weird how Chris?" Said Stevie with a bored tone to his voice, giving Andy a look as if he hears stuff like this too often.

"You're a Celtic fan, who wore the squad number thirty four, I'd say judging by her shirt it was probably a goalie." Chris asked. Something about the shirt piqued Andy's curiosity.

"Tony Warner, but he was on loan from Liverpool and only played a few games I think." Stevie said after some thought.

"Sounds interesting, what else was she wearing?" Andy said suddenly, a thought flooding into his mind.

"Well, all I will say is my Kelly rides horses and she keeps hounding me to buy her boots like the young lover has on but they cost hundreds and here is this girl wearing them, spurs and all wandering up the street with a Celtic shirt on. She must have money to burn." Chris answered and someone else at the bar, a regular by the looks of it added his own thoughts.

"She might have stole them from somewhere." the regular commented dryly.

"Or maybe she rides to Parkhead."another regular quipped, that comment got a laugh from everyone at the bar. Andy just looked intently at Chris and in a calm voice asked.

"What way did they go?" Chris gestured that they took the high street road up north, Andy walked up and snatched Frank's van keys off the table.

"They are here, the hero and the girl." said Andy, his eyes had the look he had when he found Blondie's corpse, he was wanting revenge.

"Here? The crafty... Of course, we couldn't bloody find him, he was coming here, not Strathaven," Frank was very impressed, even proud of the hero for such a tactic "Are you sure?"

"Oh yes," Andy nodded "Remember that cottage where the couple nearly caught them? Well, they said the hero had a shirt on with Warner thirty four on the back, one of the regulars saw a girl wear it and very expensive riding boots. I bet he's given her the shirt and I know roughly where they are going." he went out to the van.

"Andy, let's just leave them be, Joe will be here, we go to Newcastle, little road trip and we are in Spain, plus you have been drinking.." Frank stopped when he saw the look in Andy's eyes and got in the passenger side, They must have been the couple he saw before, he hoped Andy wouldn't find them as he started the van.

Darren and Tegan were hiding out of sight in the long grass near the Biggar sign.

"Tegan, aren't you worried your parents won't like me?" He asked " I am sure they will be grateful to me for saving you, but.."

".. How will they react to you being my boyfriend too? " she interrupted.

"Pretty much." he replied.

"Well, Dad will be a bit protective and he may be unsure at first but that's bound to happen, eventually he will see what I see in you. Mum definitely will like you, trust me on that." she said as she untied the jacket from her waist.

"Here, you really should put this on, you're cold and please don't deny it," she handed him his jacket back which he dutifully put on "What about your parents?"

"How will they feel about you? Well bear in mind they actually might not know about any of this, only my brother knows and even then I only mentioned I was going somewhere to meet a girl, that's all he knows." he replied.

"Really?" she said genuinely surprised.

"Yeah, I was worried I'd be talked out of it, anyway my mum will be very cautious at first about us in general, as for my dad, he will see it as, if I am happy that's good enough for him. I mean they are divorced and all so you would probably meet them separately, which might be a good thing, ease you into the craziness that is my family." he explained and he just looked at Tegan, there she was sitting wearing a mismatched outfit of her riding boots, jodhpurs and his Celtic top, she was dirty, hair a mess... but to him, she was beautiful.

"Tegan," he said", in the past week I have been beat up, bound, gagged, kidnapped, strangled near to death twice and had my skull caved in for good measure, the song is right."

"Oh?" she said not really following his train of thought.

"Love hurts" and he smiled and kissed her.

They heard the sound of a car stopping, a Range Rover had pulled up on the other side of the road.

"That's them." and Tegan nearly got up but Darren pulled her down, he pointed to a very familiar van that just drew up at a discreet distance behind. It was the kidnapper's van, she knew it too, yes it had a large bump and damage at the front but was the same van.

Darren realised what needed to be done, in his head anyway, if both of them got in there would surely be a car chase and who knows what will happen, no one of them... He had to stay, distract them, the chances of him surviving weren't good but no other choice, Tegan's safety came before everything.

"Tegan when I say go, run to your parents and get in as early as you can," he said, he was tense "I will be behind you," Tegan was scared but nodded. He took her head in his hands, memorised every feature and line of her face in the moonlight and kissed her "go!"

Andy seen them run across and put the van lights on the full beam just as Darren was about halfway across to the Range Rover, the light illuminating him.

Tegan ran to the Range Rover and her dad rolled his window down and was telling her to get in quickly, he sensed the danger too and had an idea who may be in the van if the terrified look on Tegan's face was anything to go by.

Darren took one last look at Tegan, looked at her dad and yelled.

"Go! Now! Get her out of here!" Quentin took a moment, Darren spoke again "Please just get her to safety, please" Quentin looked at the younger man and in a silent understanding, nodded and started the engine and drove off, the sudden movement causing the car door to close.

"Damn, well played hero but at least I will have revenge on you for screwing everything up for me." Andy said as he accelerated forward.

Darren had a chance, there was an open gate in the fence, the area was muddy, may stop the van, he ran as hard as his stiff tired legs could go, if they get out to chase him or the van is stuck in the mud he will have given Tegan enough time for her parents to get her safely home, as for Darren he wasn't thinking about his own safety as he knew that if and when they caught him, he would surely be killed.

Andy was gaining, soon the have a go hero would be under the wheel of the van and they could go after the Range Rover and then off to sunny Spain. Frank shook his head.

"Andy, stop, it's over." Andy wasn't listening so Frank grabbed the wheel and turned it hard, hitting the handbrake too.

Darren heard a screech of tyres and looked back only to see the van turn sharp and the sudden movement with what might have been a handbrake turning caused the van to teeter, then topple, it skidded along on its side as Darren jumped to the relative safety of the roadside ditch…

As soon as Tegan got in, her father accelerated away much to her shock.

"Dad, we need to wait for Darren." she said looking back.

"Tegan," his voice slow and calm as if explaining something to a child "It was him who told me to go. He kept you safe, he's done his part and I won't risk your safety.." he didn't get to finish as Tegan started lashing out, punching the back of his seat, thrashing about and trying to do anything to get him to stop.

"Quentin, what are you going to tell his friends," Olivia said, "they will want to know why we didn't help him."

"Not you too, look I'm sorry but I am not risking our daughter's safety for anyone, I'm sure they will understand. It was at his own request." he replied but Tegan was not listening to anyone, she was having a full violent meltdown, punching and kicking the back of her dad's seat.

"Stop the car now, you don't understand.We can't leave him, I promised him, I need him... I… I... I'm in love with him." she said, the words coming out felt so natural to her, felt right. But her dad, however, wasn't convinced.

"You hardly know him, you don't know what you are talking about." he sighed, believing she was saying that as much to get him to turn the car around than any real or imagined feelings, however, Tegan's mother looked around, ready to say along the same lines as her dad, to tell Tegan she wasn't really in love... Until she saw her daughter's eyes and at that moment she knew not only her daughter's feelings for the boy but also if they did continue on and just abandoned him, Tegan would never forgive either of them.

"Quentin, turn the car around... Now or she will never forgive us, never forgive you." she said with an authority Tegan had rarely seen her mother use, Quentin prepared to turn the car around, he knew better than to argue and besides he couldn't cope with the thought of Tegan never forgiving him.

As he got out of the ditch and slowly stood up with aching knees Darren watched the Range Rover drive into the distance noises from the van made Darren turn around as he heard Andy get out of the van by smashing out the windshield as he exited the van it was clear Andy was moving unsteadily. There was no way they could follow Tegan now, did he see the brake lights on the range rover go on before he turned? Must be imagining things. Of course, he realised he may face the full force of their wrath but it didn't matter, he was able to be useful one last time.

Andy was determined to have his revenge, he was going to carve Blondies name into the hero, slowly. Nothing else matters, Blondies death had to be avenged..

"You are a dead man!" shouted Andy as he pointed at the younger man, groping for his knife in his pocket he went to step forward when out of nowhere someone landed a punch to the side of Andy's head, knocking him to the ground, it was Frank.

"This stops now," he said kicking Andy down the minute he tried to get up. Frank could not allow this to go on any longer, he kid had done more than enough to be allowed to live and had earned Frank's respect, he didn't deserve to die to settle some wannabe gangsters bloodlust "It's over."

He couldn't believe what he was seeing, the main kidnapper, Blondie's boyfriend and one of the Donnelly crime family was being attacked by his partner in crime, who pointed to something beyond Darren's view.

"Go, I'll deal with him... And explain to the others," the partner said "Don't worry," Then he turned to Darren and gave a loose salute "Frank... My name is Frank." Darren was about to reply when he heard a voice behind him.

"Darren!"
He turned to see the Range Rover had returned, the back passenger side door opened and Tegan was shouting at him to get in with her. Darren couldn't believe it. She came back... He moved as fast as his tired body and knees could go, every movement hurt but he didn't care, she ran out of the car to help him.

As Frank stood, pinning Andy with a foot to his chest he observed Tegan get Darren in then get in herself, closing the door behind them, he said to himself.

"Good luck, both of you," Frank said as the car drove away, he then looked down at Andy "As for you," he kicked him in the ribs "we are staying here until the police show up and I will tell them everything, and if you or your brothers touch my Siobhan and I will kill you. That is a promise." Andy just lay there helpless and in pain, it was over and he knew he had lost.

Quentin started the car and drove off, this time with both of them. Tegan held Darren's head in her hands, staring into his eyes, tears of joy rolling down her cheeks.

"Promise me not to do anything like that again, I just got you in my life. I can't bear to lose you so soon, or ever again for that matter. I told you we are part of each others lives now and... I love you."Tegan managed to say eventually, her voice trembling. Darren just pulled her close in a loving embrace and felt her wrap her arms around him tight.

"Tegan... I love you too." he eventually said through his own tears of joy and they spent the rest of the trip back to Netherfield Manor with Darren holding Tegan, as she cuddled into him listening to his heart and smiling, whatever the future has in store, they will face it all together.

EPILOGUE

The resulting court case and the inevitable media frenzy were overwhelming for both Tegan and Darren, although the one thing they were worried about most, Blondie's death, was deemed a justifiable homicide. The Galloway family lawyer who, true to Tegan's word, represented both of them and said under the circumstances it was the best case scenario. Yes, it would be something that will hang over their heads for the rest of their lives but they won't go to jail.

Andy was convicted of kidnap, attempted murder and various other crimes that mounted up, Frank's testimony helped greatly. It seemed like the rest of the Donnelly clan did not come out in support of their youngest sibling, apparently the rumour was that they were embarrassed by Andy and how he was so easily duped by Blondie. Joe had fled the country, he was last seen on a ferry to Ireland. Andy, Malcolm and the others involved all received twenty year sentences except for Frank who only got fourteen years and was sent to a different prison, his sister Siobhan had taken the savings and already moved to Spain to set things up for when he gets released. She wanted to give him something to look forward to.

Tegan and Darren were inseparable throughout the whole thing. On the first night they had given statements and as a matter of routine were arrested for the death of Lucy, an ordeal that Tegan in particular found difficult to get through but luckily they were both quickly released on bail with conditions. It was decided to let Darren stay at Netherfield House that night in a spare room but Tegan insisted Darren sleep in her room instead as she wasn't ready to be alone at night. Initially he was to sleep on a on a fold down bed, but her parents found them in the morning both on the fold down bed asleep with Tegan cuddling up to Darren listening to his heartbeat, from then on they were allowed to share her bed as her parents saw no point in fighting it.

After that first night in Netherfield, the only times Darren went home to Wishaw was for more clothes and stuff then back to Netherfield again, after a week of him staying 'just one more night' and seeing how much he meant to Tegan, her parents suggested Darren move in proper, something he readily accepted to her delight, Olivia convinced Quentin it was a good idea by saying it would make things like court dates and lawyer appointments easier plus at least on Netherfield grounds both would be sheltered somewhat from the media, though the more he saw of Tegan and Darren together the more he realised they truly did love each other.

During the trial, the two of them were always sitting beside each other holding hands. They never stopped helping each other through it all. Some noticed on the last day of the trial as they stood outside the court with her father and his lawyer, Darren wore black dress trousers, a white shirt, green tie, plain black casual jacket with black trainers. Tegan wore a black turtleneck top, dark grey suit jacket and matching skirt with tights and a pair of her knee high boots and an engagement ring on her finger. They had gotten engaged in secret over a month before but had agreed not to make it public until after all the court drama was over. Tegan had put the ring on the minute they stepped out the court for the last time. They knew people would talk but they didn't care, they were happy and free to enjoy life together

In the aftermath, it was decided it was best for them to move from the area for a while. Tegan found Dundee University were more than happy not just to let her continue nursing there but to repeat the year she missed half of due to the trial.

Darren couldn't face going back to college but managed to get a job with Dundee Council working as a librarian in Central Library, though they both wondered if Tegan's dad helped get him the job somehow, he wasn't complaining though.

What Tegan's dad did do for sure however was buy them a little two bedroom flat near the university, it was a recent build too. They moved up immediately to settle in and accept things like furniture deliveries and get Princess settled into her new stables, Olivia came up with them for a week and was helping out, especially with Princess. Tegan had started driving lessons too and alot of stuff was coming up in a rental van later in the week.

Today was the day the rental van arrived, finally, the flat will feel like home. Tegan was on the bus back from the stables, she was also excited because it would be the first night alone together in the flat as her mum had left for Strathaven after helping unload the van. Darren would be busy putting the finishing touches by now. Her hair was in a messy ponytail, she was in her knee high rubber riding boots, her two tone grey and black jodhpurs and Darren's... well it was hers now... Warner thirty four Celtic goalkeeper top. She had taken to wearing it anytime she went to the stables, which made her feel safe for some reason. She looked at the engagement ring on her finger. It may only be a cubic zirconia but it was all Darren could afford and it wasn't the price that mattered but the commitment behind it that was important.

It was only a short walk from the bus stop to the flat and Darren was waiting at the door with a smile on his face. He had let his hair grow out just a little bit on top and maintained a nice level of stubble she felt suited him. He was wearing trainers, camouflage trousers and a plain black t-shirt, looking exhausted but happy.

"How was Princess?" He asked.

"Her usual," said Tegan "She is finally settling in I think."

"Close your eyes." he said suddenly she gave him a look but gave in when he insisted.

"Okay, okay You win." she smiled as he slowing guided her in to the sitting room.

"Okay, you can open them now." Tegan opened her eyes, the sitting room had white walls and ceiling and beige carpet with the large dark green corner sofa and large television with video and DVD player as it had since they moved in but the rest, it felt like home. On the main wall in the centre was Tegan's Runrig poster in its frame, on one side, were large Star Wars movie and Aliens posters in frames and on the other side was a gift from her dad, his prized signed and framed nineteen ninety five Celtic home shirt signed by Andreas Thom from his work office next to a large photo of Princess.

On the wall next to the kitchen were some small framed photos of various points in their relationship up until this point, including the first one ever taken of them while they were still dishevelled and dirty from the ordeal and the last day at court. On the wall behind the television was a clock with a horseshoe motif and either side of the clock had newspaper cuttings, one side had a framed cutting of Darren in his school football team, the other side was one of Tegan's photos from the Glasgow Herald.

There were various other little touches, Darren's Boba Fett and Princess Leia figurines, bookshelves with a selection of both their books, videos and DVDs, some of Tegan's awards on full display with Darren's School football league winners medal in there too. There was Darren's three CD changer sound system with their CD collections in the small unit it sat on (they had quite a few double copies due to similar taste), next to it was the computer desk with PC and office chair. She had to admit it was an eclectic taste but it felt like home.

"Oh got you something as a housewarming." Tegan said, heading to the spare bedroom and returning with a gift bag, Darren had something in his hands too a large awkward looking parcel, they exchanged gifts and opened them, In Darren's gift bag was last season's yellow Celtic goalkeeper top with Kharine and twenty three on the back.

"It's a new lucky shirt to replace this," and she pointed to her shirt "Oh and it's match worn, dad got it for me." When she opened her package it was a big cute plush fox with a note attached to him, Tegan read it out loud as Darren put the new top on.

"Hello I am Reynard, can I stay with you?" she read and hugged the fox and smiled at Darren, "thank you."

"I thought you'd want your own little Reynard," he smiled back at her and handed her a box "I little extra I got, hope you like."

Tegan opened the box and in it was a necklace that had a golden horseshoe pendant with T G + D D engraved on it and came with matching earrings. Darren helped put it on her.

"Suits you." he said and she had to agree.

"Thank you," Tegan said, placing Reynard on the

sofa and hugging Darren "Thank you so much." Darren took Tegan's hand leading her to the bedroom, as they walked past the spare room, Tegan quipped.

"I see it's ready for Linda visiting this weekend, I'm teaching her the basics of riding to impress Ellen." Linda had simply accepted Tegan into the little circle of friends and was like a big sister to her, especially during the trial.

"Linda is visiting?" Darren sounded surprised but then remembered something "Oh yes, Jason said he will be coming up any time Rangers play Dundee or Dundee United, and he says he will get Astrid to come as well, that okay? "

"Of course it is, He and Astrid are still together?" Tegan said shocked.

"Apparently, now where were we? Ah yes." he pulled Tegan close and kissed her lovingly.

"You know, this is the first night we are completely alone together here." she said playfully, in fact even when they stayed at Netherfield together someone else was almost always in the house.

"Yeah," Darren said looking at Tegan's face and seeing her playful expression "What are you thinking?" She paused for a second and lead him to the bedroom, it had a fitted wardrobe, a dressing table with Tegan's CD player on it, double bed with bedside tables and Darren's telephone alarm clock, Tegan had him sit on the edge of the bed.

"You know, might be better to blindfold you," and she took one of her old Celtic scarfs and blindfolded him "now don't remove it until I say, understood?" she said in a tone of mock authority as she went to get ready.

Darren wondered what she had in mind, he heard her go into the wardrobe for something and leave the room, about five or so minutes before he heard her come back in and was at the CD player putting something on, the song Rhythm of my heart by Runrig filled the room.

"Okay you can remove the blindfold now." when he did Darren saw Tegan, her hair down and loose, he noticed she still had the Tony Warner shirt on with the sleeves pushed up past the elbows. It was the bottom half that surprised Darren, although the leather was once again clean and polished to a soft sheen, Tegan was wearing the same riding boots she wore to the foxhunt on that fateful day they first met. He also noticed that she wasn't wearing jodhpurs at all, the goalkeeper top was just long enough to be an impromptu minidress, she looked cute, gorgeous and very sexy all at once.

"You like?" she said as she moved closer, he stood just as was within reach, and pulled her close, kissing her deeply.

"You look.. beautiful." he eventually said smiling.

"You always say that,"she said as she gestured to her riding boots and top "so, you really find this a sexy look?" Darren kissed her again and grinned.

"I think you already know the answer."he said in that honest tone of his, she smiled seductively and eased his Yellow goalkeeper top off him and pushed Darren onto the bed. Tegan, still wearing her shirt and riding boots, climbed onto the bed as well and as she did Tegan whispered into his ear she had no underwear on. Before Darren could react, she proceeded to straddle him, her boots clamped tight on his sides and she looked into his eyes lovingly.

"Darren Douglas, my hero, my protector.. and my future husband... I love you with all of my heart." she said softly.

"And I love you Tegan Galloway, more than life itself." That statement would have sounded hollow if it had came from anyone other than Darren, but she knew he meant it, and they kissed a long loving kiss…

The end... For now.

ABOUT THE AUTHOR

D.D. Braithwaite was born on the 2nd of October 1980 and grew up in the Scottish town of Wishaw where he still resides with his wife Gillian and his son Corran (who is named after one of his all time favourite fictional characters). He is dyslexic and also dyspraxic (so he apologises if any little grammar or spelling errors have crept into this work) but has not let it get in the way of his writing. He is a fan of, amongst other things, science fiction, Formula One, professional wrestling and listening to the podcasts of Jim Cornette.

The authors who inspired him the most are Douglas Adams, Timothy Zahn, Aaron Allston, Michael A. Stackpole, Karen Traviss and Harry Turtledove. He also takes a lot of inspiration for his storytelling style from director/producer Dave Filoni.

Printed in Great Britain
by Amazon

87542060R00180